THE FELEEN BRAND

Hush Feleen came out of the Tennessee Mountains with his folks. Texas was a wide, strange place to him, but Hush walked tall and spoke soft—until they lynched his father. Then he swore he'd burn the Feleen brand on every loose cow in the Brasada, and swore that the whole damn country was going to bow to Hush Feleen . . .

THE FELEEN
BRAND

Will Henry

First published by Mills and Boon

This hardback edition 1999
by Chivers Press
by arrangement with
Golden West Literary Agency

ISBN 0 7540 8052 8

British Library Cataloguing in Publication Data available

Printed and bound in Great Britain by
Redwood Books, Trowbridge, Wiltshire

HE CAME TO the sawgrass Gulf Coast country in the summer of 1873, his only friends an old mountain mule and a rusted twelve-gauge shotgun.

Inland, before his unbelieving eyes, stretched the vast brushland pastures of the southeast Texas *brasada*—the Big Thicket—the greatest natural breeding covert of wild cattle the world had ever known. Within its sunless copses and open, bright-skied savannahs grazed the countless thousands of Spanish longhorns bred and rebred without diminishment since the days of the conquistadors. And now they grazed without the mark of any man upon them. Ownerless and unbranded, they were the dangerous prize of him who might first ride upon them with the luck of the bold in one hand and a smoking straight-rod iron in the other.

So it lay there calling him onward, this sinister kingdom of black thorn, brown water and multicolored wild cattle. Virtually untrod the past ten years of Civil War and Reconstruction, it awaited only the one who first would seize its longhorned treasure and make of his name a legend to endure beyond the Alamo. The soft-spoken, gray-eyed youth from Tennessee, gazing westward across the tangled land, vowed silently that its hidden wealth of hoof and hide and horn would be his.

He would become another Lone Star prince like fiery Mifflin Kennedy, bull-voiced Shanghai Pierce, fabled Jesse Chisholm or incredible Charles Goodnight. All it would take was twenty years' hard work—or one winter's luck with the long rope and the running iron.

There were, he knew, two ways to win the golden crown of cattle king: with an honored brand burned deep and clean; or with the rustler's rope and outlawed single-iron. One way might take a lifetime, the other merely a life. But if the odds were high, so were the stakes—six feet of nameless prairie against a million acres of matchless grass. The material gain was uncertain; the moral risk, inexorable.

A man could be remembered for a full, good life marked by the monument of a decent name; or he could leave behind him nothing save an evil legend wandering forever across the plains with the coyote-lonely wind.

The choice was Hush Feleen's. It lay in wait for him within the eerie quiet of the *brasada*. He knew what it was. It was the rope against the crown.

CHAPTER 1

His mother's name was Hushton. The boy, after the custom of the hillfolk, was given her family name for his Christian one. Jupe Feleen, the father, did not like his wife's people and was not pleased to have his first son called by their name. When the christening was over and the circuit rider had written it in the Bible the way his wife wished it, Jupe Feleen took up the book, handed it to the circuit rider and said in his short, flat way:

"Read what you writ, Preacher."

The circuit rider was not surprised. He knew these hard-scrabble hillmen. It was the rare one who could read or write, the even rarer one who would admit that he could. They wore their illiteracy almost as a badge of defiance, a symbol of their separation from the outside world. They wanted to be alone and to be let alone, and they had discovered that poverty and ignorance were the best insulation against the prying charity of the lowland folks. So the circuit rider was not surprised, and he took the book from Jupe Feleen and read aloud:

> "Hushton Hatterson Feleen, firstborn son to Jupiter Aurelius and Nancy Hushton Feleen; Wheeler's Ridge, Slashpine Township, Holden County, Tennessee, Apr. 17, 1857. May he walk tall and talk soft all the days of his life."

That last was a line the baby's mother had made up for a boy, provided she had one; and although the circuit rider did not make much sense of it, he put it down the way she gave it to him. Now, having finished his reading of it for the child's father, he returned the Bible to the pine plank table and went back down the mountain.

Jupe Feleen, standing lean and dark in the open doorway, watched him go. Then he turned and tore out the page in the Bible and said to his wife:

"We uns will call him Hush."

She knew better than to question him, even when he balled the page in his fist and threw it toward the fireplace. She waited until he had taken down his gun to go up on the mountain for some meat, before retrieving the page from the ashes. Folding it, she put it away in the bottom of the cow-hide trunk which had borne her bridal things across the ridge to Jupe's cabin from the Hushton homeplace on the far side of the drainage. That done, she went on about her choring and her care of the dark-haired baby boy.

She was not unhappy. Neither was she critical of her man. The Feleen men were like that. If you were lucky enough to have one of them, you did what he said you were to do, and you remembered what he told you you were not to do.

From that day, the boy was known as Hush Feleen.

In time, Nancy Hushton came to like the name, even to think it pleasing. If for other ears it had a different sound, his gentle mother never knew it. Before the boy's twelfth birthday she died of overwork and childbearing. Between the plowing and planting of their flinty hillside forty, and the eternal carrying, summer and winter for eleven years, of Jupe Feleen's insistent seed, the poor creature was left no time for anything save to die.

For four more years the boy chored for his father and cared devotedly for the eight live-born children. In that span three of the little ones died—one of the whooping cough, one of the lockjaw, and one from the vicious tusks of the old sow in the outback hogpen. It was a mean, poor way to live, but it raised up no weaklings. At sixteen, Hush was lean and hard and clear-to-the-bone tough. At the same time, he had in him a peculiar veining of gentleness, a seemingly inborn compassion for the small helpless ones of the world about him, the ones that could not properly look after themselves, that needed a big brother.

If it was a Hushton trait, this odd touch of tenderness, it was compounded in the boy by his foster-mothering of Nancy Hushton's brood. Jupe, who did not care at all for the idea that any son of his could be soft-flawed, blamed Hush's gentle streak on the woman's work the boy had been forced into since his mother was taken off. Jupe did not like that. He did not like, as well, several other things of the same spoiling nature which were commencing to go on around the homeplace forty in Slashpine Township.

Wheeler's Ridge was peopling up. It was time to be moving on.

One sweet-smelling spring morning in April of 1873, he called Hush to him and told him to get ready.

"Put the bedding and the cook things in the wagon," he said. "I will run in the team and shoot the sow."

"Which way we going, Pap?" was all the boy asked.

"West, I reckon," was all the answer he got.

It took the whole day to get the old sow cut up and put down proper in deerlick salt. There was no halt for noon dinner. When the children got to fussing from being empty-bellied Jupe had only to murmur, "Hesh, now, cain't you see we uns got a load to tote?" and the fretting fell off and the youngsters nodded. "Sure, Pap," they said, and stood back out of the way. At five o'clock the wagon was packed.

"Wait up a spell," said Jupe to Hush, and turned and walked off up the hill toward the spring.

He was gone so long that Hush said to the little ones, "Get aboard and set tight," and he went up the hill after him.

He went quiet and did not get too close. By the old lightning-struck oak he stopped, peering along the slope to the spot where he and his father had put Nancy Hushton to rest under the wild cherries by the spring.

Jupe Feleen was on his knees beside the grassy mound, his slouch hat off and held in his hands in front of him. His head was bowed and he was praying. In the slant of the westering sun's rays through the cherry trees Hush could see the glint of the tears on his cheeks and the slow moving of his lips over the awkward words. Hush's own mouth moved a little then.

He had never known his father to admit there might be a Power Beyond. It unsettled him to think Jupe Feleen could be humble and afraid, could get down on his knees and pray to any power, for any reason. He went quickly back down the hill.

To Arnie, the next oldest boy, he said: "Pap will be along in a minute. He's saying good-bye to Ma up by the spring."

Arnie looked at him and asked, "Whyn't you say good-bye to her, Hush? We uns all did."

"I said good-bye to her."

"When? Dogged if I seen you."

"Four years gone. Yes, and times since. Down on my knees talking to Ma, asking her to show me the way to rear up you young uns—down in the dark so's Pap wouldn't see me. Now you hesh up, Arnie, you hear? You're eleven years old and near growed. It's time you got some sense."

The other boy shook his head.

"Shucks, that ain't what I mean, Hush. Four years gone don't count. I mean whyn't you go up and say good-bye to her at the mound, same as we uns? Now, I mean. In the broad day and—"

Hush put a hand on his shoulder, his voice quiet. "Arnie," he said, "shet up your mouth."

The younger lad shook his head again. "Iffen you say, Hush."

"I say."

Arnie subsided. After a bit he said, "Where we going, Hush?"

"West, Pap allows."

Lubelle, the willow-slim blonde, ten that spring and pretty as a brown-eyed jersey heifer, spoke up quickly.

"We uns hearn him say that our ownselves. What's it mean, west, Hush?"

"Out yonder," explained Hush. He flung a muscular arm toward the lowering sun. "That's west where the sun goes down; I taught you that, Lubelle."

"You mean we uns are going to live on the sun?" asked Jodie Beth, the five-year-old one with the chestnut curls and the withered leg. "Ain't that a fair piece aways, Hush?"

"It be," said Hush soberly. "But we ain't going to live there. Only going to set out in that direction."

"Well, then," put in Billie Bob, the outspoken one of the eight-year-old twins, "providing we travel a fur enough piece, we'll get there. I mean to the sun. Ain't that so?"

Before Hush could reply, the other twin, Billie Jim, taciturn and restless-eyed like Jupe Feleen, glanced up the hill and warned abruptly, "Best hesh up your talk. Yonder comes Pap."

The children stopped talking, and when their father came up Hush said to him, "You ready, Pap?"

"Most," answered Jupe. "There's one thing more."

They waited again while he went back into the cabin.

Inside, he took his dead wife's cowhide bridal chest from under the leather-webbed bedstead. Opening it, he found the rumpled page he had torn from the Bible so long ago. He put it in his pocket and said, half aloud:

"I knowed you'd want it thisaway, Nancy gal. Iffen you kin hear me, I want you should know my heart near cries for leaving you. A man don't love but one good woman in his life. You was mine, Nancy, you was mine. . . ."

Outside, he walked to the wagon, climbed stiffly to the seatbox and took the lines from Hush. In their place he handed him the folded Bible page.

"Carry it careful," he told him gruffly. "It tells who you are."

He looked once more toward the cabin. There was a great

5

loneliness in his seamed face. He made an awkward wave with his hand, as though to some unseen watcher from an empty window.

"Your Ma writ that for you, boy," he said to Hush. "She would want that you should keep it, and cleave to what it says. Remember your Ma, boy. Her kind don't come two to a lifetime."

"Yes, sir," said Hush, looking away so that his father would not see that he was crying. "Thank you, Pap—"

Jupe Feleen nodded. He clucked to the bony team and the ancient wagon started lurching down the hillside track. He kept his fierce dark eyes on the valley far below, and did not look back.

Neither did his son Hush.

They went 1400 miles by single horse-and-mule team down through Mississippi to the Louisiana Narrows and across their gathered waist to the Sabine River of Texas. Going over the Sabine, they kept angling south and west along the Gulf Coast until they struck the San Antonio River at the Forks of the Guadalupe.

There, at the Forks, they took some thought to locating on the Guadalupe. But Jupe was lured on by the talk of richer land and more plentiful game still farther south and west along the middle prairies of the Rio Nueces brushlands, down Live Oak County way. It came pretty steep for Hush to believe any soil could be loamier or any thickets more full of eating meat than those along the lush green Guadalupe. But Jupe would not be swayed. When he heard, finally, that it was far less settled up on the Nueces, there was no more to be said.

They started on, Hush thinking how beautiful it was there at the Forks and promising himself that if ever he was given the chance, he would come back there one day and live in that country.

They worked as they went, to pay their slow passage, the same as they had each day and mile of the way since leaving Tennessee. In one place—Brazoria—they made a stake of cash money scraping green steerhides and cording wood for the huge fires which burned night and day beneath the black iron vats used by the rendering plants to try out the Texas longhorn tallow. This, with the flinty cowskins, was making the inland hide hunters wealthy.

Hush was mightily stirred by Brazoria and by the stories of the "skinning wars" raging in the *brasada,* that vast wilderness of brushland stretching inland from the Gulf.

Somewhere "out there," far up the Nueces, the Brazos,

the Colorado and the Trinity, fortunes were being made by killing the wild Spanish cattle which ran everywhere along the hundred creeks and streamlets of the thicketed pastures. It seemed that all a body needed to be in the business was a fast horse, a stout rope and a handy gun. Those three things, and then maybe a little "cow hunter's luck"—or a lot of it— to go with them. Cattle were clearly not the only things being killed up on those Texas rivers. Not, at least, according to the grim stories he heard at Brazoria. Men, if they got in the way of other men who might be running the same cow or steer, were as apt to wind up dead and down in the long grass as any outlaw longhorn in the *brasada*.

Such yarns were the stuff of pure excitement to a mountain boy who had lived in the laurel tangle all his life and who could lay the sights of a Tennessee rifle so fine he could give you either eye of a fat buck at 150 yards. But Jupe would have no more of Hush's wanting to go into the *brasada* and take up hide hunting than he had had of his yearning to linger at the Forks of the Guadalupe and try ranching in the accepted Texas style, gathering and branding a herd of the wild cows for their very own, betting their muscle and grit against the other fellow's, as it were, in an honest, hard-sweating way. The elder Feleen was not looking for either hard work or easy-won riskful gain. He was not looking for a place in the Texas sun, but for a dark covert in her deepest shade. That passion for seclusion had driven him from Tennessee; it wasn't going to be stopped now by any cow-hunting or calf-raising nonsense. The little family understood that, and did not argue it.

Toward the last of their journey, getting well down into Live Oak County from Goliad County, they were forcing the tough old mule and the faltering Morgan mare which were their beginning and their ending team. They had been six months on the trail and September was gone. Overhead, great stringing V's of gray Canadian geese were moving. Their lonely cries kept Hush awake and restless during the long nights. The air, even in that south country, was taking on the feel of October. By day the cloudless skies turned gunsteel blue. By dark the blazing stars dropped lower, growing in size and whiteness until a body could hardly believe they were real. In the crisp dawns the smell of woodsmoke lay downwind of every hidden ranchhouse. In the evenings the frosty stillness would carry a dog's bark or the sound of an oxbell so clear and sharp that it would make the short hairs on the back of Hush's neck rise up and shiver him in a grand, fearful way.

It was a powerfully lonesome and wondrous country; the

folks up at the Forks had not lied about that. Hush had to admit that its spell had him breathing hard and eager, and that he wanted, at the last, to find journey's end within it just as surely as did his weary-faced father.

So it was that the mysterious dark *brasada* of the Nueces Basin beckoned to the travel-worn Tennessee clan with a welcome only mountain folk, born and bred to the furtive freedoms of the wilderness, could appreciate. And so it was that Jupe Feleen and his lank sons and slender, shy daughters disappeared into the Big Thicket as gladly as though they had been brought into the world there and had just come home to it from a long and homesick time away.

CHAPTER 2

They located in a hawk-lonely swale just below Fort Ewell, where there was a bend in the river; if you followed the river north you would climb the prairie toward Fort Clark and the buffalo country. The spot they chose was a place of rich, unbroken wilderness, and Hush and his father felt they could be happy there.

Through the late fall and the following winter they worked the short days through, putting up shelter and getting the household settled in. They had both liked the Texas "dog-trot" houses they had seen in the latter miles of their journey, and they built their place in the brushland in that pattern. With its two rooms separated by the roofed-over dogtrot and set with a north-sheltering bank to its back and the river running dark and clean in front of it, it was a better home than any they had ever known, and all of them were proud of it.

The little house and an open shed for the team and the wagon winged onto it, plus the saltmeat barrel set on cross-cradles in the dogtrot for Old Blue, their Walker and Red-bone hound who had trotted the whole way with them from Wheeler's Ridge, were all that they put up that first winter. Later they would put in a pen—folks out here called it a corral—for such stock as they might acquire. And maybe they would put up a haybarn too, something not much seen in those parts but a mighty useful thing when the wind began to blow fierce and spit blue ice the way they were learning it could occasionally do out there in the *brasada*.

It was a good-memoried time, that first winter.

Living was easy in the Big Thicket. There was meat to be had for the running, and fish in the stream before their door. The weather held mostly fine. Early mornings would be nippy, daytimes sunshiny, nights wine-sharp and sparkling. Hush was heard to laugh out loud three times before Easter, and two of those times Jupe Feleen laughed with him. Everyone was content and grew close. Arnie's guitar came out almost every night after supper and Jupe would pretty soon say, "Lord, Lord, Arn, you play to make the angels weep," and he would go fetch down his mouth harp from the mantelpiece and chord sweetly along with him.

Hush, whose voice, soft and low as a lullaby, would break the heart of Lucifer himself to hear, would take up the shivery Tennessee harmony to Lubelle's silvery lead, with the young ones just sitting by with the tears shining in their eyes, it was so beautiful and sad to hear that haunting mountain music there in the Texas wilderness.

When the final chorus of "Nelly Was a Lady" or "Tenting Tonight" had died away, maybe Lubelle, who had an ear for remembering lines, would recite "Sheridan's Ride" or "Lee's Farewell." Then everybody's eyes would be brimming and that would be the end of the family sing for that night, and full time to put the twins to bed anyway.

So the winter was whiled and sung away by dark; hunted, wandered and explored away by daylight.

The strange new land had much to teach them, and learning its many lessons—some harsh, some happy, all fascinating —was a dawn-to-dusk job. Jupe summed up their good fortune for Hush and Arnie one blustery warm April night when the three of them sat with Old Blue, snug beneath the dogtrot, watching the lightning chain across the *brasada* and burst over the Gulf a hundred miles away.

"It's a powerful grand thing," he said, "to set here and know we're free men agin. Not a neighbor in sight, north, east, south or west. Nothing but the wind and the rain to argue with. The sun and the stars to watch and wonder at. The moon to tell the months by. The critters of the thicket, big and small, to give us pelts and meat agin our every need. Water running 'fore the door, glassy clear and pure as arry mountain crick. Stovewood and starting tinder easy to hand on every side. Grass like never growed nowheres else. And, powerfullest of all, the room to rare back your head and yell out like a catamount, and have nothing come back to you saving your own echo. Oh, I tell you, boys, iffen either on you kin remember how your Ma taught you how to pray, you had ought to get down on your kneebones this night and tell Him up yonder there, that we uns down here are humble

9

beholden to the hand what led us inter this Gawd-blessed wilderness and solitude. To be free, boys, really absolute and untrompled free, there ain't no wondrouser thing than that in this here weary world. . . ."

He trailed it off, suddenly conscious of his own eloquence and embarrassed by it.

Arnie shook his head in his slow, wondering way.

"Gawd A'mighty, Pap," he said, "you kin lay it on beautifuller than a circuit rider, happen you take the notion. It's downright creepy, Pap. Most like I never really knowed you afore. Now how come you s'pose that to be, us being blood kin and all?"

Jupe Feleen had no answer. He shook his head, his words low and rough. "I dunno, Arn," he said. "I purely dunno."

Hush, listening to them, looked out over the *brasada,* waiting for the thunder to die away after the lightning had glimmered in the east. When it had, and it was still and dark under the dogtrot, he put out his hand and laid it on his father's shoulder.

"Pap," he said, "iffen you want, I'll say that prayer for you."

From the first, the greatest spell of the *brasada* for young Hush Feleen was cast by its wild longhorned cattle.

Perhaps it was that he was born to be a cattleman and that the good Lord had brought him to the one place where there were more unclaimed native cattle than the world was to know again. Perhaps it was only that in loving the wild things of the prairie thicket as he did, he must love the least tamed of them all with an intensity past ordinary comprehension. Or perhaps it was a burning combination of these forces which would not let the Tennessee youth rest until he had mastered the lore of the savage Spanish cattle and brought under his own hand, and brand, a herd of them which he could know was his own.

Whatever the reason, as late summer of the second year came on Hush was being stirred past all resistance as if by a summons. Opportunity to answer the call arose on a stifling Sunday afternoon in mid-August. Jupe Feleen had gone with Old Blue to run some meat. The twins and Jodie Beth were not yet awake from their midday naps. Lubelle was fussing with some woman's work in the cookshack side of the house. Arnie was lying up with his slingshot in the shade of the horse shed waiting out an old granddaddy brushrat which had developed a taste for the team's shelled corn to the point where he was getting more of it than either the mare or the mule. Hush himself was sitting on the

10

rise in front of the house, under the sentinel mesquite that marked the drop-off to the bottoms, listening for cow sounds in the *brasada* below.

Presently his ear picked up another and obtruding sound: the muffled walking in deep loam of an unshod horse.

Hush slipped back to the house and took down from its deer antler rack in the dogtrot the rust-brown shotgun which had come from England with Jupe Feleen's grandfather. It was a fine antique piece, with carved outside hammers and percussion locks, double-bored, twelve-gauge and cylinder-choked for market fowling.

He quickly loaded it with #2 buckshot and was ready with it when Diego Santimas shuffled his linebacked dun pony up out of the river brush and guided him across the clearing to the dogtrot.

"Buenas dias, señor," said the Mexican patriarch. "I am Diego Santimas. I have lost a trail and wonder if you might help me find it?"

Hush did not understand a great deal of Spanish, but he had picked up enough to make out that the old Mexican had called him "mister."

"Yes, sir," he answered carefully. "What was it you was running?"

"A big yellow *ladino*," replied the old man. "A real *anciano*, one who has been in the *brasada* as long as I."

"A big yellow *what*?" said Hush.

"Ah! you must excuse me," replied the other. "I forget that you are new to this land. A big outlaw steer, *señor*. A true *bayo coyote*, a yellow lineback dun like this slender pony of mine. Have you seen such a one?"

Hush looked at him, thinking hard whether he should tell him.

He had, indeed, seen such a steer, and not long before. He had been sneaking through the brush, downriver, not ten minutes gone. He had made no more noise than a white owl in the moonlight, but Hush's wonderful ear needed no more than that. Now he wondered anxiously about talking to the old Mexican, or even having let him come on the place. It was certain Jupe would not be pleasured to find him there.

"Well, *señor*?" said Diego Santimas.

"I seen him," blurted Hush, unable to bridle his curiosity. "Why for you want him? What's he did?"

"Nothing. He is a *cimarrone*, an unmarked one. Someone has castrated him long ago, but did not get to brand him. Now I would put my mark on him before the next man. It is the way we live here in the *brasada*."

11

"You mean you're a mavericker?" Hush burst out.

"But of course, señor. Are you not the same?"

Hush shook his head, but his eyes shone with excitement.

The "mavericker" in Texas was the man who rode the brush and the prairie after the war, gathering and branding with his own mark the wild Spanish cattle running free in the *brasada*, not always being too careful whether he ran his brand on clean hide, or over the existing mark of some previous user of the long rope and the running iron. From his time in Brazoria, Hush clearly understood the venturesome and dangerous connotations of the term.

Now he shook his head again and said very carefully, "No, sir, we uns ain't in it. Pap don't cotton to cows."

"But *you* do? Is that it, *niño*?" queried the white-haired Mexican, just as carefully.

"No, sir, I didn't say that," denied Hush, suddenly fearful that he was talking away too much to a man he had never seen before. "I seen the steer, like I told you. He went down the river, thataway. And I wisht you'd go arter him right off, Mr. Santimas. I surely wouldn't want my Pap should catch you on our land."

"*Gracias*, young friend," said the other, not turning his horse.

He eyed the worried Tennessee boy a moment, then added:

"When a man gets old, *niño*, his eyes are not so keen as they once were. You can tell me where this *ladino* went, but it would be a better thing for me if you could show me his track. The young eye is the only one for following a real outlaw. Will you not help me, *señor*?"

"You mean for me to run that critter's trail for you?"

"*With* me, *niño*, *with* me," corrected the old man. Then, softly, "The best time to learn a thing is when we are young. I can teach you what you want to know, *hijo*."

"What you mean?" said Hush, not daring to raise his head.

"I can read your face when we talk of these wild cattle of ours," answered the old man. "You have a feeling for them as much as I. You had better go with me, boy."

"Oh Lord, I cain't!" groaned Hush, sorely tried. "I dasn't even think of it. Pap would skin me alive. He will, anyways, happen he hears abouten me talking to you."

"Let us go, *muchacho*," the old man said again, gathering his reins. "I will tell you all I know of the wild Texas cows."

It was too much for Hush Feleen.

"Wait up!" he cried, his gray eyes sparkling now like struck flint, and he wheeled about and ran for the horse shed and Jupe Feleen's little Morgan mare.

CHAPTER 3

"To begin with," said Diego Santimas as he and Hush picked up the dun steer's trackline and turned down it along the river, "a few names and a little history. So—"

He paused, pursing his lips with that ruminative look off into nowhere which is the mark of old men about to tell a story as dear to them as the next breath of life.

"I have said already that the *cimarrones* are the outlaws of the breed. Especially are they cattle of the old, all-wild strain. Now, the *ladinos* are much the same, save for having been a little civilized. *Ladino* means crafty and cunning. They are like that, like the coyote; having had some experience of man, they are that much more difficult to hunt or trap. *Mesteños* is our name for cattle which, while unbranded, are yet to some degree herdable. They are ones which may have had a riata on them at one time, but escaped to return to the *brasada*. *Mesteños*, mustang cattle, that is what we call them. The older name for them is *orejanos,* eared, or unmarked cattle."

He interrupted his remarks long enough to stop his horse and get down to examine the dun steer's hoofprints.

"Aha!" he cried. "Exactly as I thought. He has passed this way but minutes gone. We are coming to him beautifully."

"How can you tell?" asked Hush, down off the mare and squatting beside him in the leafy mold.

"See," said the old man, pointing carefully, "there is a broken snail track across the hoofprint. The glaze is still moist. It has not had time to dry. The glaze of a snail's path sets very quickly, in only in a few minutes."

"But how did you spot the snail's sign?" persisted Hush.

"The sunlight shafting down through the mesquite caught the fresh gleam of it for me."

"You mean you saw that much from the saddle?"

"But of course, *niño.* How else?"

Hush looked a little surprised and hurt. "You fibbed abouten your eyes being bad," he said.

"No, no, boy. I only said they were not what they used

13

to be. In the old days I could have read that snail's story riding by it with my pony on a lope. Do you understand what I say, young friend?"

Hush understood, and not only about the example of a snail's glaze being brighter at thirty than at sixty years. This old man's eyes were still sharper than most younger men's. Why, then, had he wanted Hush to go with him after the dun steer?

Remounted and going forward again, Hush said what was in his mind.

"Mr. Santimas, why for you brung me along with you? You can see good enough to read a Bible under a bed."

The old Mexican thought it over. Presently he shrugged.

"I knew you wanted to go; that is all there was to it."

"No," said Hush, "that ain't all there was to it, neither. Sure, I wanted to go; and sure, maybe you could see that I did. But that didn't fetch you outen the brush and over to our place to begin with. Why for did you come?"

"To see you, *niño*."

"Me? Why, that's daft. Who'd want to see me?"

"I would," said Diego Santimas. "I have watched you for many months. Oh, you did not know that I did!" He smiled as he saw the doubt darkening Hush's gray eyes. "But then, neither did you see the snail's track. Is that not so, *niño*?"

It was so, and Hush had to grin at the sly way the old rascal had boxed him.

"All right," he smiled back. "So you've been spying on me. What'd you see?"

"A very lonely boy," replied the dignified Mexican. "A tall boy and a strong boy. Yes, and a boy *muy duro*, very tough, as well. Yet still a lonely boy. *No es verdad?*"

"What more?" queried Hush, feeling moved but not wanting to show it.

"I saw a boy I thought would make a fine *hombre del campo*, a real man of the wilderness. I thought I could help you to become that, and that you could help me in the bargain."

"Now just a minute," objected Hush. "We been all through that."

"No, no, I do not mean about the eyes, boy. That was a small lie; I admit it."

"I wisht," said Hush plaintively, "that you would admit whatever else it is that's eating on you."

"Very well," agreed Diego Santimas with a slow smile. "It is that I, also, am lonely. I had a son many years ago. An only one, about your age, *niño*, tall like you, and dark—"

14

His voice tightened and Hush murmured understandingly, "Sure, Mr. Santimas, sure." Then, after a properly decent pause, "By jings, Don Diego, iffen you're a mind to make a *hombre del campo* outen me, we'd best get a hustle on. Happen we don't stir ourselves right smart, that cussed steer is apt to drift clean inter San Patricio County."

The steer came out of the chaparral like a charge of cannister, point-blank.

Hush was riding three pony-lengths behind Diego Santimas and the yellow *ladino* did not see him. He saw only the old Mexican, for whom he had been waiting beside the trail, and when the latter had ridden past his covert he broke from it to race away along the backtrail. In midleap of his second jump he slammed his right horn into the little Morgan mare. Throwing her into the air with one thrust of his great neckcrest, he charged on and was gone from sight before Hush, clawed out of the saddle by the brush, fell to the ground and came to his feet, unhurt.

He was in scant time to dodge aside as Don Diego's dun gelding flashed by him after the steer. The lithe pony smashed into the solid wall of the thicket and was gone as instantly as the outlaw steer before him.

Hush turned to the mare. She was dying from the terrible gaping hole the yellow devil had horned into her flank. Hush kicked around in the brush and found the shotgun where it had fallen when he and the mare separated. Ordinarily a man would not waste a charge of shot and powder where a knife across the gullet would do the work as well. But he couldn't knife that mare. She was seventeen years old, being a yearling when Hush had come into the world. She wasn't a horse, she was a Feleen.

"I'm deep sorrowed, Nellybell," he whispered. "It ain't fitten you should suffer because of me." He knelt swiftly and for a last moment caressed the velvet plush of the nose skin above the nostrils. The mare whickered and sighed. "Rest easy, rest easy," said Hush, and put the left tube of the twelve-gauge behind her ear and pulled the trigger.

The blast of the weapon was still muffling off into the brush when Don Diego's voice came shrilling from the river.

"Aqui, niño! Adelante! adelante! I have him, come quickly!"

Hush turned to the sound of the voice, staring blankly. Then, deliberately, he put the shotgun's other barrel on cock. "I'm coming," he called, and stalked into the brush.

He moved, eyes straight ahead, without regard to the whip and thorn of the thicket. When he got to the clearing where

15

Don Diego had the outlaw longhorn roped and snubbed to a live-oak sapling, his face was streaming red from a dozen brush-cuts deep enough to spread open and curl back at the edges like knife wounds. He walked on past Don Diego as though he did not see him, going directly toward the steer, the shotgun hanging from his right hand.

"Cuidado!" shouted the old man. "Take a care, boy! He has the rope to turn!"

Hush did not hear him.

The dun steer was a twelve- or fourteen-year-old incorrigible. At the tip of his harsh-haired withers he stood as tall as the youth who now walked toward him. In his gaunt-flanked body, with its cat hams, narrow hips and ridgepole spine, he carried a near ton of bone and muscle. When he lifted the seven-foot spread of his moss-hung horns, his great flaring ears were almost eight feet above the ground. From the bloodied tip of his right horn a shred of the mare's intestine still dripped. The side of his head was wet and dark where it had twisted along the mare's ribcage in tossing her. He was a sight to strike the gripe of fear into the bowels of any Texas man afoot within forty rods of him. But Hush Feleen was from Tennessee. He was a stranger to Texas and her wild cattle and to the fear of anything on four legs or two when the Feleen anger was in him, as it was now.

He walked straight into that ton Texas steer, and when he was close enough he put the shotgun's muzzles into the brute's bawling mouth and blew away the roof of its mouth and the entire back of its shaggy head.

The dun *cimarrone* grunted, blew blood froth all over the dark-faced boy before him, slid to its knees and dropped its great horned head to the dirt. The gray-black muzzle came to rest six inches from Hush Feleen's left boot.

"Santissima Maria!" breathed Diego Santimas from the clearing's edge, and it was over.

When Hush came again to the grassy break in the *brasada* which was the Feleen ranch clearing on the north bank of the Nueces, the sun was an hour down.

He stood a moment at the edge of the thicket, listening to the sounds he loved in the night around him.

Upstream, he heard the deep grunting "bruh-huh-huh" of a herd bull coming to water with his cows. Down the river a ways another bull, this one without cows, answered with the more staccato "huh-huh! huh-huh!" of the bachelor announcing his irritation with the challenge, but not really offering to take it up. Deeper in the thicket a band of

16

collared wild pigs—*javelinas,* the Texans called them—were rooting for yucca bulbs and making their familiar "chop-chomp, chop-chomp" feeding noise. Other, lesser sounds of the Nueces night were laid over and beneath the main ones. In his minute of delay before going in to face Jupe Feleen, Hush sorted out a vixen's yapping, the hooting of a cactus owl, the overhead twitter of a bullbat and the raucous squabbling of a roost of wild gobblers blundered off their live oak perch by some climbing varmint, most likely a bobcat.

For another long breath or two, Hush thought about not going in at all. He considered facing about and going back into the brush and staying there. But that wasn't the Feleen way. A Feleen didn't run. He didn't turn his back on an obligation, lie about a debt, or fail to pay a levy that was due and collectable against him.

He shifted the army saddle which Jupe Feleen had stolen off an Illinois cavalry horse at Second Manassas and brought home on the mule Grant had given him at Appomattox Courthouse—the same mule that would no longer tighten a breast-tug alongside the little Morgan mare—and slung the battered hull over his shoulder and went on across the clearing.

At the dogtrot Old Blue heard his boots scrape and came roaring out of his barrel to take his leg off. He got his nose belatedly full of the family smell and was instantly on the ground squirming and grinning and urinating upon himself in abject apology. Hush didn't stop to scold him. He just stepped over him and said, "Hesh up, you damned old fool," and went in past the hanging cowhide that covered the cookshack doorway and grounded the shotgun butt on the dirt floor and stood looking at Jupe Feleen.

Jupe returned the look for a long five chews on the venison chop he was eating.

"Well, boy?" he said at last.

Hush settled himself harder onto his planted feet.

"You hearn where I went, Pap?" he asked.

"I hearn."

"You aim to hide me for it?"

"I ought, don't you figger?"

"I reckon. But you ain't going to."

"How's that agin, Hush?"

"Pap," said Hush stoutly, "I got the mare kilt today. It were my fault and I mean to work it out and to pay you for her, full price. But that's all I mean to do. You ain't going to whup me for it, nor for talking to that old

17

man and going along with him. I'm growed, Pap. You just ain't noticed it."

"No?" drawled Jupe Feleen, tossing the chopbone to Old Blue and getting up from the plank table. "What happened out yonder?"

"Me and Don Diego, that's old Santimas, the Mexican up the river, we was trailing a dun steer he wanted to put his brand on. The steer was a *ladino*, a bad one, and he laid up alongside the trail and got a horn into Nell afore I could move to stop it. I ain't begging the blame, Pap. I'm just saying you done laid the cat to me the last time. I'm man size, Pap, and I bin toting my share of the load."

Jupe was at the deerhorn coatrack by the stove now. He looked at his soft-voiced son, then at the rawhide dogwhip hung on the nearest antler tine. He took his hand away from the whip, and when he spoke his voice was as quiet as Hush's.

"You figger you're too big to whup, now, is that it, boy?"

"I don't figger nothing, Pap. Just don't come at me no more with that cat. *Please* don't do it, Pap."

Jupe Feleen was neither a mean nor a vicious man. But the Feleen code was narrow—and hard. Jupe's hand reached again for the whip.

"Hush," he said, "you know you done wrong and you know I got to whup you for it. Git yonder acrost the table."

Hush did not move.

His father's jaw twitched. "Hush," he said, "git yonder."

Hush only watched him, his last word spoken.

The elder Feleen understood, then, how it was going to have to be. He came across the room, spread his feet, set his teeth and swung hard. He hit Hush once across the body, shoulder to hip. He recovered and hit him again. On the third whistling cut, the boy's hand shot out and seized the whip-wrist. Twisting, Hush got a hip into his father's side and threw him heavily to the floor. Jupe started to his feet and Hush hit him with the stock of the shotgun. Jupe didn't move after he went back into the floor dirt.

Hush sank down beside him, the fear big in his eyes and in the agony of his low cry.

"Pap? Gawd, oh Gawd, answer me, Pap! *Please*. Pap—?"

It was then he knew his father was not going to move, was not going to answer him. He straightened, the first sense of what he had done turning him sick inside. As he rose, he caught the sound of a slight noise outside, and leaped for the cowhide door curtain.

Across the dogtrot, young Arnie stood rubbing his eyes and gaping sleepily. "Hullo, Hush," he mumbled. "Whar the hell you bin? Is suthin wrong? Seems I hearn a ruckus out here jest now."

"Speak soft, Arn," said Hush. "There's been trouble. Step out here past the trot, so's we kin talk."

Arnie followed him a few steps into the outer darkness.

"Arnie," Hush said, "Pap's yonder in the cookshack, bad hurt. I had to gunbutt him. He came at me with the cat agin, and I seen red. I was trying to belt him acrost the withers and got him alongside the head instead."

"Gawd!" the younger boy breathed.

"Arn," Hush went on, "you go get Lubelle but don't wake the young uns. I don't want they should see Pap that way, his pride gone. You and Lubelle get his head cleaned off and wropped up, and you see he don't lack for nothing it's human possible to provide, you hear?"

"Jesus, yes, I hear, Hush. You taking to the bresh?"

"I got no choice. Pap'll want to kill me sure. Now there's only two things, Arnie, that I want you should remember hard."

He waited, giving his brother time to make his slow nod.

"First, I want you to tell Pap that iffen he comes arter me, he'll want to do it with bear loads in Old Betsy. He won't be hunting no bresh rabbits. You got that?"

Arnie nodded that he had it, and Hush went on.

"Second, I want you should never forget that iffen you or the young uns suffers any grief you caint handle, you kin find out where at I am from the old Mexican up the river."

He put his lean arm quickly about the other boy's shoulders.

"Now, Gawd bless you, Arn, and don't you be afeered. I'll be nigh iffen you need me."

"Sure, Hush, sure. But what iffen—"

Arnie broke off his question uncertainly. He turtled his head forward into the murk of bottom mist rising from the river. "Hush," he called, "whar the hell air you? Quit your funning, now, Hush. Hush, you hear me—?"

But Hush did not hear him He was already gone over the bank into the eerie blankness of the river brush.

The only answer was the lonesome sound of a loafer wolf mourning down the moon far out across the Rio Nueces *brasada*.

CHAPTER 4

Hush had meant to live out in the brush and become a mavericker. But very quickly he decided the cattle were in better shape to wait than was his stomach. The *brasada* night was just turning to daybreak when he was quartering up the river looking for the telltale wisp of mesquite smoke which would lead him to the old Mexican's place. He managed to spy it out and walk it down in time for noon dinner.

Hush liked the Santimas *jacal* from the minute he got free of the thicket and saw its adobe brick and woven thatch construction. The odor of cornmeal *tortillas* being deep-fried in antelope fat for the midday meal added to the good impression. And the whiff which followed it of simmering lean beef stewed in a sauce of little red *chilipiquines* finished the decision for him. Hush went forward, hardly able to get out his "hello" for the hunger he was feeling.

Recognizing him at once, the white-haired Mexican greeted him warmly and invited him to come and partake of the food being readied by *la señora*. Glad enough to accept, Hush responded with an awkward *"Muchas gracias, Don Diego,"* which was taken favorably by Diego Santimas. The title "Don" means something more than "mister" in Spanish. Hush figured it was sort of Mister with a big M; and that was tolerably close to Spanish meanings for an American boy.

So he and the old man went around the *jacal* to meet Doña Anastasia, an agreement without signatures having already been made between them, each as happy as the other that they were come together again, each thinking how good it would be if the partnership could be made a permanent one.

The beginning toward that end was highly promising. That morning Hush moved in with the Santimases and began his life with them as the son of the house. Their days together were full of rich learning for the boy and rewards of the spirit for the childless Mexican couple.

Doña Anastasia was convent-educated. She spoke English with a Spaniard's mind but with a textbook's exactness. Gently, persistently, she corrected Hush. Gradually, in the days and weeks that followed, not even realizing the change was taking place, he came to express himself as well as most privileged folk of his day, and did it without losing any of the knife bite of his Tennessee idiom, or the honeyed edge of his hillman's drawl. She taught him, as well, to write his name, to print the letters of the alphabet, and eventually to read.

Before he had mastered the latter accomplishment, it occurred to him to have Doña Anastasia read him the writing on the Bible page Jupe had given him. Taken with the idea, he thought about it a long time, but did not ask her to do it. Weeks later, he had begun to put a few letters together to make words, and he decided he would wait until he could read it himself, just in case it contained something only a Feleen should see. Meanwhile, he was too hard-worked to worry about it.

What kept him busy was the *brasada* side of his learning. Don Diego did not fail this, his part, of the assignment. In that fall of 1874 and winter of 1875 he taught Hush all there was to know of the wild longhorn cattle and the vast thicket of thorns which was their home.

The original seedstock, Don Diego thought, must have been the Spanish *ganado prieto,* the fighting "black cattle" of Old Andalusia. A second strain, apparently derived from the first yet somehow differing from it, had developed in Mexico over the next two centuries. This produced the *ganado mayor,* called "common" or "Mexican" cattle to distinguish them from the original, or Spanish stock. They were of a uniform coloring, a deep brown or black body with light dunnish toplines and undertrimmings. The third strain was that of the "tame" or "cold-blooded" cattle brought to the New World from Old World sources other than Spain. From this latter line, some claimed, although Don Diego himself denied it, had come the bewildering profusion of color varieties found in the present-day Texas cattle.

These hues were, to mention not even half of them, brindle, blue, mulberry, slate, dun, pure black, pure white, bay, brown-splotched, gray-speckled, pure red, red-peppered, palomino, cinnamon, toast-beige and bright liver chestnut.

As to the patterning of these colors, the linebacks, yellow bellies, brindles and mealy noses—cattle with light fawn rings around eyes and muzzles—were the most common variations. Nearly all the Mexican cattle were of the mealynose marking, and it was perhaps the most persistent of all the color types carrying over into the modern Texas cattle.

There were many *brasada* beliefs about the wild longhorns, some true, some not true.

Because of their high withers and curly heads, there was the claim that the bulls were crossed with buffalo. This was nonsense, of course. Then there was the conviction that a

21

wounded or pursued animal would trail back and lay up alongside his own trackline to charge and kill his human follower, and this was absolutely true. More than one good friend of Don Diego's had died just that way.

It was said the wild cattle would fight with their feet, like deer. The Texans even had a saying, "to kick like a bay steer." Not true, said Don Diego; they were horn fighters, these cattle, nothing else. Their favorite hook was an upward cut for the belly with the master horn. This was the dreaded *saca tripas,* the "get the guts" slash.

It was a fact that the lean-uddered cows were more dangerous than the great high-headed bulls. This followed the axiom of the old country bullring breeders that if one wished to know how the bull would fight, he should flag the cow. "As the cow, so the calf," the Spaniards said. The Mexicans, Don Diego thought, said it better: "Fight the bull but fear the cow."

Much could be learned about the wily longhorn by listening to these old sayings about him, both Texan and Mexican. "He never lingers long enough in the open to leave a shadow" suggested his extreme wariness. "Lean sides make a long nose" told that his bad nerves were due to his being eternally half-starved. "He will scent water as far as a Spanish mule" demonstrated his unbelievable sense of smell. And, "By his side a tiger is as tame as a school teacher" left no doubt as to the wicked quality of his temper.

Certain other facts about the breed could be counted on. In windless air a longhorn could get the scent of the nearest waterhole at ranges of from four or five to ten miles. He could "feel" rain fifteen miles away, and would walk that far to meet a storm. Following the rain was a regular trait of the longhorns. They knew there was a certain type of grass which broke the earth within twenty-four hours of a good shower. Invariably the cattle would be there waiting for the yellowish sprouts to come through the softened earth. It was one of the ways they survived in a harsh land where drouths were an endemic disaster.

In the spring, as regular as calving, the longhorns would migrate to the salt and sulphur licks. They would travel as far as a hundred miles, returning to their home range as soon as their needs were satisfied.

The age of an animal over three years could be told by the wrinkles on its horns, counting one wrinkle for each added year. The left horn was generally more uniform than the right. Also it fitted the body curve of a right-handed man, and so was the one most used in making powder horns.

An animal with one drooped horn was common, and was called a *chongo*.

Longhorns made a hoofprint different from that of tame cattle. It was neater and sharper, deeper and less splayed. And hoofprints varied, according to whether made by cow, bull or steer. All four hoofs of the cow were sharp. Only the front toes of the steer were sharp. The bull was notably blunt-toed all around.

Distinguishing marks by which a man could, at a glance, tell a longhorn from all other cattle were the wolf-high withers—"thin enough to split a hailstone," the Texans said—and the extremely long, heavily tasseled tail, which dragged the ground when the animal was at rest. In good light a man could always determine the longhorn blood by the coarse brown hair growing fiercely bristled about the huge ears. The same sort of harsh hair often grew in a ridge, or roach, like that of an angry dog, along the crest of the withers.

The ways of the Texas cattle when confronted by the danger or the actuality of capture were devious and desperate. Ringed about by riders in a gather, or "surround," the brutes would literally crawl on their knees through brush so low a child's head would show above it, and so escape to grow wickeder and wiser another year. Forced to hide out in the driest growth, they could exist up to eight weeks without a drop of surface water, chewing the scant moisture out of the prickly pear cactus. Confirmed outlaws of the breed would fight to the death to stay free, charging a man on horseback as quickly as one afoot. When roped, they frequently had to be shot to save the life of the rider who had put his riata on them. If brought to bay, subdued by terrible brutality and dragged off toward imprisonment, they possessed the strange power to will themselves dead. They would suddenly stop, slump to their knees, shudder and be gone.

"Sulling," the old man told Hush, was what the Texas cowboys called this peculiar trait. The Mexican vaqueros, as might be expected, had a more poignant name for it. The brave bull or valiant steer had died *acolambrao*, of a broken heart.

With these lessons in wild-cattle lore, Hush was given equally careful instruction on the thicket which nurtured and protected them.

He came to know as old acquaintances the mesquite and black chaparral, the fernleaf lesser catclaw, the true catclaw, called wait-a-minute, the little treelike colima, the evergreen granjero, the coma with its winter-born white flowers of jasmine sweetness, and the huisache, that spectacular spring bloomer of golden, aromatic clusters.

Besides these, there were the sun-yellow bursts of the retama, the green- and black-spined palo verde, the gray cenizo which burst into glorious lavender bloom after each rain and which was, for a wonder, thornless.

By the second spring in the *brasada*, the Tennessee boy could point out, as well, the iron-fibered guayacan, the velvety leather plant and the agrito, whose currantlike fruit made the superb wine-red jelly the tangy elegance of which, as brought out by Doña Anastasia's secret brown-sugar recipe, he would remember as long as he lived. He also knew the riotous nopal, or "devil's head," with its multicolored waxen flowers and red and purple prickly pear apples, the spiked tasajillo and pitahaya cacti, the Spanish dagger, the sawtoothed maguey and the jonco, called the "cursed jonco," which had only thorns and no leaves whatever, and of which, Mexican legend insisted, the crown of the Crucifixion was woven.

All these things old Diego Santimas taught him about the savage cattle and their thorny covert in the shinnery, the great brush-thicket pastureland of southeast Texas. By early spring of 1875, Hush was as ready to take up the riskful trade of mavericking as skilled instruction could make him. He knew how to braid the four- and eight-strand, sixty-foot rawhide Mexican riata, and in the use of this he had become a real *hechicero de cuero*, a real "wizard of the leather." He could horn, heel, break, snub, stretch or bust his cow with the best of them, and he was a real artist, too, with the *peales*, the short strands the maverickers carried for "tying down" their captives to take the sap out of them.

There were other vicious ways, to tame the wild cattle. Recalcitrant bulls were "towed" by a rope around their cod bags. Incorrigible fighters had their eyelids slit and sewn up with rawhide thread. A bullet fired through each horn close to the skull, where the quick was, would take the anger out of the fiercest steer. Hamstringing a rear leg slowed down the wildest runner. Wrapping the hocks to stop the circulation would cripple any resister. And a very bad one, *un ladino puro*, with horns like an oxyoke and a heart full of murder, could be made to walk like a pet lamb by slashing open his nose, nostril to nostril, with a castrating knife. Don Diego told Hush of these ways but taught him only the tying-down technique, for he would not practice the greater cruelties of the other cow hunters.

Finally, there was one remaining thing about the wild-cattle trade which was the most important of all.

Before a hide, or an animal, could be sold it must be marked with the brand of the man who was the seller. This had been the law of Texas since the 1840's. The man who violated it was gambling with his life. If caught marking a calf sucking a cow that had upon her another man's brand, or if come upon while altering some other man's brand to resemble his own, or burning his own mark on cattle he was being paid to put another man's brand upon, the mavericker faced the rope.

Such justice was never referred to courts of law, but administered at the scene of the crime.

Just recently—Don Diego thought it was in 1870—the state had set rule and dates for working the wild cattle. A man now had to wait for these dates before he could heat his iron. Then, on the dates, everyone went out and branded at the same time. Thus it was a fair thing. Men who anticipated the legal dates were known as "sooners." The fate they faced was the same as that of the brand changer or calf stealer.

Nevertheless the temptation to evade the law was strong. The dry-humored Texans had two good ways of saying it: a man's branding iron worked faster than a billy goat; or, his cows always had quadruplets.

Such easy gains, Don Diego warned, must be eschewed as the very kiss of Judas Iscariot. To die by the rope was a disgrace upon any house. Hush must always remember that.

He, Don Diego, was poor. He had, in all the world, no more than a good wife, a dry roof, and a few things to eat and wear. But he had never coveted his neighbor's ox, nor branded his cow, nor stolen his calf. In this way he would die without wealth, but with honor and in peace. If his foster son would do likewise, let him remember well the Biblical law of life in the Nueces wilderness: *Thou shalt not steal thy brother's cattle nor their increase.* To violate that law would lead inevitably to the mesquite limb and the shadow of boots which dangled but did not move.

This final word was sealed in Hush's memory by an exchange which took place between the old man and himself upon his query as to what all this talk of the rope had to do with him, Hush.

When the question was put to him, Diego Santimas got that faraway look in his eyes.

"There was once," he replied, "an Apache chief named Delgadito. He was famous among his people for his ability to elude the American soldiers who were sent out to bring him to justice for his many crimes of robbery and murder among the white settlers. He was, in a word you now know well, a human *ladino*.

"It was said by his friends and by those who knew him

25

when he was a young brave, that he had been handsome and well-formed, with never an evil thought nor act remembered against him. It was his terrible sense of avenging wrongs that had been done him which led to his downfall. He could not control his dark anger, his passion to punish those who had harmed him.

"Gradually, even his own kind grew afraid of him and turned against him. It was then he became the hunted one.

"There is no need to tell you how his story ended. Where a man will seek to be a law unto himself, there can be but one end for him. God has written it so. It was no different with Delgadito."

He let his words fade, and the silence grew until Hush said, "But I still don't understand, Don Diego. What is it you would say to me?"

The old man pursed his lips, nodding slowly.

"The name of that Apache chief has come to have a special meaning—a very bad one—here in the *brasada*. The most cunning and dangerous of the longhorn outlaws, the ones that will put the horn into you for no reason save that you are in their way, we call *delgaditos*."

He paused, moving his shoulders helplessly, and Hush had to prompt him once more. This time when he answered he took fewer words. But Hush did not have to question him again.

"You will recall what you did with the shotgun to the dun steer, *niño*?" he said. "The one that gored your small bay mare? Be careful, my son. Discipline your dark angers. Do not think always of an eye for an eye."

Then, with quiet dignity, he added: "Do not hook blindly for the guts, my son. Remember the story of Delgadito."

CHAPTER 5

It was a day in May, lovely with high clouds and a balmy tropic wind drifting in from the Gulf, when the time came for Hush to leave the Santimas *jacal*.

He had determined to set out toward the northeast, exploring for a place to maverick closer to the coast and the Brazoria tallow works, where he hoped to market his poor-quality carcasses. He had in mind the Guadalupe River country, the beauty of which hung in his memory undimmed from his first sight of it twenty months gone.

His plan was that, after finding a suitable location, he would return and fetch out to the new place old Diego and Doña Anastasia. It was in his mind to fend for the elderly couple in their advancing years, so repaying them in some small measure for their kindness to him.

He was eighteen now, a month past. Taller than ever, he had developed his hill-country heritage into a prairie man's vitality.

As was natural with a youth growing up in the mountain-laurel country of the Cumberland watershed, and then among the chaparral of the Nueces basin, he had developed characteristics peculiar to the wildlife which was his constant environment. Animalistic comparisons were inescapable in the case of Hush Feleen.

His distrust of other human beings was that of the out-settlement coyote. At the same time, his insistence on watching them, but from afar, was wolflike. He had an eye only a little less keen than that of the red-tailed hawk, and his tendency to leave his lookout perch and glide away to safety was no less swift. His ear was tuned to catch and translate sounds, even down to that of a muskrat sliding into slough water. His nose was trained to sort out the slightest shadings of scent. He could walk as quietly as an ocelot, run with the tireless energy of a mustang stallion, lay a trail or backtrack one as cunningly as a black brush bull.

Yet with all these acquired traits of wariness, Hush was a young man of good heart. As he set out from the Santimas homeplace that May morning in 1875, armed with his excited hopes and his old rusted shotgun, there was no thought in him of anything save hard work, high ambition, and minding strictly Don Diego's parting injunction to "tend to your own troubles and the troubles of your neighbor will tend to themselves."

But life is not governed by well-meant advice.

Hush had not traveled an hour from the house of Diego Santimas when he swung, whistling happily, around a bend in the shinnery trail and came face to face with Jupe Feleen.

Hush was afoot, having no horse of his own and having refused Don Diego's parting offer of Gato, the old man's tawny dun cow-hunter. Jupe, too, was afoot, but not because of being without a mount. Andy Jackson, the one-eyed mule from Appomattox, stood droop-eared on the other end of the rope which ran from Jupe's saddlehorn to the left hind foot of a big brindle *ladino* stretched and tied down alongside a tiny branding fire over which Jupe was crouched as Hush came around the bend.

27

The father came slowly upright, he and his dark-haired son locking eyes across the smoke of the mesquite coals.

Seconds passed. Neither spoke, neither moved. It was Jupe, finally, who bobbed his head.

"Hush, boy," he said.

"Pap, good old Pap," responded Hush.

They stood there, and kept on staring. Hush felt an ache in his throat. He didn't dare try to talk.

"You wintered good, Hush," said his father, after a long heart-filled time of looking.

Hush only nodded, still mute.

"Growed some," said Jupe. "Filled out a mite, too."

"Pap," Hush blurted, "I'm plumb sorry about what I done to you. It was a wicked thing. I've been meaning to come home and take my whupping ever since."

"It's did, boy, and you ain't never going to take no whupping from me, not ever again." Jupe dropped his gaze. The silence returned, lengthened, grew awkward once more. Finally Jupe looked up. "Reckon I'm some sorry, too, Hush," he said. "Yes, and some wrong, likewise. We uns all been mightily hongry to see you, Hush. Happen you'll come home, we'd sure be pleasured."

It was a hard thing for his father to say that, Hush realized, knowing the fierce Feleen pride the way he did. "Thank you, Pap," he said. "I allow I'll not forget that. And, Pap, I'm beholden you don't hold no ill against me. I was moral wrong, you know." Then, after another painful wait: "How's little Jodie Beth and the others, Pap?"

"All tolerable, thank you, Hush. Jodie Beth she come up a mite peaked this spring, but she'll gain with the warm weather."

"Sure," said Hush, "sure she will," and silence fell again.

"Pap." Hush shifted his eyes to the ash-gray tip of the running iron in his father's hand. "What you doing with that straight-rod iron?"

"Marking cows for old Avery Hudspeth. Gitting fifty cents a head for all I kin burn. It ain't fast, but it's cash money."

Hush looked narrow-eyed at the flank of the brindle steer.

"Hudspeth's brand is a Rocking H, Pap," he said.

Jupe dropped his eyes again, but Hush did not.

"Pap," he said, "that's a Lazy J, and it's still smoking."

The older man shook his head obstinately.

"I cain't make it no other way, Hush. I got to do it. I burn one for Hudspeth and one for me. It ain't exactly honest, but it ain't as bad as burning over another man's brand, or mavericking a calf offen a already marked cow."

Hush looked at his father straight and hard.

28

"It ain't no different, Pap, happen they catch you at it."
He glanced swiftly around the clearing, and hurried his next
words. "Pitch that damned iron into the brush. Kick out
that fire and cut loose the steer. We got to get out of here."

"A good idea," said a dry, flat voice from the edge of the
brush, "but a little late in the day."

Jupe and Hush did not hurry to turn. They knew what
the words meant, and to whom the voice belonged.

"This is my boy Hush, Mr. Hudspeth," said Jupe. when
they had come around with slow care. "He's been away."

The mounted man's expression did not change. "He should
have stayed away," he said.

"Howell," he added to one of the three riders with him,
"shoot that steer. We got to get on."

Hush felt the small hairs rise along his nape.

In that country it was the custom to kill the animal with
which the cheating mavericker was caught, leaving it, with
the mavericker, as evidence of guilt at the scene of the capture. Also, the branded carcass was intended as a warning
to other ambitious thieves who might ride by it. The connection between the sprawled steer and the swaying corpse
above it needed no footnotes of legal explanation.

"By God, Mr. Hudspeth, you wouldn't do it!" he muttered aloud, unbelievingly.

Hudspeth looked at him. He was a hard-fat, gray-bearded
man, no seeming kindness nor generosity in him.

"You know the law, boy," he said. "You've been here better than a year."

"But it ain't no law excepting what's been made up right
here in the *brasada*, Mr. Hudspeth. You know that. It ain't
the *real* law." Hush had been well taught by Diego Santimas
and he was right in what he said. But men of Avery
Hudspeth's kind were not interested in rights, only in reckon-
ings.

"It's all the law we got," he answered, without expression.
"And it's all the law we need. Howell, gun that steer. We
don't get started back, we'll be late for noon dinner."

The pulse in Hush's throat nearly choked him. He shifted
his grip blindly on the ancient shotgun.

"You mean to tell me," he gasped, "you'd hurry a man's
death to be on time for your dinner, Mr. Hudspeth?"

Perhaps a shadow of doubt stirred on the rancher's heavy
face, but he did not answer.

"It's blowing up to rain bad, boys," he said to his men.
"Let's get on with it."

Hush stepped back and brought the barrels of the shotgun
up on a line with Avery Hudspeth's belt-buckle.

In this country, if a boy was old enough to carry a gun, he was old enough to use it.

"Mr. Hudspeth," he said, "you ain't getting on with anything. Now you call off your men and you get out of here. I'll see you get paid for every steer Pap's marked. But if you don't do as I say, this minute, I will blow a hole in your belly you could run a yearling heifer through. Move out, Mr. Hudspeth."

"Howell," said Avery Hudspeth, "hold up."

The lean rider checked his pony, slewed around in the saddle.

"Yes, sir," he responded. "What'll it be?"

"You hear what the boy said?" asked the owner of the Rocking H.

"Yes, sir. You want I should persuade him different?"

Hudspeth only nodded and the cowboy turned to Hush.

"Boy, drop that shotgun," he said.

Hush quartered around so that he could see the speaker while still covering Hudspeth.

The rider was thin, thin all over. He had a sallow, dark face; eyes deep-set, quick, never still. His pony was angled toward Hush so that its rider's left leg was cleared. On the thigh of that leg, low and laced down, was a bone-handled .44 Colt.

"Drop the gun," repeated the rider quietly.

Hush was on the point of doing it, then realized the monstrousness of what these men intended. It was his father, Jupe Feleen, they were meaning to string up. The thought of that terrible thing—the mean, small unfairness of hanging a decent man for a pitiful thing like branding a handful of wild cattle to feed himself and his four kids by—brought the dark blood rushing into Hush's desperate face. He suddenly had no fear of the varmint-eyed rider, or of his fat employer.

"Sure I'll drop the gun," he said softly to the leather-faced man. "I'll drop it on you, you murdering bastard."

He did not see the movement of the man's left hand. Yet the orange flame burst from that hand the instant Hush spoke. The .44 slug struck the bunched muscle of his right shoulder-cap with the force of a lightning bolt. It blasted him off his feet and back onto the ground hard enough to bounce his whole body like a slammed-down rubber ball. He saw a thousand pinwheel lights, then nothing but an echoing blackness.

The light returned slowly. He was not lying on his back now. He was turned over on his stomach, hands pinioned behind him. Beyond him, similarly stretched and tied, he saw his father. The older man caught the movement of his son's head, struggled to turn his own so that he might look directly at him.

"I'm turrible sorry, Hush, boy," he told him. "I explained how it was for them, but they wouldn't have the truth. Remember, we're Feleens, son."

It was only then that Hush realized Hudspeth and his men had assumed he was working with his father, and were going to hang them together. The shock of it brought him acutely conscious.

He bowed his spine to raise his head, straining to locate Hudspeth and the others.

The Rocking H men were twenty feet off, standing by their ponies, talking in low voices. There appeared to be some argument going on about how the execution was to be carried out. Hush heard the gunman, Howell, say he thought the thing to do was put a bullet through the head of each of the captives and save the waste of two good ropes. Hudspeth, however, was adamant. For a cow thief, hanging was the only remedy. Let Mason and Pettigrew get their rope over yonder mesquite limb as ordered, and no more talk.

Mason and Pettigrew shook their heads. In the end they had decided they couldn't do it.

"All right," rasped Avery Hudspeth. "Cut and ride. Draw your pay at the homeplace and don't let the sun rise on you in this country."

The two men got their horses. They hesitated, at the last, as though they might yet side the boy and his father. Jupe saw the doubt on their faces and cried out to them.

"Fer Gawd's sake, boys, don't let them hang the kid! I swear afore Christ Jesus he didn't have nothing to do with it. He just come upon me burning the steer, same as you all. He's been away from home all winter and you kin prove it from that old Mexican up the river. Tell 'em, Hush, boy. Fer yer Ma's sake, son, speak out and save yourse'f!"

Avery Hudspeth pushed past his two hesitating hands. He came to stand over Hush.

"Is that so, boy?" he asked him. "That you wintered in with old Diego Santimas?"

It was his chance, his last chance. But Feleen pride would not let Hush take it. How could Jupe Feleen's son whine and crawl to save himself, then stand by and watch his father die alone? Hush stood taller and set his jaw. His heart pounded so wildly it jarred his sweat-soaked shirt, but his voice came soft and unafraid.

"You go to hell, Mr. Hudspeth," he said.

The cattleman's broad face paled. He turned to the thin-lipped gunfighter and said, "Howell, bring the ropes. The kid was in on it."

"Now wait, Mr. Hudspeth." It was Mason, the smaller of the two discharged riders pushing his pony forward. "Maybe you'd ought to check for sure with old Diego. It'd be a turrible burden on your mind to find out later you was wrong."

The paunchy rancher stared at him, expressionless.

"Howell—" he said.

The gunman dropped his left hand.

"Git," he told the two men.

The latter exchanged helpless, guilty looks. They glanced at Hush and Jupe, each man making a gesture like a pointless little wave, as though to ask their forgiveness. Then they looked back at Howell to make sure they had read the sign of the dropped hand correctly. They had, and they turned their mounts and were gone, with their shame, into the shinnery.

Howell and Avery Hudspeth got on with it quickly. They walked their captives to the mesquite limb. Hudspeth fixed the ropes about their necks, while Howell and his left hand stood guard. When the rancher had the nooses rove to suit him, he threw the free ends of the ropes over the limb and ordered Jupe and Hush to mount his own and Howell's ponies.

Jupe moved his head from side to side and said they would have to put him up on any horse. Hush said quietly, "Double that for me."

Hudspeth stepped to his pony, pulled his Winchester from its scabbard, relieved Howell of the guard. The latter walked up to Jupe and kneed him in the groin. Jupe twisted forward, writhing in agony, and Hush, crying out like a wounded animal, crouched to spring at Howell. The muzzle of Avery Hudspeth's carbine barrel bit into the small of his back, bringing him upright.

"I wouldn't try it," said the fat rancher, and Hush, not wanting a bullet-smashed spine, didn't make the move.

Instead, he turned to Jupe. "Good-bye, Pap," was all he said. "I'm mortal proud to have been your boy."

"Good-bye, Hush," Jupe Feleen answered. "I'm fitten proud to have had you."

It went still more quickly then.

Howell forced the groaning Jupe onto one of the ponies, Hudspeth doing the same for Hush on the other. The gunman then made fast the ends of both ropes to live oaks on the far side of the gallows limb, taking up all slack in his tying-off. This done, he took his quirt, stepped behind the horses, nodded to Hudspeth standing at their heads.

"Hang onto the bastards."

With the words, he yelled out and cut viciously with the whip at the rumps of the mustangs. The ponies jumped as one, lifting Avery Hudspeth off his feet in holding onto their headstalls.

Jupe Feleen and his tall son fought against the strangulation with all the hard, mountain strength that was in them. They jerked and kicked at the ends of the knotted ropes, making muffled, terrifying sounds in their struggles to breathe.

Howell and his employer got on their ponies, the rancher unable to watch the slowing life's fight of the Tennesseeans. Howell, however, proved willing enough. He studied the suffocating men, then wagged his head in grudging wonderment.

"Jesus Christ!" he said. "They sure quit hard. Look at them lash out. God Amighty, they'll last another full minute."

Avery Hudspeth gritted his teeth.

"Put a bullet into the poor devils," he said to Howell. "It's not Christian to let them kick that way."

The gunhand shrugged, palmed out his Colt, threw three shots from the hip at each of the twisting figures. He saw both bodies buck to the impacts of the big slugs, then holstered the .44 and swung his mount easily around.

"All right," he nodded. "We can go now—it's Christian."

The two went swiftly out of the clearing. Not even Howell looked back at the slumped weights spinning slowly at the ends of the ropes. It was as well that he did not. Jupe Feleen was dead, but the third of the shots fired at his son Hush had missed its human target and clipped into the rope which supported the unconscious boy. Before the last breath of life had gone from him and before the last hoofbeats of his would-be stranglers had faded away into the *brasada,* the weakened rope lengthened at the break and began to spin backward. It jerked haltingly, and gave way.

CHAPTER 6

The stars were out. It was very quiet in the *brasada.* Hush lay on his back where he had fallen beneath the hanging tree. The return of awareness was slow. It was some time before he realized he was alive, and then a long time before he gathered the will to do anything about it. When he tried

33

to move he felt a great torture in his left shoulder and right hip. He lay still again, trying to think.

He made out a few things. The strand of rope hanging from his neck had been cut. How, was not yet clear. There was a sound behind him—the grinding of the cusps of an old horse or mule grazing. He said, "Ho, Andy, is that you?" and the old mule grunted and blew out through his nostrils in recognition of his voice. He knew, then, that Hudspeth and Howell had not troubled to cut the mule free from the dead steer, and that he had a mount if he could reach him. But he had been shot and was badly wounded. It felt as though both bullet holes had gone clear through; but, bad as they were, both had caked over with clot-blood. Provided a body was painfully careful, he might move without breaking them open.

Past these simple facts his mind refused to go. He only knew he was hurt, and that he must somehow get to the mule.

It took him an hour. An hour in which each inching motion was a nightmare of sickness, a belly-sinking ebbing away of his tiny strength. But at the end of the time he had reached Andy Jackson and hauled himself up. With the last fragment of will in him, he found the handle of his beltknife and cut through the riata binding his mount to the stiff-legged steer. He did not remember falling forward along the mule's roached mane, nor the wise old animal's careful, slow start off through the downriver tangle of the shinnery.

Arnie Feleen went into the sleeping side of the dogtrot house and told the twins to hold down their rumpusing in bed, before they woke up Jodie Beth. Then he blew out the candle which he always left lighted for Jodie Beth to go to sleep by, and went back outside, where he had been sitting with Lubelle.

They watched the stars and listened to the river for a considerable spell; then the boy said:

"I don't like it, Pap being gone so long. You figger I'd ought to go out and cast around for him?"

"No," answered his sister. "Why fer? You cain't see to blow your nose out thar."

"That's so, I allow. All the same, I got the fantods. Suthin's went wrong."

"Nothing's went wrong. He'll be along directly."

Arnie shook his head, not convinced. "I'd ought to be out working with Pap these days. I'm going on fourteen."

"You ain't been going on it long," said Lubelle drily.

"Long enough," countered the boy. "Hell's fire, Hush was

34

hunting meat back home when he wasn't no more'n twelve."

"We uns ain't back home, and you ain't Hush," the girl reminded him. "Besides," she added, wanting to take the sting out of what she had just said, "hunting meat ain't the same as hunting cows. Not by considerable, it ain't."

"Reckon that's so," agreed Arnie, mollified.

They sat another spell, but before long Lubelle said, "Arn, go fetch yer gittbox. I crave a tune."

The boy got the instrument and hit two or three chords. "What'll it be?" he asked.

"Play Pap's favorite. Could be it'll toll him in outen the bramble patch. Or leastways cheer us up."

"I don't cotton to that song just now," complained Arnie. "I got a funny feeling about Pap."

"Arn," said his sister patiently, "suthin'n allus giving you a funny feeling. You got the fantods half the time. Play Pap's tune."

The boy bent his shaggy head over the rosewood box of the guitar. He began chording softly. As he went along, he flowed into picking the melody, single-noted, blending chords and lead notes smooth and easy. There was not much Arnie Feleen was apt at. But when it came to fingering the frets of a six-string guitar he could, Lubelle allowed, make an overseer throw away his whip and kiss the nearest nigger. There was nothing he couldn't play, and no tune he played better than "On Top of Old Smoky," Jupe Feleen's favorite.

But now the boy ran through only two choruses before he stopped with a discordant plunk of his thumb across the strings.

"The hell!" he said glumly. "It ain't the same without Hush to sing harmony, and Pap to play the mouth harp."

"No," sighed Lubelle, "it surely ain't." Then, after a moment, "Arn, why for you suppose Hush never come home arter closing with Pap? You reckon he was feared of Pap?"

"Not him, Lubelle. Not Hush. Hush never was feared of nothing in his hull life."

"All right, take Pap, then. Why for you figger he never went arter Hush and brung him home? Because of Hush warning him not to try it, you reckon?"

"No, hell, no! Pap don't know no more fear nor Hush. That ain't it, Lubelle, not fear. Never. I figger it was more a kind of love."

"Of *what*?" exclaimed the girl.

"Love, I said," nodded Arnie soberly.

"Well, hardly!" snorted Lubelle. "Not them two."

"No?" insisted the slow-voiced boy. "Well, now, I dunno. You know what I think, Lubelle? I think Hush and Pap was

35

hungering suthin' fierce to clinch hands and make up agin. I allow Hush was mightily took with pride in Pap, and I *know* Pap was secret fond, and special, of Hush."

"So? How come you to know that? Warn't he allus riding Hush abouten him being like Ma, softlike and gentle with critters and kids?"

"It's what I mean, Lubelle," said Arn. "To Pap's thinking, Hush was most like Ma, and Gawd knows Pap loved Ma more'n he done his own life."

"Reckon that's so, Arn," murmured his sister. "Reckon that's mighty certain so."

They sat quiet again, listening to the night, and were still sitting there without talk when Arn suddenly raised his head.

"I hear Andy Jackson a-coming down the river," he announced, getting up and going out from the dogtrot. "Tarnation, he's grunting fit to bust his cinchbuckle. Must be packing a full buck, or a half of Rocking H beef."

Lubelle heard him move away from the house and call out.

"Great Day, Pap! What you toting home this time?"

Then she heard his gasp and sharp cry.

"Pap! Pap! Gawd Amighty, Lubelle, come a-running. He's hit mortal bad!"

The girl leaped through the darkness, coming to Andy Jackson's sweated side in time to help ease the lank figure of his rider to the ground. "Leave him lay till we see how desperate he's hurt," she said to Arnie. "Fetch out the candle and some rags to wipe him clean afore we tote him in," she added. "He's sopped with blood. Gawd, smell it! Like a fresh-stuck shoat."

When Arnie got back he couldn't light the candle, his hands were shaking so. His sister took it from him, her hand steady as her voice. Reaching in her apron pocket, she dug out a lucifer and scratched it across her hip, like a boy. It flared, sputtered, burned steadily.

"Jesus save us, it's Hush," she said, and dropped the match.

They got him into the cookshack and cleaned him off.

By the time Lubelle got the shoulder tied up and a cowdung poultice put to the hole in his right side, Hush was sitting up drinking chicory coffee. He was still showing the gray of shock in his face, but the worst time had passed. The bladebone of the shoulder wasn't broken and the wound in his hip seemed to be nothing worse than painful, though the hip was stiff. With a sling for the left arm and a night's rest, he would be able to travel by morning. Trouble was, he didn't have until morning.

36

"Lubelle," he said, "I got to get on tonight. They'll be here tomorrow to see about you kids."

"They?" Lubelle's voice had the Feleen softness in it. "Who's they, and how come they'll be here?"

Hush told them about their father then, sparing them what he could of it. There was a minute of quiet when he had finished, then Lubelle nodded.

"I knowed he was doing it," she said. "He was trying to git up the cash money to take Jodie Beth inter Fort Worth. Thar's a new cutting doctor thar. Feller come down from the North just recent. Pap was told he was skillful fine."

"Well," said Hush, "Pap done wrong, according to Texas law. The doctor will have to wait a spell on account of that. But I'll promise you we'll get Jodie Beth to him one day soon."

"Hush," said Arnie plaintively, "what you aim to do right now? Skin on down the river and hide out in the brush?"

Hush stood up, the effort whitening his face. He had to push the words out between his gritted teeth.

"I ain't going to skin nowhere, Arn," he said. "Get the spade. Lubelle, lead the mule."

They left the children sleeping, and set out through the shinnery. Hush was on Andy Jackson again, Lubelle and Arnie walking on either side to catch him if he fell. They had not far to go. When they came near the dark savannah where Jupe was Hush called a halt.

"Wait here," he said. "I'll go ahead."

He rode on to the clearing and across it to the mesquite tree. Leaning from the saddle, he sawed at the riata until it parted and Jupe's body thumped to earth. He got down off Andy Jackson and cut the noose free of his father's neck, throwing it from him violently as though it were a hoe-chopped snake. Only then did he call softly to the others to come along in.

Arnie dug the hole, and Lubelle spelled him. As they worked, Hush limped around in the grass, hoping his old shotgun had been overlooked by Howell and Hudspeth, and it had. He found it where it had fallen from his grasp, behind a silvery quebradora bush. Using it as a cane, he made his way back to the grave.

"That's deep enough," he muttered. "The Mexicans say the coyotes won't uncover what's guarded by the cross."

His brother and sister looked at him quickly.

"You fixing to put a cross over Pap?" said Arnie. The idea struck him as mighty strange. "Him feeling like he done about preachers and all?"

"Preachers ain't God," said Hush Feleen.

"I dunno," put in Lubelle anxiously. "Seems to me Pap might not rest easy under the sign. He was powerful agin the Bible—you know that, Hush."

"The Bible ain't God either," said Hush. "I seen Pap praying over Ma's grave when we come away. He was talking to God. He believed. Arnie, take his head."

There was no more argument. Between them, Arnie and Lubelle rolled the body of Jupe Feleen into its shallow last resting place beneath the sandy loam of the Nueces bottomlands. When they had patted the final spadeful of dirt into place, Hush planted atop the mound the mesquite-branch cross he had bound together with the rawhide *peales* from the dead steer. Then he stepped back, saying quietly, "Can anybody pray decent?"

None of the Feleen children had been inside a church. The family Bible had not been read since the death of Nancy Hushton. Lubelle shook her head.

"Me nor Arn cain't, Hush. How abouten you?"

Hush glanced up at the broken sky. For just a few seconds he watched the low-lying clouds drift across the face of the waning moon. Then he began.

"I know that Jupe believed," he said slowly. "I seen him once on his knees and talking like I'm talking now, with his face turned up to you. Happen you heard him then, maybe you'll hear me now."

The tall boy paused and looked down at the grave of his father. He added in a low voice:

"God help him that rests here by the river."

Then, staring out across the crowding stillness of the great thicket, he said so softly that neither Arnie nor Lubelle caught the whispered meaning of it:

"And God help them that put him here."

CHAPTER 7

It was four o'clock in the morning when they left Hush at the edge of the brush on the downriver side of the Santimas clearing. By his order they did not tarry, but climbed on the mule and rode double back into the night. There was need for hurry. Hush had told them to get Jodie Beth and the twins and hide out in the thicket until Avery Hudspeth had come and gone in his looking for them. If the rancher found them they would be taken away and raised in foster homes, after the frontier custom. The folks in that country had had plenty of experience taking in the orphaned young ones of their neighbors. "Comanche kids" were the commonest kind, but there were many other ways, such as bad horses and mean cattle, by which a man's children could be left to local charity.

Hush had no intention of seeing his family parceled out up and down the river. He was the eldest son; it was his place to look out for the others. So he had told Lubelle and Arnie what he wanted them to do—lay up in the brush until he sent for them—and so they now urged old Andy Jackson down the river to do just that.

True, it was a hard thing to lose their Pap. Especially to lose him in such a wicked, wrong way. But it was a grand thing, to have old Hush back again. With Hush, a body never had any doubts. You could take Hush's hand in the darkest night, walking with him with your eyes wide open, and never need fear for your shins nor your face nor anything in between.

These thoughts comforted Lubelle and Arnie Feleen as they rode Andy Jackson through the night in the race to beat daylight and Avery Hudspeth to the twins and Jodie Beth.

Their brother Hush, hesitating on the edge of the *brasada* east of Don Diego's *jacal*, had no such faith to buoy him up. He shivered as the dawn wind whipped up from the river and struck into his hunched form. The fever was raging in his wounds now. He was running sweat like swamp rain. The bite of the wind shook him until his teeth chattered. He was sick, very sick.

He spread his legs, lurching forward, forcing his head to stay up and his eyes to remain fixed on the *jacal* door.

Halfway to it, he knew he would not make it. His insides were swimming again. He heard a voice, faint and far away. It was calling for help in Spanish: *"Socorro! Socorro! Ayudame! Ayudame!"* but no one was listening to it, and he realized it was his own voice, crying inside his whirling mind, making no outside sound at all.

He did not feel the ground when it came up and smashed him in the face like a great, black-loamed fist.

It was there Don Diego found him at five that morning, huddled twenty feet from the *jacal* door, face-down and not moving.

It was many hours later, nearing mid-afternoon, before he stirred and a little of the color of the blood of life

39

flowed back into his waxen features. But from that moment, Hush began to mend.

His recovery was aided by the insistence of Don Diego and Doña Anastasia that the other Feleen children come to live with them. Not upon any temporary or charity basis either, but as their own flesh, with all the honors and privileges of the home.

Some lingering pain and weakness aside, the following weeks were memorably happy ones for Hush. During that time he saw that the *brasada* adoption of his brothers and sisters was going to take. It was particularly cheering to watch Jodie Beth. The long-motherless baby of the family followed Doña Anastasia around like an orphan range colt with an aging foster-dam. It was not so much that she showed any marked outward sign of improvement, as that something had taken flame inside the lonely little girl and its radiance shone out of her eyes like candlelight.

This alone would have rewarded Hush, but Doña Anastasia meant equally as much to the other youngsters—and, indeed, they to her. And also important, she gave them of her education, providing them the same opportunity to improve themselves which she had granted Hush. They loved her for the chance. All of them, that is, save the slow-smiling Arnie. The others took to the alphabet book, the goosefeather quill and the precious store-bought paper like dusty ducks to a summer rain.

Sober Lubelle especially, being older, appreciated the gift of learning. She proved quick, too, much quicker than Hush, and well before the latter was strong enough to travel she was writing fluently and reading aloud to the twins at a clip her embarrassed older brother couldn't begin to match with his full year's headstart of practice.

In all this, naturally, Don Diego was not idle.

The twins were now ten, Arnie fourteen. All three were old enough to be shown the facts of *brasada* life, the only art of existence known to the silvery-haired *brasadore*. Although none of them took to the lore of thicket and longhorn the way Hush had, their willingness to try was payment enough for Don Diego. The old man and his wife, so long childless and so long full of the love for children, began to dream a little and to talk guardedly of "their family." It seemed not improbable that in their old age God meant to bring them a happiness for which He had been preparing them, by denial, all the years since the death of little Diego. If this were so, *Dios lo permita*, then the blessing for it must go to the tall, soft-talking boy who had come to them out of the *brasada* these many months past, and

40

who had changed their entire world into a place of reborn hope and new purpose.

For his part, Hush shared this sentiment, and he was, thereby, more than ever determined to make good in his search for a new home, in a new country, where they might all make a fresh start.

So it was that when the time came, late in the summer, for him once more to set out on his interrupted journey to the Forks of the Guadalupe, he was able to do so with a free mind and a sure heart.

It was late in the darkness of his last night on the Nueces. There were the beginnings of a good rain slanting in from the upriver country. The wind was on the rise.

In his snug bed beneath the slope of the loft room shared with his three brothers, Hush let his limbs go slack, let himself drift off to the drowsing dance of the rain on the roof thatch above him. The stillness of the house beneath the patter of the summer storm was broken only by the gentle breathing of the young boys sleeping beside him. Hush sighed, and drifted gratefully deeper into sleep.

The sudden raging clamor of the two Santimas cattle dogs on guard at the stock corral brought him up out of his blankets, his heart pounding. Before he could move to leap for the loft ladder, a series of rifle shots—at least half a dozen—blurted through the rain. There was a sharp yelp from Lupe, the bitch of Don Diego's fierce brace, and a crying snarl from Lobo, the dog. Then there was nothing, no sound whatever outside the Santimas *jacal*, save only the increasing whip and drive of the wind.

Hush went down the ladder without his boots, running for the gunrack beside the front door. Don Diego was there before him.

"It is no use, *hijo*," he said, putting his hand on the shotgun. "Nothing can be changed by adding your life to those of my two old friends out there. The dogs are dead, my son. I forbid you to join them."

The low-spoken words stopped Hush as no argument of force could have. He dropped his reaching hand.

"*Quien estan?*" he asked quietly.

"*Los Indios,*" replied the old man.

"Indians?" said Hush, surprised. "What Indians?"

"Comanches, if they came for the horse only. Apaches, if they also took the mule."

"How does that make sense?" Hush asked.

"The Apaches prefer roast mule to antelope or fat cow," explained Diego Santimas. "The Comanches would not step down from the ponies to steal such a lowborn mount. If

41

your shaggy-eared friend is there in the morning, and Gato is not—" At the unhappy thought he broke off, letting the pelt of the rain take over. Quickly, Hush put out his hand in the dark, finding the old *brasadore's* shoulder.

"If Gato is not there in the morning," he said to him in Spanish, "do not despair."

Then, with a chilling gentleness, he added, "If the Indians have taken your horse, I will trail them *a la muerte*, to the death. You have my word on it, *padre*."

With first light, Hush was outside. Despite the early hour, he found that Don Diego had come ahead of him to the high adobe wall of the stock corral. And he found that he had already translated the story of last night's tragedy.

The Indians had been Comanches. For proof of that, there was the old mule grazing over there beyond the small *magote* of huisache, that small island of golden flower.

There had been seven of them, but only six horses. This explained why such a band would stop at a poor, one-pony dwelling. No doubt they had been raiding in the settlements and had lost one of their mounts in the process. They had seen the good horse in Don Diego's corral, and they needed that one pony very badly.

They had gotten Gato out of the corral by whipsawing the wet adobe with a knotted riata, cutting a hole in the rear wall wide enough to pass the horse out and never going near the gate in front, where they might have been shot at from the *jacal*.

The forms of Lupe and Lobo told their own sad stories, the bitch sprawled at the edge of the *brasada*, the dog stretched out with his nose just touching her paw, to which position he had dragged himself a hundred feet after being shot four times through.

Now the best thing to do, the old man told the scowling boy, was to forget this evil thing which had happened. Forget, too, he urged, the dark vow made in the excitement of last night's emotions. In no situation whatever was it safe for a white man alone to go after seven Indians. In this case, where the man was but a boy riding an old Tennessee plow mule, and the Indians were Kwahadi Comanches mounted on the finest Texas mustangs, it would be sheer insanity. Besides, was not one adopted son worth a thousand stolen cowhorses?

"Come now," smiled the old man, putting his gnarled hand on Hush's arm, *"que dice, hombre?* What do you say?"

Hush brought his eyes up from their study of the Indian pony tracks. He took Don Diego's hand gently off his arm, patting it reassuringly between his own two callused palms. "I say go catch up the mule, *padre*," he told him. "I will get the saddle and the shotgun."

"The shotgun, *hijo*? Why would you take such a weapon?" The old man waited, his surprise showing in the quick squintlines at the corners of his eyes.

"Porque no?" asked the tall boy, pausing in his stride toward the *jacal* door. "Is there a better weapon for getting the guts?"

Hush had never seen a wild Comanche, but this did not deter him. He could trail anything that left tracks, and these Indians were leaving tracks. As for what they looked like, he was satisfied he would know them when he saw them.

He was right. When he came up with the Kwahadi raiders —it was the third night out, in a cottonwooded swale along a nameless creek just north of the Rio Grande—it was abundantly clear to him that he was spying on Indians, and that, moreover, they were the Indians he was looking for.

There were seven of them, as Don Diego had said. It had rained and turned off chill that afternoon. They had a great fire going—none of your little Indian blazes for them —and were drying out their shirts, leggings and breechcloths. They were, squatted to the warming flames, stark naked.

Their ponies, Gato among them, were being grazed on horsehair *cabestros*, staking ropes, rather than being loose, or hobbled, as would be the case with familiar stock. From this, Hush was certain that Gato was not the only stolen mount among them. It was another certainty that the band had run into shooting trouble somewhere down the Nueces. Best hazard in that direction was that the Texas Rangers had jumped them. But Rangers, or whoever, the Indians had taken on a load of somebody's lead not long ago.

Four of them were wincingly stiff with new wounds. Of these, one had an arm in a bowstring sling. Two others could walk only if helped. The fourth couldn't walk at all. As Hush watched, two of the Indians had to cross their arms and carry this one away from the fire to relieve himself. Three of the Comanches seems to be uninjured.

So far, so good. What now?

Hush had wisely left Andy Jackson a mile back, tied and nose-wrapped in a dense *magote* of black chaparral. The land hereabouts was not like the Nueces *brasada*. There was a lot more grass—the open stretches just went on and on. What brush there was, was in the draws and arroyos. And

43

there was none of it between the Comanches' fire and Hush's hiding place.

Down by the creek were cottonwoods and willows flanked by a scattering of live oaks and jack oaks. But in the line of any sneak-up that Hush could take directly toward the camp, there was not a solitary tree. If he went in flat on his belly the high grass would hide him maybe, but grass had a nasty habit of waving at its tops when nudged at its roots. Unless a man was hankering to get himself harvested by a hail of rifle bullets, he would do well to forget about belly-sneaking any seven Comanches in tall grass.

Well, what then?

The daylight was going fast. Autumn was only around the corner of August, and the light wasn't lasting as it had only a few weeks ago—especially on a drizzly afternoon. Hush scowled anxiously. Full dark would be down in half an hour. It didn't give a body much time to make up his mind.

He stayed there in the wet grass, shivering, twenty minutes, thirty minutes . . . still no idea came on how to do it.

At the end of almost an hour all he had accomplished was a set of the bone-chill shakes. For three days he had been riding hard on a mule that was gaited like a hybrid buffalo. The weeks of convalescing hadn't toned his muscles any. He was cold and wet, and if he lay any longer in that grass, he was going to wind up with nothing but double pneumonia for his vow to bring Gato back to Don Diego. True, he had promised he would trail the cussed horse *a la muerte,* but he hadn't been thinking of that "muerte" in terms of catching his death of cold.

Suddenly the idea did come. . .

Down by the fire, the three uninjured Indians were starting to tend the wounds of their four brothers. Watching them, Hush was struck anew with how seriously hurt were three of the four. In any kind of a surprise face-out, those three could be pretty sure counted out of things. On the other hand, if you gave them any warning and let them get into the trees, the hurt Indians could fight as lively as the well ones. The picture was fairly simple. If you wanted to cut your odds to four-to-one, there was a way to do it: belly in as close to that fire as you could, then stand up and walk into them, cold turkey.

In the last minute of turning the plan over in his mind, Hush thought of Don Diego and the story of Delgadito. He hesitated, strangely uneasy.

In getting back that dun horse the way he was figuring,

somebody was likely to get hurt, most likely mortal hurt. A man didn't like the idea of that, naturally. But then, honestly and fairly, was it Hush's fault things had come to this pass? He couldn't recall inviting any Comanches to come along up to the Santimas' *jacal* and help themselves to that prize lineback cowhunter of Don Diego's. No, sir, Don Diego needn't worry. Hush wasn't hooking blind. The red devils had brought it on themselves; they had it coming.

The lean white boy nodded to himself with the decision. He was in the moral right.

Rolling carefully to one elbow, he broke the breech of the shotgun, checking its loads. He set both triggers then and there. To do so any nearer to the Indians would be to risk them hearing the cocking clicks. The gun ready, he eased back on his stomach and started inching forward. He took his time. There was no hurry now. He knew what he had to do. He was absolutely certain that he could do it.

CHAPTER 8

The Indians were talking.

"I do not agree," said Crow Horse, the brave with the wounded arm. "This was a good fight, but not the best I have been in."

"Yes," said Roan Calf, his closest friend, "there was the time we went all the way to the Big Water."

He meant the Gulf of Mexico and, indeed, in that late day it was a very daring thing for Comanches to raid so far east in Texas. It could be believed the Kwahadis might have encountered more trouble that time on the Gulf than they had just run into on their venture down toward San Patricio on the Nueces.

"Say what you will," said Tall Walker, the brave who had opened the argument by contending that their San Patricio raid should be listed among the tribe's more difficult exploits, "we took great chances, and for very little gain."

"I do not say that," broke in Big Belly, the badly wounded one. "Look at the ponies we have gathered. That *bayo coyote* we took from the Mexican's corral back there on the river, that one will go a week on wind and water, and finish stronger than he started. He is a real *kehilan*, a real one of the old pure blood, that yellow Spanish horse."

"I will take the black mare," said Tall Walker. "She is

45

more of the size. The yellow horse has too much leg under him. Remember what the *vaqueros* say, 'Praise the tall but saddle the small.' I will take the black mare."

Sand Crane, who had ridden Gato from the time of the theft, spoke now. "And who is to get the *bayo coyote*? I agree with Big Belly. The yellow horse is the one I want."

"I, too," said Roan Calf. "Let us see who will take the tall yellow horse."

"Do not bother to see," said a soft voice in white man's Spanish from the misty dark beyond the fire. "I will take him."

The seven Indians froze like red squirrels at the sound of the hunter's footstep cracking a twig underfoot. They seemed almost to flatten to the ground without visibly moving a muscle. Not one of them turned his head.

"Quien es? Who is there?" said Tall Walker in Spanish after a careful wait. *"Amigo o enemigo?"*

"Enemy," said the voice.

"A donde esta? Where are you?" asked Tall Walker, stalling for time.

"Here," said Hush, and he stood up in the matted grass fifteen feet from the fire.

His appearance so close to their fire, the face he could have crept in so near without the least sound to warn the acute Comanche ear, was disconcerting to the Indians.

"What do you want?" said Tall Walker, his wild nerves in no way quieted by the fact that not one of his companions had his weapon to hand, while their visitor's shotgun was wandering their circle with a slow sureness which at once put in question the first thought that here was only a boy to contend with. He was a boy, yes. But such a watchful-eyed, quiet boy as Tall Walker could not remember seeing among the white men's children. One might expect an Apache youth to do such a thing as this one had done, but it was scarcely like a white boy to crawl up alone on seven Kwahadi Comanches. Much less to stand up out of the wet grass and calmly say that he came as an enemy. There was something very wrong here, and Tall Walker and his friends would do well to go slow until they found out what it was.

"Estamos a la mira," he side-mouthed to his companions. "Let us be on the lookout. I do not think he is by himself."

To Hush, he repeated with deliberate loudness: "What is it you want, boy? Why do you come here?"

Hush shifted the shotgun.

"I want that yellow gelding. He truly belongs to my

46

father, who is Don Diego Santimas, and I intend to return with him, or to die. *Comprenden Ustedes?*"

It was surely not the way Hush would have said it in English, but Spanish was another tongue—and the only one in which he could communicate with Comanches, who generally spoke it.

"Yes," the Indian leader answered him, "we understand what you say, but we do not understand how it is that you have the courage to say it."

"Test me," said Hush.

Tall Walker thought about this. He thought about it hard. And the more he thought about it, the less he thought of it.

"No," he said, "I do not believe I will. Sand Crane, go and get the yellow horse."

"Get the black mare too," said Hush.

Sand Crane, who had started to do as Tall Walker told him, stopped short.

"The black mare?" he said.

"The black mare," nodded Hush.

"Why is that, white boy? Why will you also take the black mare?"

"To teach you never again to steal from me, or mine. Get the mare."

"I won't do it," vowed the brave angrily. "She is ours."

"Yes," said Tall Walker, coming slowly to his feet. "Why should we give you the black mare, boy? What is this talk of stealing? She was never yours. We have given you back your yellow gelding, now take him and go. Better hurry too. We might change our minds about testing you."

"Stay away from that gun," warned Hush, as the tall Comanche moved his feet six inches nearer the live oak against which his Winchester leaned. "And don't change your minds about testing me."

He paused, searching for the proper way to say it. He didn't like talking right and wrong with a bunch of naked red heathens, but neither did he want them, any more than anybody else, thinking Hush Feleen didn't know the difference between outright horse stealing and what he was proposing to do. Finally, he did the awkward best he could.

"If you steal from a man and you are caught," he told Tall Walker, "then you must pay back more than you took. There must be some extra repayment made for the wrong you have done him. You took a horse from my people; I am taking a horse from your people. Now I want that horse, and no more talk about it. Do you understand me, *hombre?*"

47

Tall Walker looked at him with a long, hard stare. At last he nodded.

"Bring the black mare too," he said to Sand Crane.

It was then the whole gamble came to where Hush had feared it might when he cocked the shotgun and started in. But he had made his ante and seen their raise. If the Indians were going to raise him back, he would have to call, or get killed.

Sand Crane hesitated. That was a beautiful black mare, and there were seven of them against one skinny white boy, who did not look too well. Tall Walker was within hand's sweep of his rifle leaning against the little tree. Sand Crane's own gun was propped on that cottonwood log, no more than a rolling dive away. Back by the fire, Roan Calf, the third of them without a wound to slow his speed, was squatting only a pony-length from where his fine Sharps buffalo gun lay on a flat rock by the little stream.

Sand Crane's glittering eyes shifted to Tall Walker, who made a little nod with his head, a nod which no one but a Comanche could have noticed. Sand Crane flicked his glance to Roan Calf. Roan Calf inclined his dark locks an inperceptible degree. This was the time.

"Eee-yahh!" yelled Sand Crane, and made his leap and roll for the cottonwood log. In the same instant, Tall Walker and Roan Calf made their separate moves.

Hush shot with the double twelve at hip level.

He caught Sand Crane with the left barrel at less than thirty feet. Swinging to his right, he got Tall Walker and Roan Calf in a line and pulled on the crossing. The charge opened up the right side of Roan Calf's ribcage and went on to strike Tall Walker with sufficient force to knock him to his knees. He staggered back up to his feet, still trying to get to the live oak and his Winchester. Hush bounded past him, seized the rifle, whirled and crashed its steel-shod butt to the side of his head.

This time when he went down, Tall Walker did not get up.

Hush stepped over his huddled body. Leveling the Winchester on the four wounded Comanches at the fire, he said to the one with the armsling:

"Bring the black mare too."

Crow Horse considered the order briefly.

Over there behind that cottonwood log lay Sand Crane, instantly dead of a wound which would have killed a running buffalo. By the small stream, Roan Calf, the friend of his childhood, moved yet a little as he died of the fearful hole in his side from which the blood poured. Down in the bank loam, not moving at all, was Tall Walker. He could be either dead or alive. It mattered no great amount which . . . not at this moment.

Crow Horse got up from the fire. "Yes, I will bring the black mare too," he said, and went to untether the two mounts.

The other Indians said nothing, did nothing; they only sat there looking at their youthful threatener. It was as well for his future ability to sleep at night, that he did not comprehend the nature and intent of the red men's still-eyed regard.

In the Indian philosophy relating to the laws of such events, trails always crossed again. They never ran forever parallel from the point of origin. Tonight's trails would be no different. They would meet again.

Against that time, in preparation for that distant, certain happening, the Comaches were doing a very simple thing. They were memorizing the face of Hush Feleen.

CHAPTER 9

Hush never told Don Diego about the dead Indians, yet somehow the old man knew.

When he returned with Gato and the slim black mare, the venerable *brasadore* said only, "Was there trouble, my son?" and Hush replied, "Yes, a little, *padre*. Nothing really."

At that, Don Diego cocked his white-maned head.

"Well, my son," he said, "I am glad you have returned safely and that you have brought back to me my good dun horse, but I hope the price you paid for the black mare was not one which left you in debt to the Indians."

"I settled with them," answered Hush, and there the matter was allowed to remain.

After a few days' rest he felt surprisingly strong, and decided it was time to get back on the road for the Forks of the Guadalupe. The weather was turning and the hint of fall in the September air put a stir in his blood which would not permit of further lingering.

On the day he rode out, Don Diego saddled Gato and went with him a ways up the trail. It was evident to Hush that the old man had more on his mind than saying good-bye out of sight of the others. Accordingly, he halted the mare and broke out one of his rare, quiet smiles.

"Padre," he said, "I know I deserve the *lectura* you are

about to deliver, but pray do me a favor. Make it short. I want to see if the mare will go fifty miles today."

Don Diego nodded.

"Let me see now," he began, running his eyes speculatively over Hush's outfit. "You have a fine saddlemount, a trusted old friend in the mule to carry your pack. The dog"—he pointed to Old Blue, who sat waving dust circles with his tail in the shadow of Hush's mare—"clearly means to share your journey and should provide good companionship until you are ready for the family to join you. Ah, that will be a proud day for me, my son, when you send for us. *Ay de mi!*"

"It will be a proud day for both of us, *padre*," said Hush, genuinely pleased. "But you were examining my *equipaje*. What is it? Have I forgotten something?"

Don Diego squinted carefully.

"No, I think not. There is the fine rifle and the big buffalo gun which you acquired from the Comanches. They should keep you in meat. You have the shotgun as well, another old friend. You have your blankets, your cornmeal, your coffee. *Quita!* It is enough. A good horse, a good gun, a good dog; what more does a young man need to conquer the world?"

"A little advice perhaps," said Hush.

"Ah yes," sighed the old man. "Ah yes—"

He grimaced, tugging at his snowy beard.

"My son," he said, "I will be brief. You have but one enemy to fear in this world. It is he I would warn you about."

"*Que enemigo es eso?* What enemy is that?" asked Hush, curious.

The old man was direct with his answer, and succinct. "What enemy but yourself, my son?"

Hush studied him, gray eyes dark with worry.

"*Padre,*" he said, "you must tell me exactly what it is you mean to say. Don't lead me on a blind trail."

Don Diego sighed again, waved his hand in acknowledgment.

"All right, my son, I will tell you. Many of us have hot blood when we are young. That is a known thing, and accepted. But if our wild anger leads us to take a life and then our fierce pride makes us argue that the taking was right and just, we are going fearfully beyond bad temper. It is not the crime, *hijo*, which makes the criminal. It is the failure to understand that God's law has been violated. No man may commit murder and then say no murder was committed. It is not man's place to judge, but to be judged. This is all

50

I am saying to you, my son, or that I am meaning to say: *Do not take God's law unto yourself."*

Hush dropped his eyes. He knew what the old man meant, and he knew he was right in meaning it to apply to him. But his words had opened an old wound in Hush—one that had nothing to do with those dead Indians out on Nameless Creek above the Rio Grande, one that had left a question which had rankled a long time in the soul of Hush Feleen.

In the end, he had to ask it.

"Padre," he said, low-voiced, just before he turned the black mare quickly away, "where was God's law when Avery Hudspeth hung my father?"

It was a good winter on the Guadalupe.

There was plenty of rain, very little cold, and an amazing number of big, unbranded steers in the brush.

Hush worked daylight and dark. Headquartering on the river just above its confluence with the San Antonio, he stayed in the thicket weeks on end. It was he and the black mare and Old Blue against the *brasada*, and it was his determination to have the new home ready for his folks when the spring grass came.

His mark was the HF connected, and by the time the first faint green was showing he had it burned deep on the left flank of fifty longhorn steers. He had, of course, been "soonering" all winter to do it; beating the legal branding dates in southeast Texas and knowing he risked his neck in so doing. Yet he could see no real wrong in the act. He was not stealing anything with another man's mark on it. He was breaking local law, yes—but what kind of law was that?

In reviewing his Texas life that winter, he could not see where he had transgressed any laws that really mattered, either of the Lord's or anybody else's. Actually, the same could be said of his Texas life from its first beginnings in the Nueces *brasada*. It seemed to Hush that people, no less than plain animals, had a right to live their own lives and set their own laws, provided they just minded their own troubles and didn't put off any grief on their neighbors. He believed, for a fact, that if things were let to run their natural course, the wrongdoers, man and beast alike, would bring down their own punishments on themselves.

Had not that *ladino* steer killed the little Morgan mare to earn his brain full of buckshot? Had not those thieving Comanches robbed a kind old man of his only horse, to bring about what happened to them out yonder on that lonely creek? And wouldn't the same kind of rightful lightning catch up one day with Avery Hudspeth and that hired gunman of his for what they had done to Hush's Pap? And had tried to do to Hush?

The answer to all these things was yes. The steer and the Indians and old man Hudspeth and that hawk-faced Howell, they had all brought undue grief on innocent parties, and had been, or would be eventually, made to pay for it.

That was natural law.

What difference did it make whether it was delivered by Hush Feleen, or somebody else? If they had it coming and they got it, that was what counted. If he, Hush, ever stole anybody's horse, or branded his cow, or hung a man from a mesquite limb without waiting to find out if his story was true, he would expect to get paid off, and paid off deep, for the wrong.

No, sir, even with all winter to think about Don Diego's lecture on God's law—and he had thought much about it, for he knew the old man loved him and was a very wise old man, as well—he had not been able, by the time spring came in the shinnery, to see that Don Diego was right, and he, Hush, was wrong.

With the first of May, however, all second thoughts on the bothersome subject were put behind. His soonered gather of HF-connected cattle could now be recorded in the brand books at Goliad. The legal roundup dates were safely past and a man could ride into town and register his new mark without suspicion.

Hush ran in the black mare and whistled up Old Blue. He put the pack on Andy Jackson, nailed shut the door of his brush hut, let down the bars of the pole corral. *"Hee-yahh!"* he yelled at Andy Jackson, and the history of the Feleen brand was begun.

CHAPTER 10

It would have been hard for a man to stay in the saddle and not float right off into the balmy May morning had he felt any better than Hush felt when he set out from his Guadalupe brush hut that spring of 1876. He was three weeks past nineteen years old, he would fight a ringy steer on foot or spit in the eye of a mossyback bull, and if there was a cloud bigger than a cottonboll in all that grand sweep of horizon between him and a triumphant home-coming at the Santimas *jacal*, Hush could not see it.

But you can't trust bluebird weather in Texas.

In Goliad the weather changed for Hush. It came on to frost in the middle of a sunny morning.

"An HF connected? On the Guadalupe, above the Forks?" said the county clerk, frowning at the opened page of the brand book, then eying the tall youth suspiciously. "There's already one registered from out there."

"An HF connected?" asked Hush wonderingly.

"An HF connected," echoed the clerk unsympathetically.

Hush felt a strange panicky fear start up in him. "Who by?" he said uncertainly.

"Feller named Hudspeth."

Hush blanched. It wasn't possible. It had to be wrong.

"From down Live Oak way?" he inquired carefully.

The clerk glanced at the book.

"Yep."

"Avery Hudspeth?" Hush couldn't, he wouldn't believe it.

Annoyed, the clerk referred again to the book.

"No," he said abruptly, "Howell."

Hush felt the force of that hit him in the belly like a balled fist. But still he fought to reject the blow. To accept it meant to face the loss of his long winter's gamble on the Guadalupe; and worse, to face that deadly enemy about whom old Don Diego had so earnestly warned him—himself.

"*Howell* Hudspeth?" he heard himself ask numbly. "You certain sure, mister?"

"Look, youngster," the clerk began testily, then got a look at Hush's face and thought better of it. "What I mean," he said, "is that I'm tolerable busy. Was there anything else?"

Hush waited a minute, then nodded quietly.

"Yes, sir. When was this Hudspeth in here?"

"This morning. About an hour gone."

"Thanks. I reckon I won't have no great difficulty catching up to him. Probably still in town somewheres."

Hush was turning for the door, actually talking more to himself than to the clerk. A man got that way living all winter in the brush. But the clerk was neither a bright nor a feeling man, and he was, after all, an official of the local government.

"I wouldn't make no trouble if I was you, mister," he called out. "We got the law here in Goliad."

The tall youth stopped in the doorway, turned and stared again at the clerk.

"I know you have," said Hush Feleen. "It just rode in on a black mare."

53

He stood on the sagging plank stoop of the county clerk's office looking off east toward the Gulf. The horizon over that way was piled high with fleecy clean cloudbeds made up since he had left the Guadalupe that morning. To the south and west the sky was as sparkling clear as a quartz crystal. Hush shook his head unhappily.

No man in his right mind could fail to feel such beauty, nor could he make it square up with the dark urge in his heart to walk on down that dusty street and commit murder. God knows, there had to be a better answer to his trouble than killing Howell Hudspeth. But what? The burdened youth shook his head again, and turned to survey the town.

Goliad was a fair-sized settlement in 1876. It was no Dallas, but it would do. Main Street was lined both sides with gaudy rawboard fronts advertising everything from free eats with your whiskey, to twenty-four-hour legal advice.

It was the latter sign—*G.B. Prescott, Atty. at Law*—that now caught Hush's worried eye.

The law. The legal law. Could that be his answer? Well, now, maybe it was.

He had never been able to see made-up law as a real, enforceable thing—something which would actually work; which would protect the innocent and punish the guilty —*actually*. But now, of a sudden, and hopefully, it struck him that possibly Don Diego had been right all along. Maybe it was wrong for a man to take the law into his own hands. Maybe the law would work by itself, if a body stood back and gave it room. It was worth a try anyway. Hush owed that much, at least, to the old man. And, by damn, he would pay it to him!

Straightening up, his face cleared and he felt better.

He untied Andy Jackson and the black mare, led them across the street, dropped the mare's reins in front of the dingy shack of Attorney Prescott.

"Wait up, Muchacha," he said to her, and went into the lawyer's office.

The black mare blew out through her thin-veined nostrils, stomped a trim foot, whickered demandingly.

She was a *kehilan*, a pure-blood descendant of the old Arab stock of the Spanish colonists of two centuries gone. Tough as Toledo steel, intelligent as a trained dog, sensitive as a woman, she adored the tall boy with the soft voice and gentle, steady hands, and she was not completely happy when he was gone from her.

In the present case, however, she scarcely had time to register her uneasiness before her master was back again. And the look on his face was not of the sort to encourage

54

either an intelligent young horse or a wise old mule to take any frivolous liberties with a valued understanding. Muchacha stood as quietly as a plow mare to Hush's mount-up, eased off down the dirt street walking a chalkline and stepping on eggs. Behind her, Andy Jackson did likewise.

The instinctive caution of the two animals was deserved.

Lawyer Prescott had been brief. There was nothing he could do for Hush, no legal action the law could take in his behalf toward recovering those cattle or punishing the man who had stolen them from him. The brand registry statutes were iron-clad. They were not subject to interpretation in the courts. They were stronger than the U.S. Constitution in Texas. Those fifty steers with the HF connected marked on the left flank belonged to Howell Hudspeth. He owned the brand. Hush Feleen owned nothing but his black mare and his old mule and his blue-ticked Tennessee hounddog. Those three things, and his short memories of being a big rancher on the Guadalupe—that was all.

But Hush knew better. He knew he still owned one other thing.

He still owned Jupe Feleen's rusted Sheffield shotgun.

It was 2 P.M. in the afternoon of May 10th, 1876, when Hush caught up to Howell Hudspeth in the Red Steer Saloon in the San Antonio River town of Goliad, Texas.

It was 2:03 when he finished his business with him.

Hush saw his man the moment he came in through the slatted doors looking for him. He was seated at a poker table twenty feet away, his back turned three-quarters to the street entrance. The game was one of those hot and noisy ones, the kind that build up from drinking red liquor for breakfast. Whiskey in the daytime was like love before noon dinner. It worked fast and rough. A man who could hold a quart after sundown would spill all over the place on half a pint taken by broad day. This game had started early. It was a good four fingers past the half-pint mark.

Hush got behind Howell Hudspeth and put the muzzles of the twelve-gauge between his shoulder blades with just the least chilling pressure.

"Stand up slow," he said.

Howell stiffened. The other players looked up at Hush and froze. There was a long silence; then Howell got to his feet.

"Turn around," said Hush. *"Muy cuidadoso."*

The other did as he was bid, making his turn very carefully, the muzzles of the shotgun following around the curve of his ribs to end up resting against his breastbone.

55

"You Howell Hudspeth?" said Hush.

"You know it," answered the dark-skinned rider.

"Avery Hudspeth's son?"

Howell let a grin twist his thin mouth and nodded.

"Hard to believe, ain't it? You never know what you're gonna get when you gamble with an Indian on a blanket, though. My mother was a pure-blood Comanche. It's where I get my gentle nature."

Hush was not amused. "You know why I'm here, I reckon," he said.

Howell glanced down at the shotgun.

"Well," he shrugged, "it ain't to wish me no happy birthdays, nor to change your will .in my favor, I allow."

"One thing," said Hush: "How did you know about me?"

The Indian grin lit up the dark face once more.

"I got a Comanche cousin. Big Kwahadi buck name of Tall Walker. Good-looking Indian, but a hell of a poor horse trader. What was it you paid him to get that yellow gelding back, Feleen? Two dead braves, plus that black mare outside?"

Hush was glad to hear that the third Indian had not died, and said as much. Howell took it for a sign of weakening.

"Me and Hudspeth, we got to thinking after we had chinned some with Tall Walker," he said. "Rode over to that place where we caught your old man burning his beef on our time. Seemed kind of lonesome there with only one hump in the grass."

Hush held his silence. Howell went on, not so sure now.

"The Indian had already trailed you up here to the Forks country. I come after him and talked him into going home and leaving me settle with you, half-breed style."

"And from there," murmured Hush, "you saw me building up my HF brand and got the idea of letting me work all winter for the Rocking H outfit."

"You might say," nodded Howell. "Sort of giving you the chance to pay back the steers your old man stole offen us."

"That all you got to say?"

"It's all."

The two stood, eye-locked, across the length of the shotgun's barrels. The men at the table began to shift their feet, ease back their chairs. "Sit still," said Hush, and they sat.

"All right, Hudspeth," he told Howell, "now I'll say something. You know that HF connected is my brand. You know I got the moral right to it. If you want to go with me up to the county brand office and sign back the *legal* right, we'll go right now and no more said nor owed on either side. Me, I want to stay in this country, and I want to start right.

That's your good luck, if you want to ride it. *Que dice?*"

Howell Hudspeth wasn't buying any lucky rides that morning. Not from Hush Feleen.

"I say go to hell, you Tennessee son-of-a-bitch," he snarled, and let his left arm go loose.

Hush nodded, and cocked the hammers on the twelve-gauge.

"Boys," he said to the white-faced players, "this is a personal matter; stay out of it." He kept his eyes on Howell as he asked quietly, "Is this feller into any of you for chips?"

"Me, for ten blues," answered one of the men.

"Take 'em out of his pile," directed Hush. The man did so.

"Now," said Hush, "I'm going to step back a ways. This feller will take three steps to the left, to clear the table."

"For God's sake," said the pudgy man who had taken the chips, "let us get up and out of the way!"

"No," said Hush. "Sit tight. You won't get hit."

He took his steps backward. Howell slid three catlike paces to the left.

"When you say so," Hush instructed him. "If I down you, I don't mean to swing for it."

Howell stood with his left hand brushing the butt of his bone-handled .44. Hush waited with the rusted shotgun dangling at the full length of his right arm. It was a fair and equal face-out; if anything, favoring the revolver fighter. The crouching players at the table would not have bet a full house, hidden, into two deuces showing, that the fierce-eyed boy from the riverbrakes would survive his calling out of the rail-thin gunman with the tied-down, left-hand holster.

"I'm waiting," breathed Hush. "It's still your call—"

"All right," said Howell Hudspeth. *"Now."*

He moved as he had on that other day in the *brasada* of Live Oak County. His pull with the big Colt was startlingly fast. Yet this time his shot did not hit Hush Feleen. It went into the sawdusted floor of the Red Steer Saloon. The reason it did, was that Hush did not move as he had that other day in the *brasada*. He did not swing with the shotgun, trying to bring it up before he fired; he merely tipped up its twin muzzles, as it hung in his hand, and fired both barrels at once. The unsupported recoil of the double pull nearly broke his wrist, but the speed with which the shot got off was quicker than the eye.

Howell Hudspeth made no sound beyond a gasping, single breath.

He fell slowly, knees first, then folding over and twisting to lie on his back, glazing eyes straining upward to focus on the face of his killer.

57

Hush stepped forward and stood over him.

"I didn't think you could do it again," he said, looking down at the dying man, and turned to go out of the Red Steer.

At the door he seemed taken with a belated thought, and faced back into the room for a still five seconds.

"My name is Hush Feleen," he told the motionless players at the poker table. "Tell that to anybody who wants to know who killed Howell Hudspeth."

CHAPTER 11

Arnie Feleen was fifteen, a grand time in the life of any boy. He had shot up and was strong, but he had not changed with the hard muscle nearly four years in the *brasada* had laid over his rawboned frame. Inside he was soft. Inside he was a Hushton.

Among the intense Feleen brood, his Hushton homeliness and crinkly, sunburned smile made him stand out like an orphan buckskin in a corral of linebred bays. Without meaning to, the other children regarded their blond brother more as a family pet than as a fellow Feleen. They all doted on him, but they spoke to him in the same tone they would use to Old Blue or, if put out with him, to Andy Jackson.

For his part, Arnie didn't mind this. He never really thought much about it, or about the other children. There was only one thing in the world which mattered for him, and that was his big brother Hush.

As much as one boy ever worshiped another, Arnie worshiped Hush. The others, in their various ways, had all given him a hard road to travel. But Hush had never raised a hand or said a hard word to him in his whole life. There was, actually, more to this than Arnie knew.

Nancy Hushton had provided for him beyond the others. When she knew her time was near, she had called Hush in and charged him with "looking special to little Arn." Hush had taken the charge willingly and had never shirked nor resented it. He felt about Arnie as he did about Jodie Beth; both were handicapped creatures, needing extra help to make their way in life.

In view of this attachment of the two brothers, it was not strange that when, on a dew-fresh morning in mid-May, the younger one saw his older brother jogging up the Nueces on his slim black mare, the reunion should be a heart-jumper.

Hush was as glad to see Arnie as the blue-eyed youngster was to see him. He slid to the ground and threw both lean arms around the big youth and went into a Tennessee bear-hugging contest, which turned, quick enough, into a mountain wrestle to see who could still pin who. Hush had his troubles putting down the grinning towhead, and might never have made it had not Old Blue leaped in and begun licking Arnie's face and nipping him in the side till he hit his ticklebone. That got Arnie to giggling so hard he couldn't fight, and Hush was glad to press the boy's shoulders flat into the dirt of the trail and quit while he could.

They got up, knocking the dust and twigs off themselves to cover the awkward spell that was bound to set in when big boys had carried on too catnippy for their ages.

Curiously, it was Arnie who got to talking first. As they walked up the trail toward the *jacal* clearing, with the younger boy leading Hush's mare as a high privilege, and with Old Blue still nipping his shanks and pawing for attention to the fact that he, too, was home again, Arnie chattered a blue-tailed streak. He brought Hush up on everything which had gone on in his long time away—not much had—and started in on the prospects for the approaching summer, all before Hush could do more than get in a pleased grin sideways.

By that time they were at the clearing, the others had spotted them, and the homecoming was on.

Arnie lay in the loft bed staring wide-eyed at the low-pitched thatch above. He could not sleep, any more than he had been able to eat, hours ago, when Hush had broken the news at the supper table that he meant to take Arnie along with him on his new start in the cattle business.

They were to go far, far away, Hush said, to a place where the brush thinned out and the true grass set in. Taking a route he had heard about on his way home, they would angle up to the Forks of the Frio in Atascosa County, then north and west along Atascosa Creek to where it headed up near Bexar, and then cut over and pick up the Medina River west of San Antonio and follow it out to the open grazing of the Pipe Creek country in Bandera County. There they would get the Feleen brand going again and, this time, do it legal, according to Texas law, and not trusting to rustlers' luck.

The grand plan had been buttressed by two gifts which would have put a lump in the throat of any *brasada* boy alive. The first, from Hush, had been the old Sharps buffalo gun he had got from the Comanches. The second, from Don Diego, had been the wonderful yellow cowhorse, Gato. With a gun like the Sharps and a horse like Gato, a boy was almost fit company to ride with Hush and his black mare and his lever-action Winchester, also traded from the Indians.

The entire prospect was more than most fifteen-year-olds could have closed their eyes on short of daybreak and the starting hour. It was, in fact, long past midnight when Arnie Feleen relaxed and began to breathe rhythmically and deep.

Hush, by his own declaration having outgrown the sleeping loft, punched restlessly at the pillow of his straw pallet in the *ramada,* the brush-covered outside porch of the *jacal.*

The moon was shining in his eyes, the coyotes wouldn't let up yelling out in the thicket, and the lizards were falling out of the roof-thatch to land in his face. He got up and went to the water *olla* hanging on the post nearest the *jacal* door. He drank, then spat hurriedly. It was a new *olla* and still tasted of clay. He walked out into the moonlight.

At the corral he had a look at Muchacha, the black mare. She came over and talked to him with small grunting nickers, then shied away and kicked at Gato as the latter came nosing up to get his share of the petting. Hush scratched him under the jaw, spoke softly to Andy Jackson, and said, *Hola amigos. Que pasan?"* to Guadalupe änd Golondrina, Don Diego's two wise gray wagon burros. It was no good. The wandering around made him only more restless.

He went down and sat by the river, listening to the *brasada.* The night sounds, as always, comforted him.

He heard the deep bass of the big longhorn bulls in their grunting brushtalk to one another. He heard the wild pigs squealing far off in the thicket. He heard *lechuza,* the owl, hooting forlornly; *zorra,* the red vixen, bickering spitefully, and *zorro,* the dog fox, scolding yappily in return. To him came the distant coughings of *el tigre,* the spotted Mexican jaguar. And from somewhere, far off, he heard the minor-keyed complaining of *lobo cano,* the gray dog-wolf, baying to the stars his discontent with doing all the meat hunting for a nursing bitch and five furry whelps.

Hush stirred uneasily.

The *brasada* had been his happiest home. It had become what the Mexican's called his *"querencia,"* his place in all the world where he felt most secure. Tomorrow he would be leaving it. There was a feeling in him that he would never see it again.

It was a lonesome, sad thought, and he was afraid. . . .

Don Diego turned his face to the abode wall, muttering that it was no simple thing to sleep in one small room with three women. If it was not Doña Anastasia saying her Rosary out loud between snores, it was the eldest girl getting up to bring the little lame one a drink. Or it was the poor little one herself trying to find her own way to the *olla* and stepping on the old hound's tail, to bring on an outcry which would have resurrected a saint.

Ay de mi, there was no rest for the ancient. If a man's kidneys did not get him up, his conscience would.

Had he advised the just-returned eldest son correctly? Had he been right in agreeing with him that it would be best to go away, to leave the *brasada*? To go north and west, far out upon the beginnings of the great *llano*? To do this, so that he would not be known, and no man's hand would be raised against him, in his second try to make a new home for all of them? Yet what other thing could he have told the boy? That it was perfectly safe for him to stay on the Nueces, after the misfortune he had just suffered on the Guadalupe? Would not the older Hudspeth persecute him to the grave for the unfortunate affair in Goliad? Of course. These Texans were fiercer than Corsicans in their family loyalties. There was no other way; the dear son must be gone with daylight.

It saddened the old man's heart. It made him lonely in the middle of the night. He loved this boy, this dangerous, proud-hearted *delgadito*. No natural father could feel more than he felt for this soft-spoken, gray-eyed foster child who had come to him out of the *brasada*. Nor could any natural father fear more for his future. It was no easy thing to be old and to have been sent a son you cared for so deeply and yet who you knew had already killed three men. God forgive him, God go with him, God guide him upon another, and brighter, pathway.

"*Pater Noster qui es in caelis, sanctificetur nomen tuum: adveniat regnum tuum: fiat voluntas tua sicut in caelo, et in terra. . . .*"

CHAPTER 12

The Pipe Creek ranch was a success from the start.

It was in good grass country in a good grass year. There were plenty of unbranded wild cattle to be picked up. Moreover, there was a new outlet for them opening to the north.

In that spring of 1876 the Great Decade of the Kansas trail drivers was beginning.

The little maverickers on the Pipe Creek range—there were five others operating there with Hush and Arnie—held that a quarter of a million cattle would go up the trail by the end of the coming summer. They were saying that before the thing was done, and the northern markets played out, ten million cows and a million horses would have swum the Red, the Cimarron and the North Canadian. And every last head of those ten million cows would have come out of the Gulf Coast brush thickets and the more westerly *llanos* of middle Texas.

That kind of a stock drive, they were telling the Feleen boys, would take as long as twenty years and make ten millionaires a year among the Texas cowmen going up the trail. Pipe Creek, they said, was as good a country as there was for a fellow to try putting his brand on his million of those cattle-drive dollars. Hush and his young brother, moreover, were welcome to join the cow hunting going on along the Pipe. There were slick ears, and to spare, for all five original outfits, plus the Feleens, and even for the big new outfit rumored to have moved into the Hondo Canyon country to the south.

This last news had spooked Hush, for he was naturally thinking in terms of having been followed out from Live Oak County by Avery Hudspeth and his Rocking H riders. But he was talked out of his worries when Travis Bowen and Beck Pearsall, two of the Pipe Creek maverickers, reported this was no scouting bunch but a big-scale move of an established outfit bringing in its own cattle and meaning to settle down and stay put.

Relieved, Hush relaxed and went to work.

For the first time in his life he felt that he was wanted and welcomed by other men. But to know that their friendly neighbors on the creek didn't resent their presence wasn't to say that Hush and Arnie turned, overnight, into tailwaggers, and they didn't. But neither did they reject the frequent visits of what Hush began smilingly to call "the friendly five." Bowen, Pearsall, Owens, Grant and Fenton were all received at the HF brush hut, at first with cautious mountain reserve; then, after a proper time, with genuine if still guarded pleasure.

The Pipe Creekers understood that. The Feleen brothers were, after all, Tennessee boys. Southern hillfolk were simply that careful, close-mouthed kind. You didn't hold their early wariness against them. It was certainly no novelty in that part of Texas for new neighbors to want to "move wide" for a while. Half the best families in Bandera County were on the dodge from something they were hoping wouldn't catch up to them. It was what brought folks to the *llano* country, mostly—that chance for a fresh start with no questions asked, no answers expected. Perhaps the Feleen boys were looking for that chance; and their good neighbors along the Pipe meant to see they got it.

Hush and Arnie could feel this welcome, and it made the summer work go even more swiftly and well.

When the last days of August were gone and the first ones of September were crisping the air, they had gathered a hundred head of good mixed market cattle; a small bunch, true, but big enough to mark with the HF connected and throw in with one of the trail herds making up to go to Kansas next spring. They figured to clear $30 a head on them, and that would net them a sizable stake to start spreading out their operation next summer. They could hire two riders, and by the fall of '77 be ready to— But why talk a year ahead? This was the fall of '76 and they hadn't even branded the precious nest-egg herd that was going to give them that running start in the cattle business.

They got to the branding on September 15th. It was a good clear day, warm and with that smoky look to the distance that comes with the prairie autumn.

They had purposely let the branding go, figuring to make out better doing it all at one place and time. The neighbor boys did it that way and it worked fine. Throwing a critter, building a fire, heating the iron and putting the mark on him where you came up to him was all right if you were soonering or changing somebody else's brand into your own. But where you were mavericking legal and open, with nobody keeping tabs on you and no chance of getting into any kind of law scrape, then this idea of putting your whole gather into one pasture and holding it until you were ready to burn it all at one time made real cow sense.

Right now, with the cattle all fat and sassy, the weather good and promising to stay that way, there was nothing to it but to build the mesquite fire, prop up the stamp-irons in it, shake out your loop and start cutting them out.

Hush and Arnie were sitting their mounts having a last, deep-pleasured look at their cattle standing ready inside the brush corral they had rigged to hold them so both riders would be free to work the fire—Arnie to rope, Hush to brand.

Arnie grinned and said, "Well, Hush, we done it. It like to broke our butts, but we done it. Ain't it a grand feeling? I vow I was never so took with unnatural pride in my whole life."

"They're good cattle," said Hush. "We've been mighty lucky."

"Scandalous lucky," agreed the blond youngster. Then hopefully: "How long you reckon it'll take us to get a trail-herd of our own together, Hush? I mean one whar we kin make our own drive with nothing but HF-connected stuff? And with our own hands and roadbrand and cook and chuckwagon and all?"

Hush scratched his chin, frowned thoughtfully.

"Doing it honest, like this, it ain't going to be tomorrow."

"Yeah, but how soon, Hush?"

"Well, Arn, it's hard to say. By trailing with the big outfits, not losing any cattle to Indian Nation stompeders, Jayhawk trail cutters, or Kansas quarantines for the Texas fever, and granting the market holds up—why, then another two, three good years like this one ought to see us somewheres close to throwing our own herd on the road."

"Seems like a powerful long time, Hush."

"It'll pass, Arn, it'll pass. Meanwhile, we're doing tolerable well. We can bring the kids and the old folks up next spring, I reckon. Shucks, we can even do it yet this fall, if it would pleasure you, Arn."

Arnie's face lighted up.

"You mean it, Hush? Go get the kids and the old man and Mama Santimas, right off? Lord, that sure *would* pleasure me, Hush. It'd pleasure me most to tears."

"I guess it would me, too, Arn," said Hush soberly. "You know I've learned some things up here this summer. I want the old man to know that. I want him to know he was right about a matter we talked of one time. I reckon we'll ride down, sure enough, boy. We'll do it soon's the branding's over."

"By Gols, that's good! Thanks, Hush!" The light in Arnie's wide blue eyes made a glow inside Hush, but it embarrassed him too. He straightened, very businesslike.

"Forget it," he said gruffly. "We got a herd to mark. Go get me that brockle-faced bull yonder. The one that's chousing up those cows. Drag him up and bust him"—Hush made a mark in the branding-fire dust with his boot-toe—"right there."

"One brockle-faced bull for the HF connected!" sang out Arnie, and dug his heels into Gato's ribs.

The buckskin went into the bawling herd of longhorns as if he were diving blind into a bramble bush. But he came out the next instant driving ahead of him the trouble-making bull. Arnie shook out his riata and yipped, high-voiced.

The yellow gelding shot forward, turning the bull in a

64

shower of dust, cutting him straight toward Hush and the fire. Hush laughed and cussed all in the same breath that took him leaping wildly aside. Arnie dropped his loop over the bull's horns with a shouting laugh of his own. Gato squatted like a rabbit, forelegs stiff, haunches and hocks doubled under him.

The roped longhorn went up in the air, turned end to end, and crashed to the ground flat on his side, squarely over the X Hush had marked in the dust. He didn't offer to move.

"Burn him!" yelled Arnie. "I ain't got all fall to wait!"

Hush, still grinning, stepped back to the fire and pulled one of the two stamp-irons out of it. He rapped it expertly on a rock, knocking off the wood ash to see the color underneath. It was a rose-gray, just right.

"Hold him!" he yelled back, lost in the pleasure of excitement. "Here goes HF connected number one!"

He laughed again, startling Arnie, who had never before heard him laugh twice in the same five minutes. Then, with a flourish, he started the smoking tip of the stamp-iron toward the bull's rough-haired flank. He never finished the motion.

"Drop that iron," said a dry, tight voice behind them.

Then, with bitterness dripping from it, the voice went on: *"Reach high and pray hard, Hush Feleen."*

CHAPTER 13

Hush neither reached high, prayed hard, nor dropped the iron.

Instinct kept him still until the first wave of blind anger had swept over him. When it was past, he turned slowly, the iron held low in his right hand.

"If you want this iron, Mr. Hudspeth," he said, "you come and get it."

He let his eyes wander over the riders siding the owner of the Rocking H. There were seven of them—six ordinary hands, one not so ordinary.

"You're not armed, Feleen," Avery Hudspeth's rasping voice said. "I would advise you to do as you're told. You'll be obliged to do so in any case. So I'll say it once more. Drop that iron."

"Arnie," Hush warned his younger brother, ignoring Hudspeth, "hold that gelding still."

Arnie, his hand dropped toward his riflebutt, had been edging the buckskin clear of the fire. Hush read his intent as plainly as though the boy had sent him a printed note.

"Don't you be a fool, you hear, Arn?" he said. "Every man has got to kill his own snakes. These here are mine."

"Sloat," said Avery Hudspeth to the seventh rider, "you had better see to the boy."

Sloat grinned. He was a gray-skinned man, not healthy-looking—certainly no cowboy like the others. He wore two guns crossbelted in a *buscadero* rig. With his old-style Confederate coat and black string tie, Hush decided he was trying awful hard to get himself taken for a gunfighter. He decided, at the same time, that he was going to take him for one. Any man who went in for killing as a steady kind of work had to be a little loco. Play-acting went natural with the breed. You didn't low-rate them because of it, either.

"Sure," Sloat now answered Hudspeth, his own survey of the situation concluded. "You're the man with the money."

He moved his horse around the fire. Coming up to Arnie, he was still grinning. "You going to make trouble, boy?" he said.

Arnie looked helplessly at Hush.

"No," the latter answered for him. "He ain't in this."

Sloat glanced over at Hush and nodded. "Reckon we'd best make sure he ain't," he said, looking back at Arnie. "Boy, get your hands up."

As he gave the order, he palmed out his right-hand Colt and put it in the big youth's belly. Reaching over with his left hand, he took Gato's reins as they slid from Arnie's reaching grasp. When the boy's hands were clear up, Sloat hit him across the head with the Colt's seven-inch barrel.

Arnie collapsed forward across the horn of his saddle. The gunman kicked his own left boot free of the stirrup, placed its sole in the unconscious boy's side and showed him off the yellow gelding. His slack form went into the sunbaked earth at a bad angle. There was an audible giving of bone, and Arnie lay loose and still.

Hush made an animal sound deep in his chest and came for Sloat with the stamp-iron.

"Stretch him!" snapped Avery Hudspeth to his other hands, and the riders spurred their horses forward.

It was like running a steer out of a chute. The riders had their loops shaken out on the first jump, built on the second, laid down on the third. Hush got no more than halfway to the grinning Sloat before the first rope was whipped tight around his ankles. His own momentum threw him flat on his face. The force of the fall shook him hard, but in-

66

stinctively he fought to get up. The second rope sang out and settled over his shoulders, pinning his arms and stretching him between the two crouching cowponies.

His head roared. His eyes were full of dirt and he could not see his enemies save as blurred, shadowy forms which had no faces. But he could hear the unhurried voice of Sloat saying to one of the riders, "Shake off your loop, seems he's still got a little fight left in him."

At once, Hush felt the second rope slacken and whip free of his shoulders. Then the first one changed hands and tightened ominously about his ankles. Dimly, now, he could see Sloat tying the ankle rope to his saddlehorn, and could hear one of the cowboys blurt out, "Jesus Christ, Ben, you ain't going to drag him!"

Keeping the rope tight between his horse and Hush, Sloat dropped his gunhand.

"You boys get paid for handling cattle," he told the Rocking H rider. "Don't try to earn my salary."

There was a moment of embarrassed indecision, then the objector, a homely little cowhand with curly brown hair and a broken nose, moved his pony forward.

"No man had ought to be drug lessen he's a hoss thief or a murderer," he said stoutly.

Before anything could come of this nervy stand, Avery Hudspeth heeled his chunky bay into the debate.

"This man is both," he declared righteously. "He killed my son Howell, and he stole that black mare he's riding. Besides, in stealing her he killed two other men."

"They was Indians, Mr. Hudspeth," countered the little cowboy. "You told us that your ownself. Added to that, they had stole this here buckskin hoss from old man Santimas. I reckon the boy had a right to go arter them for that."

But Avery Hudspeth was not listening. "Get on with it, Sloat," he said to the waiting gunman.

Hush, his head clearing, felt the rope clutch again at his pinioned ankles and the ground begin to move beneath his outstretched hands. The last thing he could remember hearing was the little cowboy yelling, "Pull in your wings so's they won't git broke, fella!" and the last thing he could remember doing was trying to obey the shouted instruction.

When Hush could see and hear again, and could think, it was late afternoon and the last of his and Arnie's cattle were being brought to the fire for branding. The mark being put on them was not an HF connected. It was a Rocking H.

Avery Hudspeth, sitting his cobby bay nearby, glanced over and saw that he had regained consciousness.

"We just bought you out," he said. "We figured you would want to be moving on to a new range."

Hush didn't answer him. He tested the bonds which shackled him to a dead mesquite stump. There was no give in them. He looked around for Arnie and saw him lying motionless on the ground alongside a mesquitale bush. He swung his eyes back to Avery Hudspeth.

"Is he dead?" he said.

"No," answered the rancher, "he ain't. Eyes are open but he can't seem to talk."

"Or move?" asked Hush quietly.

"Or move," replied the other uneasily. Then, hardening: "He'll loosen up after a bit. It's only the shock. Hurry it up, boys. We got to get on."

Hush measured him, a coldness growing in his belly.

"You're always in a hurry, aren't you, Mr. Hudspeth?" he said. "Seems like I remember another job you wanted to get done with in a rush."

"Your father was a thief; he was stealing my cattle."

"My father had four kids to feed, and a little crippled girl to get doctor money for."

"We meant to look out for the kids, Feleen."

Hush nodded very slowly, spacing his words like beads of snow-melt water falling off the end of an icicle.

"Well, Mr. Hudspeth," he said, "I will tell you something else you had better look out for from now on, and that's me. I don't care where you go, or what you do, I'll be there behind you. You understand me, Mr. Hudspeth?"

Before the Rocking H owner could reply, Ben Sloat rode over from the far side of the fire.

"Sounded like you was making quite a speech," he said to Hush. "Never figured you for a talker. Go on."

"I'm done," said Hush.

"No doubt of that," said Ben Sloat, and he turned back to watch the last of the HF steers being thrown and branded with the Rocking H.

When the animal had been burned and let up, Avery Hudspeth said to Sloat, "Get their horses. Hurry it up."

Hush watched the gray-faced gunman catch up Gato and Muchacha and lead them back. They were still saddled and bridled, with Hush's Winchester and Arnie's Sharps still in the scabbards. By the time Sloat drew up with them, the other hands had mounted and started over from the fire. One of them—it was the little broken-nosed cowboy again—veered his horse toward the huddled form of Arnie Feleen.

Hudspeth stared down at Hush.

"We'll turn your horses loose two miles up the trail," he told him. "That's so you can get the boy quick to the neighbors for decent care. Nearest one's Travis Bowen. His place is ten miles out on the Hondo Canyon trail."

Hush stared back up at him.

Hudspeth knew that he knew where Bowen lived, and how far he lived. The rancher was letting his conscience talk out loud for him, out loud and away too late. On the ground yonder lay Arnie Feleen, paralyzed from the eyes down. He might be fit in a few hours; he might never move again. Either way, it would not alter Hush's debt to Avery Hudspeth.

As though he read the thoughts going on behind the gray eyes below him, Hudspeth cleared his throat gruffly.

"I'm sorry about the boy, Feleen. Sloat shouldn't have done it."

"Sloat didn't do it, Mr. Hudspeth."

Hush didn't say it angrily, but the very easiness of the words deepened their meaning for Avery Hudspeth.

"We won't argue it," he said shortly. "I didn't want the boy should get bad hurt. He wasn't the one killed Howell."

"No," said Hush, "he wasn't."

Then, ever so careful and slow: "*You* were, Mr. Hudspeth."

The big rancher turned pale. The cords in his thick neck stood out like cypress roots. But whatever he would have said in guilty denial of Hush's quiet charge was never said. The moment's stillness was broken by the shuffle of pony's feet and the creak of saddle leather. It was the little crooked-nosed cowboy coming back from his look at Arnie Feleen.

He pulled up his roan gelding in front of Avery Hudspeth, and when he spoke the twang of his southwestern drawl was taut as a fiddlestring.

"The boy's dead, Mr. Hudspeth," he said.

CHAPTER 14

At sunrise of the next day, Hush buried Arnie on a grassy headland overlooking the creek.

His own hurts from the dragging Sloat had given him made every movement an agony. He had to lock his teeth on a piece of old bridle-strap to keep from crying out with the pain of the digging. He fainted twice before the hole was deep enough to take the body of his young brother. And then he couldn't lift him into it, but had to roll him into it, like a dead animal.

He covered him up, making the ground level, putting back all the sod, leaving no mark at all that Arnie Feleen slept there. When he was done, he raised his head.

"Ma," he said aloud, "I did the best I could for him. He was the best there was of us, and the one most like you. I cherished him, Ma, like you always wanted. God keep him safe with you."

Saying that, Hush dropped the shovel, and went back to the *jacal* he and his brother had built on the banks of Pipe Creek, in the far southeast corner of Bandera County. At the *jacal* he saddled Muchacha, put a pack on Gato and took up his Winchester.

The Sharps he had buried with Arnie. The boy had been so proud of the big gun that to leave it with him seemed fitting. Flower wreaths, a wrapping sheet, laying-out clothes, decent prayers—these things Hush could not offer. The old rifle was his best good-bye. He hoped that somehow it would comfort Arn.

When all was ready, he brought the boy's guitar and hung it on Gato's pack. Then he smashed the coal-oil kitchen lamp against the *jacal*'s brush wall and set fire to it. He turned away as the black smoke began to climb. Picking up the rusted twelve-gauge shotgun from the chopping block by the stovewood pile, he swung up on the restless Indian mare.

"Vamosnos, Muchacha," he said. "We've got a long ways to go."

At the house of Travis Bowen, he stopped his horses and called for the rancher to come out. The latter appeared in the door, shading his eyes into the morning sun.

"Quien es?" he said uncertainly.

"Hush Feleen. I want to talk with you, Mr. Bowen."

Bowen came out. "Hello, Feleen," he said. "What's the matter?"

Hush took the guitar off Gato's pack.

"That little girl of yours still like music?" he inquired.

Bowen had a daughter of thirteen. She was a giggly wisp of a thing with bluebonnet eyes and cornsilk hair, and she had thought hearing Arnie Feleen playing that guitar was the finest thrill to be had short of a Saturday trip to Bandera Town. Arnie had loved to play for her, and Hush himself had enjoyed having the little tike around. But now her father looked half suspiciously at Hush and answered guardedly.

70

"I reckon she does. Why for you ask?"

"I'd like her to have this guitar, Mr. Bowen. Happen it would pleasure her to have it, that is."

"Ain't that your brother's guitar?"

"He'd want she should have it, Mr. Bowen. It's why I come by with it."

The rancher's eyes narrowed. "Feleen," he said, "what's happened to your brother?"

"He's dead," replied Hush, and he told Bowen what Hudspeth had done.

"You mean," muttered the latter unbelievingly, "that you're heading down to the Rocking H all by yourself?"

"Mr. Bowen," asked Hush, with a slow smile, "you know anybody wants overwhelming bad to go with me?"

"Yes," the other surprised him by saying. "I'll go with you."

"You *will*?" echoed Hush.

"Me," nodded the rancher, "and the others too. Grant, Owens, Pearsall, Fenton—they'll all go. We're your friends, Feleen. Don't you understand that yet?"

Hush dropped his eyes.

"Up to now," he said, "it looks as if I hadn't." He held out the guitar again, gesturing with it awkwardly. "You reckon the little girl would want to have this, or not, Mr. Bowen?"

"Sure," said Bowen. "Sure she would." He took the guitar. "Come on along in, Feleen. The old woman can fry you up some venison chops while I'm getting ready."

"What you mean, while you get ready, Mr. Bowen?"

"To go with you, like I said."

Hush set his jaw stubbornly.

"No, thanks," he said, "I'll skin my own skunks." He turned the black mare for the road, but Bowen was at his stirrup.

"Wait up, Feleen!" he said sharply.

Hush checked the mare, and the rancher looked up at him.

"I'm going to tell you something, neighbor," he said, "and you can take it or leave it lay."

He paused, gathering his words.

"Now you may not need friends, Feleen," he began, "but the rest of us do. We depend on each other. It cain't be no other way out here. It's stick together or get starved out. Or rained, or hailed, or brush-fired out, or whatever. So when you come to me and tell me a man rode up and put his mark on a hundred head of your cattle, killed your brother and like to killed you, what you expect me to do? Throw you off the place?"

71

Hush dropped his glance again, and Bowen went on quickly.

"You can skin your own skunks all you're a mind to, boy, we'll never horn in on you. But when them same skunks might be hoisting on us next trip, they ain't exactly your skunks."

Hush brought up his head.

"I ain't never thought of it just that way," he admitted.

"Well, you think of it then," said Bowen. "And while you're at it, here's something else you can think about right along with it. We all liked you and your brother, boy. Man to man and no favors asked. Now what do you say to that?"

Hush looked down at him, face muscles working. He swallowed hard, and waited until he was sure he could talk steady.

"I say go get your horse, Mr. Bowen," he answered at last. "Me and my brother would be mortal proud if you would ride along with us."

They weren't names you would remember—Bowen, Pearsall, Fenton, Grant, Owens, all long gone—but they saddled their horses and got their Winchesters or their old Sharps rifles and they rode behind Hush Feleen down into the Hondo Canyon country on the border of Medina County, and in forty-eight hours the six of them gathered 350 head of Avery Hudspeth's unmarked cattle and put them on the drive for the branding corrals at the Rocking H homeplace above Medina River.

Ahead of the bawling herd rode Hush Feleen, his shotgun barrel across his saddlehorn.

When he came to the homeplace clearing he was amazed at what he saw. The main house was like nothing in that country: a regular plantation house like they had in the loblolly pinelands of southeast Texas, lacking only white paint to make it the equal of anything west of the Sabine. Back of it, set like the slave quarters in the cotton states, was a dogtrot bunkhouse sixty feet long. Toward this, Hush now guided the black mare.

It was deep twilight, almost full dark. Hush stopped the mare at the edge of the lamplight, holding her, and himself, in the bordering darkness.

"Hello the house," he called out carefully.

There was a quick scraping of chairs inside, a subdued hum of voices. The door opened a crack.

"*Quien es?*" asked a vaguely familiar voice.

Hush could not see his questioner. Behind him, the other men had blown out the lamp.

"Hush Feleen," he said, and waited.

The door creaked another few inches. The little broken-nosed cowboy stepped out.

"Howdy, Feleen," he muttered. "What you want?" He was obviously nervous, and did not know what to add to the bare greeting. Hush helped him out.

"I want Ben Sloat," he said.

"Ben ain't here. He's in town with the Old Man. They've went to pick up one of them mail-order brides for the old devil. Squaws ain't good enough for him no more."

"What town? San Antone?"

"Yep. She come acrost the Gulf to Indianola, and up from there by stage. She's a St. Louie gal."

Hush raised his voice to reach the other men in the darkened room.

"You boys in there stop moving around and stay away from the windows. You come easy, you won't none of you get hurt; you hang tough, there'll be big trouble. You're surrounded."

The men in the room held still, whispering their doubts back and forth, trying to talk up the courage to call Hush's bluff—if it was a bluff. But they weren't Ben Sloats. They were working cowboys, glad to get their $20 a month and found, but not ready to get killed for it.

As they hesitated, the yelling of the Pipe Creek riders bringing the Rocking H herd along the river road below the big house, arose suddenly. Hush had told them to do the best they could to sound like fifteen men instead of five. They were making a pretty good job of it, and the Hudspeth hands threw in quick and cold. They were all standing outside in the dogtrot meek as sheep when Travis Bowen rode up and called to Hush, "We got them moving up the rise out front, Feleen. Where you want them held?"

"You," rasped Hush to the little cowboy who had stood up for him against Sloat. "How many head will that main corral hold?"

"Four hundred maybe."

"Open it up. We got three hundred fifty coming."

"Three hundred fifty what?"

"Avery Hudspeth's best. Go set those wing gates like I told you."

"You'd best hop it, little fella," added Travis Bowen. "We been chousing them steers plenty. They're set to run."

"Reckon I ain't got no choice," apologized the small cowboy to his fellow Rocking H riders.

"You got one," said Hush quietly, "but I wouldn't recommend you taking it."

73

"No," said the other, eying the cocked shotgun across the saddlehorn, and edging hurriedly out from under the dog-trot. "No, neither would I, Mr. Feleen. Not nohow."

Hush watched him go legging off through the dark toward the corral, then turned to the other men.

"Get back inside and stay there," he told them. "The one sticks his head out before daybreak gets it blowed off. Just be smart and polite like the little feller."

There was no argument. The men went back in the bunk-house and Hush turned the black mare away. He pointed her toward the approaching herd, the sound of the little cowboy's parting respect as loud and sweet in his ears as the bellowing of the Rocking H cattle.

It was a small thing, but Hush never forgot it. It made him a man in one word. It established the fact that he was somebody to be reckoned with; and it hinted at a power for the future which made him feel all at once as tall as the moon.

From the night when a nameless, broken-nosed little ranch-hand called him "mister," the life and fortunes of Hush Feleen made their swift and singular turning.

CHAPTER 15

Leaving Pearsall and the others to stand guard over the Rocking H hands, Hush took Travis Bowen and the little cowboy and went up to the big house to wait for Avery Hudspeth.

The night was a beautiful one. They sat on the long veranda in the wicker furniture freighted all the way from New Orleans, and watched the moon sail across the prairie and listened to the wind stir the cottonwoods and willows of the river. Bowen and the cowboy smoked; Hush just sat there and enjoyed the smell of the tobacco.

Presently Bowen's pipe went out and he knocked its dottle loose on the veranda rail.

"I wish to hell they'd get here," he said.

"I guarantee you they will," promised the bandy-legged rider. "If that horny old goat wasn't hotter to get to that young gal than a hungry dog to grab a knucklebone, my name ain't Iota."

"Iowa, you say?" asked Hush.

"Nope. *Iota*. The ninth letter and smallest symbol of the

Greek alphabet. You see, my mother was an eddicated woman, Mr. Feleen."

"I would have guessed Curly or Shorty," said Hush, interested. "What's the rest of it?"

"Jones. Iota K. Jones."

"I reckon I oughtn't to ask you what the K stands for."

"I wish you wouldn't. It's embarrassinger than Iota."

"Don't see how it could be," put in Travis Bowen.

"It is, damn it, it is," muttered the small cowhand unhappily.

"What is?" asked Hush, his thoughts elsewhere.

"Kathleen."

"What the hell's Kathleen got to do with it?" demanded Bowen.

"That's what the K stands for, Kathleen. Ain't that sinful!"

The other two men thought it over.

"You mean to set there and tell us," said Hush at last, "that your actual true name is Iota Kathleen Jones?"

"Yes, sir. Wrote square in the Bible and all. You see, Pap he wanted a gal. When he seen me he cussed and said, 'Well, goddam it, it didn't come with the right plumbing, but it's got curly hair and it's cute and sonofabitch we'll just keep it covered up with a double set of wet-pants and call it Kathleen anyhow."

Hush grinned and thought it was pretty funny, but Travis Bowen was a literal man, and besides, he was getting a little edgy.

"Your folks wasn't educated," he growled, "they was crazy." Then he added nervously, "Damn it all, I wish they'd get here."

Hush said nothing. He was thinking again of that mail-order wife of Avery Hudspeth's. He had never had the leisure for a woman of his own. As Jupe Feleen had always said, "There ain't no better cure for itchy pants than hard work," and God knew Hush had proved that. Since the day Nancy Hushton had tired out and quit trying, Hush hadn't had time even to think about a woman, let alone look one up. Now, the idea of this Missouri girl coming all the way from St. Louis was building a strange excitement in him.

"What's she like, I wonder?" he mused out loud. "The mail-order girl, I mean." Then, to Iota, hopefully: "Sometimes they send pictures, don't they? I mean actual real-life pictures. Like in the catalogues, and all."

"Sure," drawled Iota. "Set tight and I'll fetch you one of this here filly." He was back out of the house in a moment

75

with a framed daguerreotype of a handsome, full-bodied woman, which he handed to Hush.

"Here," he said. "You hold it, I'll strike a light."

Hush took the picture, his breath coming faster.

When the match flared, all three men stared so long and intently that the match burned down to Iota's fingers and went out unnoticed.

"Wheee-yooo! St. Louie woman!" murmured the little cowboy, after a proper respect of silence. "Here, you better gimme her back. If the Old Man caught us gawking at his lady love, he'd have us all horsewhupped."

"It's not a bad idea," said Hush, surrendering the picture.

"What ain't?" asked Bowen.

"Horsewhipping," answered Hush. "But I'll think of something better."

"Better for what?" queried Bowen.

"For Avery Hudspeth," said Hush.

The Pipe Creek man, accepting at face value the tall boy's bitterness, only nodded and fell silent. Iota Jones, on the other hand, had more natural curiosity.

"What about Ben Sloat, Mr. Feleen?" he asked.

If Hush was going to answer, he did not get the opportunity.

The sound of buckboard wheels grinding in river gravel came up from the ford of the Medina.

"It's them!" said Travis Bowen, reaching for his Winchester.

"Be still," said Hush, and didn't move.

They could hear the horses breasting the rise now. They were pulling without any snap or dig, the way used-up horses will. Voices floated up ahead of their blowing and snuffling. The girl laughed. Hush shivered to the thrill of it. In an instant his want of a woman was threatening to rise over his need for vengeance on Hudspeth and Sloat. Then he heard the gray-faced gunman laugh back at the girl, and the moment of confusion was gone.

"Get the lantern," said Hush to Iota Jones.

He heard the answering scrape of lamp metal, and added tersely:

"Remember, do it just like you would regular." He moved to the veranda rail, Bowen following him. "Light it up!" he muttered to Iota, and stood at the veranda rail with Travis Bowen. The lantern flared behind them, then steadied. Iota went down the high steps, holding it out in front of him.

"Welcome home," he called out as the buckboard slewed to a halt. "Have a good trip, folks?"

"Mind the horses!" snapped Avery Hudspeth. "We had a hell of a trip. Here, damn the horses, give me a hand with Mrs. Hudspeth."

"What's ailing her?" asked Iota in a worried tone. "She buggy-sick?"

"Not hardly," Ben Sloat leered at him. "We not only had a hell of a trip, we had a hell of a wedding!"

He stumbled down off the driver's side, not wrapping the lines and half falling into the near horse's rump. The woman, stepping out on the same side, and unsupported, lurched into him, took two steps and fell down. By this time Hudspeth, none too steady himself, was out of the buckboard. Between them, he and the cursing Sloat got the girl to her feet and, with Iota lighting the way, started her toward the veranda steps. As they reached the bottom of the flight, two soundless shadows melted out from the deeper shadows on either side of the steps.

The wavering flare of the lantern shone dully on the rust-brown barrels of the shotgun in the hands of the taller of the hard-faced strangers. The wedding party came to a staring-eyed stop. Even the weaving girl from far-off Missouri had instinct enough to stand still and say nothing, awaiting the orders of the rough-coated intruders as obediently as did her two companions.

Those orders came now in a voice as softly chill as the September midnight.

"Sober up," said Hush Feleen. "The honeymoon is over."

CHAPTER 16

The work began in the four A.M. darkness.

Sloat and his employer were lashed to snubbing posts, faces to the smoke and smell of the branding fires, so that they were forced to witness the marking of the Rocking H cattle precisely as they had arranged for Hush to watch the rape of his and Arnie's HF-connected gather.

There were three fires. Hush, Travis Bowen and Iota Jones handled the irons. The Rocking H riders were released from the bunkhouse to help with the cutting out and roping. Pearsall and Fenton sat shotgun guard at the corral gates. It was still not five o'clock when the first steer bawled and the stink of burning hair went up at Hush's fire.

By noon 250 cattle had gone to the fire. By four o'clock

the entire 350 head had been burned and turned loose: 100 head with Hush's HF-connected brand; 50 each with the brands of his five Pipe Creek neighbors. It was four-thirty when the Rocking H hands were locked back in the bunk-house, the fires kicked out, the stamp-irons hung up in the dogtrot. Hush was ready for Ben Sloat.

"Get his horse," he told Iota Jones. "His best one."

While the little cowboy was bringing up Sloat's pony, Travis Bowen cut the latter down from his snubbing post and walked him around to limber him up. Sloat didn't talk, and neither did his captors.

Iota came up leading the gunman's dapple gray gelding and Hush said, "Take him and my black mare into the small corral yonder. I'll be along with Sloat." Then he turned to Avery Hudspeth.

"You watch close, Mr. Hudspeth," he told him, easy-voiced. "You're next."

He wheeled to motion Sloat ahead of him toward the corral, but stopped short.

Unseen and unheard from, the long day through, the St. Louis woman had just come out of the house, and she went up to the tense group by the two snubbing posts. Uncon-sciously, the Pipe Creekers took off their ragged hats.

"Evening, ma'am," mumbled one or two of them, while the others simply stood and stared.

The woman warranted the stares, if not the respectful uncoverings. Tall, brown-eyed, taffy-haired, and needing no aids to nature, she was an eyeful which lonely men, used at best to slatternly, leather-skinned women, would not soon forget. She was certainly thirty years old, yet, seeing her, hungry men would still think of her—as Hush had the night before—as more girl than woman.

The appraisal was scarcely accurate. Whatever she was, the new Mrs. Avery Hudspeth was not a girl.

And she was a long way from the sodden bundle of champagne bubbles which her husband and Ben Sloat had helped away from the buckboard the previous evening. Re-freshed by fourteen hours' sleep, a change of frilly St. Louis clothes, and a new coat of cosmetics, she was quite a bit more than the gawking Pipe Creek ranchers had come prepared to see.

For her part, she had eyes only for Hush Feleen.

She greeted him levelly. "Don't you ever take off your hat to a lady?"

"To a lady," said Hush, "always."

He saw the blush spread upward from the revealing cleavage of her white breasts, but he did not drop his eyes, nor his ideas. Poor and hard as his life had been, Hush was mountain-reared. He had not been brought up with the impression that ladies got drunk. Or that they clung to and giggled with other men than their husbands before the ink was dry on their wedding papers. This woman he had seen hanging onto Sloat, and falling on her face in the dirt, not twenty-four hours gone. He remembered that.

"Now, ma'am," he instructed her, his voice gentle, "you had best go back in the house, for you won't care to see what's going to happen out here."

Her color had cooled and her voice was easy again. Too easy.

"On the contrary, Mr. Feleen," she retorted, "I might very much care to see it. What you mean is that you would not care to have me see it. Your kind never does."

"My kind never does what?" asked Hush.

"Want witnesses, Mr. Feleen."

"How's that, ma'am?"

"Witnesses, sir. Testifiers to the crime."

Hush shook his head slowly.

"Your husband will tell you better than that," he said. "I demand witnesses." He shifted his eyes to the snubbing post. "Isn't that so, Mr. Hudspeth?" he asked softly.

"Damn you, Feleen," answered the shaken rancher. "God damn you to everlasting hell."

Hush angled his lean head, bringing Ben Sloat into view. "Move out," he said.

Sloat went ahead of him into the small saddlestock corral. Iota brought their two horses forward and Hush said to Sloat, "Mount up." The other did so, and Hush called to Travis Bowen: "Shut and bar the gates."

When the wing gates had been swung in and fastened, the dark-faced Hush nodded to Ben Sloat and pointed to the riata coiled in its saddle-ring beneath the latter's right hand.

"That the one you used on me?" he asked.

"You know it," said Sloat.

The gunman did not yet know how this was going. The only thing he could think of was that the hard-tailed mountain boy meant to hang him, and he knew the Pipe Creek men would not stand by and let him do that. But he was not lacking in the principal tool of his trade—a case-hardened nervous system.

Blank-faced, he waited Hush out.

"Shake loose your rope," said Hush, and as he said it he was uncoiling his own braided strand of *brasada* rawhide.

Now Sloat's face unfroze. "Why?" he asked.

79

"Well," replied Hush slowly, "you're a revolver fighter. Me, I'm better with the shotgun, or maybe a skinning knife in a dark room. Now, we couldn't make a fair match any of the three ways, could we?"

"I reckon not. What's your play?"

"Riatas."

"Riatas?"

"That's what I said, *hombre*. Riatas *al brasadore*, right now."

"*Al brasadore?*" repeated Ben Sloat, losing another shade of color. "You mean one of them crazy Mexican rope fights?"

"With one piddling change," said Hush. "The Mexicans quit when one pulls the other out of the saddle," he explained, flat-voiced. "We'll drag it out a little—"

They circled their horses, hands free, guiding them with their knees and with the lean of their bodies, the reins knotted and dropped over the saddlehorns. The wiry mounts, both trained in the brush and quick as cats, had never played this game before, but it had the feel of a good one. The men on their backs had their ropes free and on the ready-swing, and that meant action was hanging on the next knee-squeeze.

The black mare was slender, silken smooth. The gray gelding was muscular, willing, very wise. The mounts were, in fact, nearly exact complements to the men who guided them so silently around and around the deep dust of the stock corral: both quick, both strong, both alert; but the one older, steadier and perhaps just a little smarter at the deadly game of decoy now going forward inside the fence.

Outside that fence, the riders from Pipe Creek and the tall blonde mail-order wife from St. Louis, stood and watched.

Sloat shot his loop without warning, almost nailing Hush on the first cast. Muchacha, the black mare, saved him, her swift ducking of the flung coil making it miss the head of her rider and slide from his left arm and shoulder. In the instant of its falling away from him, Hush snaked his own rope at Sloat, shooting it underhand and aiming for Sloat's roping arm, still extended from its missed cast. The gunman batted the throw aside, his eyes never leaving Hush's upper body. Both men retrieved and recoiled, letting their horses make their own moves meanwhile.

Now Hush drove the black mare suddenly inward, full into the gray gelding, shoulder to shoulder. He stood high in his stirrups, his small loop overhead, literally trying to drive it down over Sloat's hunched shoulders. The drive slanted off and Sloat grabbed the rope as it hit him, jerking on it and kicking out his horse. The move almost took Hush out of the saddle, and he had to drop his rope to keep it from doing so. In the moment of his imbalance, Sloat shot his own loop. It caught and hung on Hush's left arm, and Sloat yelled at his gelding and put the steel into his flanks.

Hush went with the rope but the black mare stayed under him and he did not leave the saddle. Spared for the necessary instant, he doubled a length of his trailing riata and slashed it across Sloat's face. Sloat threw up his hands to ward off a second slash and Hush saw the blood spurting from his right brow and cheekbone. In the same move of protection, Sloat had to slacken his hold on his own rope, and Hush shook it off his left arm and was free again.

He drove the black mare into the gray horse, but the gray met her this time at a bad angle, his broad chest taking her in the flank and knocking her over. She went down in the rear, sitting like a dog. Hush lay along her off side as Sloat's rope lashed the space over his saddle where he had been the moment before. Then the mare was staggering up, getting her quarters under her, leaping away and outdodging the gray.

In Hush was a sense of losing. The thing was not going according to pattern. He had made bad moves and was lucky to be still mounted. Moreover, the mare was hurt, and would not carry him as well from here on. He could feel her going rough under him, and knew his next move had to be for blood.

He spun the mare around as Sloat pulled the gray off to come back from a better angle. The gunman sensed the fact his opponent's horse was hurt, and he felt that her rider was no longer so sure of himself. Hush let him believe this.

When the gray started at him again, coming across the corral like a flung buffalo lance, Hush sent the mare directly in to meet him. But at the moment of passing, he did not try to put a loop on Sloat; instead he dove flat behind the black's lathered neck. He felt the cut of Sloat's rope across his back, and came twisting up and around in the saddle as the gray hurtled on by. He had his riata on full coil, and threw it to use all forty feet of its sinewy length behind the rolling ground loop he sent humping across the corral floor toward the gray's flying hooves.

The loop went in under the gelding, snaked up his right rear leg to the hock, grew suddenly small and closed like a strangler's cord on the slender bone just above the fetlock. Muchacha squealed, sat down on her haunches and slid to a dead stop. The gray went out to the end of Hush's rope, hit it, jerked into the air and went down into the dirt of the corral.

Sloat threw himself clear of his mount in falling, landing heavily, but with no bones broken. He rolled to his feet, clawing at the dirt in his eyes, snarling like a wounded animal.

Hush flipped his rope off the downed gelding's foot, and shaking out a six-foot loop, dropped it over the staggering gunman's head. He snapped it tight around his body and left arm, the right having thrown itself free in an instinctive effort to force off the rope when he felt it settle over him.

"Open the gate!" yelled Hush to Travis Bowen. "I'm bringing him out!"

Bowen, thinking, as did the others, that Hush meant that the affair was over and that he was towing its loser back to his snubbing post, threw open the gates to give Muchacha passing room. But Hush put his spurs in the mare's glossy belly, hard and deep. She jumped for the exit, banging the gates aside and pinning Travis Bowen to the corral fence.

Forty feet in her rear the trailing riata jerked Ben Sloat off his feet. The gunman's body bounced ten feet on its first carom off the packed earth. It twisted violently, bounced again, and smashed into the snubbing post. Then it went limp and began to drag at the end of the riata like a buffalo paunch full of cooking stones.

And that is the way it stayed—at the end of the riata—all the long fearful way that Hush rode the black mare on the dead run to repay the broken hulk which only seconds before had been a human being named Ben Sloat.

Hush walked the mare slowly up to the silent group by the snubbing posts. He was coiling his riata, the body of Ben Sloat left somewhere mercifully out of sight behind him.

"Well, Mr. Hudspeth," he said to the Rocking H owner, "you ready?"

Hudspeth looked at the Pipe Creek riders beyond Hush.

"My God," he gasped, "you men wouldn't let this madman—"

Travis Bowen held up his hand. "No, Mr. Hudspeth," he said, "we wouldn't."

He turned to Hush.

"We mean it, Feleen," he added grimly. "You've killed your man and got your cattle back. Now let's go."

"You're turning pious a little late in the afternoon, aren't you?" asked Hush quietly. "Seems to me we marked a few head in your brand, too, Mr. Bowen."

"That was to teach Hudspeth a lesson. We came along

with you because we felt a hard example had to be set. Well, we've set it and we're done here. We mean to cut Hudspeth loose and clear out. We've backed your play as far as we're going to. You understand that, Feleen?"

"Sure," said Hush. "You don't actually think I was going to drag an old man, do you? Go right on ahead. Cut him loose and clear out."

"That," said Travis Bowen sternly, "is not what we mean."

"Go on," said Hush.

"That poor devil you drug on your rope, that could have been an accident. We'll testify it was."

"But—" suggested Hush.

"But," Bowen went on steadily, "whatever happens to Hudspeth, once we're gone, we'll call it by its right name."

"I'm waiting," said Hush wearily.

"So will the rope be for you, Feleen," warned the Pipe Creek rancher, low-voiced and resolute.

"What in hell are you talking about?" demanded Hush, his irritation neither an act nor a pose of innocence.

He was bone-tired, blind with fatigue, and honestly confused by the sudden coldness of his Pipe Creek friends. But the reply of their spokesman to his question straightened him in the saddle like a gobbet of spit hitting him full-face.

"Murder," said Travis Bowen, and wheeled to free Avery Hudspeth from the snubbing post.

CHAPTER 17

Hush watched the Pipe Creek men go around the big house and down the slope to the river road. As he did so, the realities of his position began to grow upon him.

Behind him the occupants of the Rocking H bunkhouse were already showing signs of restiveness. They had seen the Pipe Creek branding party ride away, and they must know there had been some disagreement. They had started moving around and talking, and Hush knew he could not let their case go long unattended. There were six of them, not counting the dour-faced cook and the Indian horse wrangler, a one-eyed pure-blood Lipan Apache. Hush understood they were a hard crew hired to do hard work, scarcely the kind he wanted running loose behind his back while he tended to his settlement with their employer.

83

That brought his thinking down to Avery Hudspeth.

The owner of the Rocking H was still sitting on the ground at the foot of the snubbing post waiting for the circulation to return to his cramped limbs. Hush looked at him, frowning, trying to figure in his mind what best to do about him.

He had never entertained any serious notion of killing him, no matter what Bowen and the others thought. But now he must actually take care that *nobody* harmed the old bastard. Bowen's threat had not been an idle one. If anything happened to Avery Hudspeth, the Bandera County sheriff, and after him the U.S. Marshal from Austin and the Texas Rangers from San Antonio, would be hounding Hush Feleen to the last turn in the trail.

Still, the old man was a murderer. There might have been some technical stretch in the Texas cattle law to cover what he had done to Jupe Feleen, but there was nothing in any law of God or man to excuse his persecution of Hush and his offhand order which led to the killing of Arnie Feleen. No, he had to be punished, had to be made to pay, destroyed if possible.

But how did you go about destroying a man without killing him—a man like Avery Hudspeth?

The moment the question posed itself in Hush's mind, he saw the solution, the second part of the problem suggesting the answer to the first.

Hudspeth had grown rich on hides and tallow and trail drives. Like seven in ten *brasda* cow bandits, he had built his herd by applying the old Texas axiom of the branding iron working faster than the billy goat. He had gotten his start doing the selfsame thing for which he had hung Jupe Feleen, only doing it better. Now he was rich, now he wanted to forget his rustler's luck. To do it he had put his entire stake into the land and buildings and livestock of the big new ranch on the Medina.

But the ranch and its buildings were no part of Hush's thinking. He did not want them. He wanted only to destroy Avery Hudspeth without a gun, and now he knew the way to do it: it was to take away from him, without so much as touching him, every solitary thing for which he had gambled his grasping, fat-faced life. That meant the Rocking H Ranch. But not in the sense of land or bunkhouses or plantation mansions. No, it meant the real wealth, the *living* heart of the Rocking H; it meant Avery Hudspeth's cattle.

Hush would take from him every longhorn head of Texas beef he owned—every cow, bull, yearling, stag, heifer, steer, weaner, sucking calf, *ladino* stray, dogie, slickear, mossy-horn or black Spanish *mestena* that grazed the Rocking H grass—including every single calf now in carry for the spring of '77 drop.

Hush moved his dark head with the thought, and was content with it. It was a fair settlement of the debt.

Glancing at Avery Hudspeth, he saw that the old man was coming around more strongly. At the same time, looking toward the big house, he noticed Iota Jones approaching. On a snap hunch, he walked out to meet him.

"Hello," he greeted the little man. "What happened to you? You and Mrs. Hudspeth disappeared kind of sudden, didn't you?"

"She got a mite upset, Mr. Feleen."

"Don't blame her. I asked her to go up to the house."

"Yeah—well, she's there now. I told her a little of what you've been through with the Old Man. It calmed her some. I don't think she rightly blames you too harsh."

"No?" said Hush. "How about you, Iota? You rightly blame me for what I've done?"

"No, sir, not so far, I don't. I seen what the Old Man set still for Sloat doing to your kid brother. And to you."

"What you mean by 'not so far'?" asked Hush warily.

Iota squinted, set his bristly chin.

"I had a talk with that Travis Bowen feller," he said manfully, "and I got to tell you, Mr. Feleen, I don't hold with outright murder neither."

"You figure I do, Iota?"

"I dunno, Mr. Feleen, I purely don't. You got a bad eye."

"Iota," said Hush, pleased, "I like a man who says what's honestly in his mind. I'd like to have you stay on and ride for me. What do you say?"

The wizened cowboy squinted again.

"Well, there's no use flirting my tail. I could use the work."

"I haven't got a cent," Hush warned him. "You'll have to wait and pray for your money."

"I ain't much on praying, but I'm hell on waiting. Where you aiming to start, Mr. Feleen?"

"Right here on the Rocking H," said Hush.

The little cowboy studied him, his homely face twisted in thought. Iota Jones was a drifter. He had been and seen the dodo bird several times over. He was forty-four years old and beginning to get kinky on cold mornings. The tall boy in front of him was maybe twenty. He looked to have the gait and wind to go a long trail in the least trackline. If a man wanted to chance going with him, he might make his life-stake in one winter, or maybe two. It was a mighty hard temptation.

"You mean to take over the Old Man's spread, lock, stock and gunbutt?" he inquired uncertainly.

Hush had a special feeling for this small, brown-faced man who had dared Sloat and Hudspeth in his defense. But the day was getting short and he could not let gratitude distract him from the unfinished work.

"I asked for answers," he said.

Iota studied him, nodded, knuckled his hatbrim.

"Sign me on, Mr. Feleen," he muttered. "Autumn's almost gone, winter's coming on. It ain't no time to be looking for work in Texas."

"All right," said Hush, handing him the old twelve-gauge. "Go set shotgun on your friends while I take Mr. Hudspeth up to the house. Tell them they can work for me on the same terms I set you, or cut and drift. They've got till I get back."

"Yes, sir," Iota said. "I'll tell 'em."

"Turn the cook loose," Hush added. "See he gets a good hot supper going. Tell him I like plenty *chilipiquins* in my beefsteak sauce. *Comprende?*"

"Yes, sir," Iota Jones said again.

Hush dismissed him with a wave, and walked back to Avery Hudspeth.

"Mr. Hudspeth," he asked, "can you hear and understand me?"

"Yes, yes—"

"All right, then, on your feet. Easy now."

Hush helped him up, gave him a few seconds to steady himself.

"All right, Mr. Hudspeth," he said, "let's take a walk."

"Walk? Walk where?"

"Up to the house. We got business, you and me. From a long time back, Mr. Hudspeth. Remember?"

"I've got no business with you, Feleen."

"I reckon you have. Now lead gentle, don't balk."

The older man mumbled something under his breath and broke away. He grasped the snubbing post and leaned against it, legs braced.

"Mr. Hudspeth," murmured Hush, "if you want, we can leave our business go till morning. I can hang you on that post again. Likely the night air will clear your head."

"I can't think," complained the other, putting his hands to his temples. "I just can't seem to think."

"It's been a trouble of yours right along. Let's walk."

Again the old man refused, shaking his head in bewilderment.

"What is it you want of me?" he asked. "I don't know what it is you expect me to give you, or how you mean to go about getting it out of me."

"Come along up to the big house," said Hush, "and I'll show you."

"You'll what?" queried Hudspeth, pressing his temples again.

"I'll show you what I want of you, and how I mean to get it out of you. Now you move, Mr. Hudspeth. Last call *nice.*"

The other stared at him dully. "I'm an old man," he began, "you wouldn't—"

"I wouldn't *want* to," Hush interrupted him, and let it stand at that.

Avery Hudspeth nodded weakly. It was clear to him that he had to obey this black-haired boy with the soft voice, although it was not clear to him why he had to. He started off toward the big house, trudging along head down, shoulders sloped, thick arms dangling lifelessly. He was a beaten man before ever he heard the terms of his surrender to Hush Feleen.

CHAPTER 18

There were two pieces of furniture in the forty-foot main room, an enormous upright piano at one end of it, a battered rolltop desk at the other. Two buffalo robes decorated the oak puncheon floor, one in front of the piano, one in front of the desk. The walls were of Louisiana cypress, the beamed ceiling of Texas red cedar, the huge fireplace of caprock and river stone set in adobe. A scattering of calfhides and varmint pelts were nailed to the wall paneling, a set of seven-foot steer horns adorned the cottonwood mantelpiece.

Hush, who had never been inside a house whose entirety was half that of this single room, was stunned. To a mountain boy reared with eight brothers and sisters in a fifteen-foot-square cabin with only a sleeping loft and a cooking lean-to for extra space, the vastness of the Rocking H's *sala grande* seemed like all the prairie closed in and roofed over.

He felt the lure and meaning of owning a house like that begin to glow within him. The man who lived here would never be surprised to be called mister.

For the first time Hush wondered what the rest of Avery Hudspeth's mansion in the wilderness was like. Of a sudden he was taken with the idea that he must see it, and the thought burned in him like a fever—that he would not only see it, but that he would seize it! He would make it *his* house. It would be called the Hush Feleen house, and all the wide acres around it would be called the Feleen land. Yes, and still more. People using the river road to go up to Bandera or down to San Antonio would whip up their horses and say, "This here is all Feleen range; we had best get on acrost it. They don't like sunset to catch you on it."

Up to that moment Hush had meant only to force the old man to transfer to him by bill-of-sale the Rocking H cattle. It had been in his mind simply to take the herd and clear out. He would move it north to winter on the Red near Doan's Crossing. In the spring he would throw it on the trail for the Kansas railheads, cashing it out fast and coming back to Texas with the hard money to make a last clean start for himself and the HF connected away out in some new country where the wind blew free, the grass waved thick, and the name of Hush Feleen was as good as that of any man.

It was a worthy plan, and it would work. Yet, now, Hush hesitated, tempted by the chance of the still greater stroke of taking everything from the old man—not only his cattle, but his kingdom of grass and his unpainted rawboard palace as well—thus leapfrogging the risk of wintering on the Red, and landing, instead, square in the all-out ranching business of the Rocking H, already flourishing on the rich Medina River range.

Hush looked at Avery Hudspeth, standing all the while dazed and putty-faced by the oak desk, and he said to him, gray eyes gleaming: "Sit down, old man, I've got to think."

Hudspeth found the chair, eased into it with a wordless groan. He stared up at Hush a wavering moment, then dropped his head on his crossed arms on top of the desk and did not move again.

Hush's frown deepened.

The risks were considerably greater in the second plan. Were the rewards worth the risks? Specifically, it was the big house which held the answer. Was this prairie monument of sideboard and shingle and southern plantation columns, together with what little of upstairs furnishing might prove to be in it, of sufficient added value to warrant the bigger gamble?

There was a prolonged pause then, while Hush fought against his greed. At last, he forced his inflamed ambition back to the reasonable, even justified, level of his original decision to take only the old man's cattle. It was in the act of leaning to inform Avery Hudspeth of this final resolve, that he heard the slight rustling sound behind and above him.

He spun around, hipping and levering the Winchester on the turn. At the head of the banistered stairway to the second floor, stood the St. Louis woman. For a long moment she and Hush watched each other. Neither of them spoke, neither of them moved. Then Evelyn Hudspeth smiled.

Hush shivered and glanced over his shoulder, thinking she meant it for her husband. But Avery Hudspeth was still head-down on the desktop, and the shiver came back on Hush.

"What do you want?" he said uncertainly to the taffy-haired girl.

She moved on down the stairs and across the long room to come up to him, close enough that he could get the scent of her perfume, before she answered him.

"You," she said.

Hush's breath stopped. The fire in her dark eyes jumped the space between them, blazed up in Hush. He fought it down, smothering its wild flame by sheer Feleen will. When he spoke to her, his lean features were set in the old *brasada* mold of animal wariness.

"Get out of here," he ordered her. "And in the future keep away from me. You understand me, Mrs. Hudspeth?"

She was in a feather-and-silk dressing gown, a flimsy thing even by St. Louis standards. She saw Hush's eyes flick to the swell of her breasts and the curve of her belly. Deliberately, she moved her hips and shoulders so that the garment opened above and below the loose sash which had held it closed.

"The future," she said, "is what I'm talking about."

Hush was staring now. The soft whiteness of the long thighs, the hard bareness of the high breasts, were driving the blood up in him thick and dark. It was suddenly difficult for him to speak.

"What do you mean?" he muttered.

She straightened, the movement closing the gown again. She was at once all seriousness, the seductive smile and the body shifting gone.

"I mean *our* future, Hush Feleen. Yours and mine. I go with the place—*or it doesn't go.*"

Hush studied her for thirty seconds. Then he nodded.

"Thanks for the offer, Mrs. Hudspeth. If I decide that's the way I want it, I'll let you know."

She smiled, returning his curt nod, and moved sinuously across the room. At the foot of the staircase she turned, one satin slipper poised on the first step to open the gown and show the wicked curve of the thigh again. This time the gown parted higher up, almost to the shadowed joining. She could hear the sibilant indrawing of Hush's breath cut the silence between them.

"If you decide that's the way you want it," she said, "I'll be upstairs."

The unpleasantness with Avery Hudspeth did not take long.

Twelve hours hung on a snubbing post in the hot September sun, that ordeal preceded by the buckboard journey from San Antonio and topped by the sight of a man roped and dragged to death before his eyes, had done what no amount of bodily beating could have done to the tough old mavericker.

His nerves were shattered. His will was gone. He knew what he was being asked to do, but he could not command his leaden limbs to rise up, nor his exhausted mind to rebel. When Hush told him to write, he wrote; and when he told him to sign, he signed. There was literally no more to it than that.

The dark-faced, gray-eyed boy had not touched him. He had only told him what he wanted him to do, uttering not even a hint of what might be his fate if he did not do it. Avery Hudspeth, not in any way deceived, had drawn the document giving over title to the Rocking H, its lands, livestock, equipment and improvements to Hush Feleen. Having himself dispensed summary justice in his time, he knew its image when he saw it in the face of another executioner. *All that a man hath, will he give for his life*—and Avery Hudspeth had understood he was trading the Rocking H to Hush Feleen for a saddled horse and a twenty-four-hour start.

When he had scrawled his name on the bottom of the paper, Hush led him outside and across the corral yard to the bunkhouse. Guiding him to the cook's woodpile in the dogtrot, he sat him down upon it and said to Iota Jones, "Make a light and bring the men out here."

The little cowboy lit the dogtrot lantern, unhasped the bunkroom door, called into the darkness beyond it.

"I guess you heard Mr. Feleen. Come on out."

There was a whispering in the room, and a muffled scraping of boots. Then stillness again.

"Give me that shotgun," said Hush, and started for the door.

"Now hold on, Mr. Feleen." Rafer Henderson, a lanky

rider, came out hands high. "We ain't aiming to put off on you."

"See you don't," advised Hush, and counted the rest of them out as they filed into the dogtrot.

"Seven, not counting the cook, is that it?" he asked Iota.

"Yes, sir. Six and the Injun bronc-stomper."

"All right," said Hush. "Now you men listen to me. Hudspeth has sold me the Rocking H and it's the HF connected from tonight on. That HF stands for Hush Feleen. Remember it. If you want to work for me, get over by Iota. If you want to clear out, stand over by Hudspeth." -

The men looked at one another. They looked at Avery Hudspeth. They looked at Hush.

"Move," he said.

Rafer Henderson eased over to side Iota. "I'll stay," he said.

Another man, Tate Lockhart, followed him. The next four all moved across the dogtrot to Hudspeth. The last man, the one-eyed Indian horse wrangler named Nocero, looked the two sides over and said:

"Sumbitch, me stay in middle. Injun got no friend."

Hush eyed him a minute, grinning despite his tenseness.

"You know what happens to the man that straddles the fence, don't you?" he said. "He winds up with a sore crotch."

Nocero laughed loud and startlingly.

"Goddamsumbitch," he declared, "you good man. Think like Injun. *Enthlay sit-daou!*"

Hush cocked a questioning eye at Iota and the latter bobbed his head quickly. "He says he'll stay with you." Then he added apologetically, "I talk a little Apache. Learnt it in school."

Hush was better mannered than to ask what school. But Nocero, anxious now to please the tall white boy, gave his horse-whinny laugh and leered. "Him learn in squaw school, on Apache blanket. Best way catchum lesson heap fast."

"Shut up, you one-eyed idiot," growled Tate Lockhart, a thick-set man with a baling-wire beard. "Mr. Feleen ain't done yet."

"Yeah, cease and decease," drawled Rafer Henderson. "That loony laugh of yours would make a snake nervous."

"Me know what me say!" defended the Indian stoutly. "Broken Nose him borrow my blanket."

"*Amigo,*" said Hush softly in Spanish, "*callate.*"

The Apache thought over the situation. Shortly he decided he liked the sound of being called "friend" by the black-haired boy, even if it came coupled with a blunt suggestion

91

to "shut up." Accordingly, he tossed his ragged bangs affirmatively.

"Si, patrón," he said, and stepped to Hush's side.

Strangely pleased, the latter now turned to Avery Hudspeth and the four hands who had remained loyal to the Rocking H.

The men shifted uneasily under his regard. Hush thought he knew why.

He had them—all of them—by the short hair. From Iota he had learned that Hudspeth and his hands had left Live Oak County for more reasons than to hunt down Hush Feleen. The old man had mavericked the country raw. Feeling down there had been running to talk of the rope if the law didn't act soon. So he and his riders could not turn south for help. If they went north, they would run into the Bandera sheriff and five self-interested witnesses from Pipe Creek—witnesses who would have to stand against Hudspeth in their own defense and who, although they might threaten to protest a murder on Hush's part, would certainly not hesitate to commit a little perjury in their own behalf.

No, sir, the simple fact was that Avery Hudspeth and his hands had gotten out of Live Oak County just the way Hush figured to get out of Medina and Bandera counties—after mavericking the life out of the local *llano* for as long as he dared, then making one last wholesale gather of everything his cowboys could surround in a week of hard riding and throwing it on the fast drive for a new ranch and a new range, far away.

Hush had never heard the term poetic justice, but it would have fitted perfectly his idea of what he was doing. And it would have complemented, exactly, his excited certainty that he was going to get away with the dangerous gamble, where Avery Hudspeth had not. It never occurred to him that the fatal weakness of the Rocking H adventure lay in the method, not the man.

To him, life had always been a business of betting on Hush Feleen, all the way. He saw it no differently now, as he at last nodded to himself and spoke to the waiting men.

"All right, boys, you've named your choice; now saddle it. Get your horses and clear out. Take the old man with you and take this final little piece of advice along with him."

He waited then, letting them get nervous again, before he continued carefully.

"Those of you who know how Mr. Hudspeth built his brand, know he ain't going to see any law, nor any lawyers, about getting it back. Any of you don't know how he done it, ask your friends down in Live Oak. Or ask the old man when he gets his guts back. Meanwhile, here's the advice: take my word for it, this sale is final. Get aboard your horses and don't let sunrise catch you on Feleen land."

Again he broke off, waiting them out, narrow-eyed.

When he saw, or thought he saw, that one or two of them were still unconvinced, his mouth corners whitened.

"If any of you've got any unresolved questions," he said, "go ask them of Ben Sloat."

The implication proved convincing.

The four riders moved quickly and with no further muttering. They brought up their horses and saddled them, not forgetting the extra animal for Avery Hudspeth. The last cinch tightened, they legged up and struck out for the river road at a bit-jingling trot. When they got out of sight over the rise, they kicked their mounts into a rocking lope. On the road below, the lope became a hammering gallop. And that was the gait which Hush, having followed them on foot to the crest of the rise, heard dying away in the Hondo Canyon darkness.

He came about then and stood staring for a considerable time at the stable lantern blinking from the bunkhouse dog-trot. From that, his gaze shifted to the red-chimneyed Rochester handlamp set in the upstairs bedroom window of the big house. He knotted his fists, put his head down, and tried hard to make the right and sensible choice. He was tired. God knew he was aching, marrow-bone tired. And God knew he didn't want to add adultery to his vengeance against Avery Hudspeth. He and the old man were quits. The St. Louis woman was no part of their deal—and no part of Hush's plans.

He brought his head up, turning his face to the silent stars, seeking a strength that was greater than his own. But his eye caught again the red gleam of the Rochester lamp, and he felt his belly go tight and his breath grow short, and he knew which light he was going toward.

He did not remember the veranda steps creaking under him, nor the panels of the front door swinging inward beneath his hand. He did not even remember crossing the *sala grande* to stand, awestruck, at the bottom of the banistered staircase.

He only remembered—and remembered always—the bedroom lamplight flooding the landing above to bathe in its rose-red wickedness the satin cream of Evelyn Hudspeth's unclad body.

CHAPTER 19

Hush had no background of experience for coping with a woman like Evelyn Hudspeth. He had never been through the painful adolescent hungering after the sight and feel of a girl's body. Too work-pressed to worry about sneaking looks and feels, he had always reasoned that when he was ready to be a man, he would be one. In consequence of his innocence, Evelyn Hudspeth devastated him.

Beginning with that night, he could not get enough either of the pleasures of her body, or of her company. She was an enjoyable woman, taken any way—young in flesh and spirit, old in wile and wisdom. She was the incarnation of the lucious young schoolmarm whose ripe buttocks and breasts the eyes of every older boy pupil followed incessantly.

Hush could not keep his hands off her, and it was only with the greatest effort that he refrained from pawing at her the livelong day. As for his thoughts, they followed every movement of her sinuous figure, awake and asleep. When he could not have the flesh of her, he could have the image, and that is what he held to the point of obsession. He was not the first youth to be enamored to sickness of his first woman, but in his case the emotional disorder was multiplied by the obvious physical attractions of Evelyn Hudspeth and her practiced art in using them.

As the weeks went on, September passing into October and November, Hush's malady deepened; and in the end, fiercely and with a desperately unreasoning hope, he seized upon the conviction that he could be, finally, at peace with the world about him through being content with the taffy-haired wife of Avery Hudspeth.

For her part, Evelyn Hudspeth also wavered. For a time the affair might have gone either way. For a time she forgot that she had not come to Texas to wither and grow sere while a boy waxed and grew green on the nourishment for which she had decided to gamble the last, fading bloom of her golden beauty.

Born Evelyn Fay Hollister in the *Vide Poche*, the notorious "empty pocket" district of St. Louis' old French Creole quarter, she had inherited from her Gallic mother the gutter-born savageness to survive which is nowhere more vicious than among the transplanted poor of Paris. The quick good humor, ready laugh, drift-and-let-drift philosophy bequeathed her by her American mountain-man father, had never been enough to overcome the European heritage. His gifts of easy laughter and surface good nature made her only the more able to earn her way in the world of men; they did not compensate for her grasping, hungry, maternal inheritance.

Yet in Hush she seemingly found her equal. He was as hard as she was, and as much a man as she was a woman.

Not yet twenty, he stood six feet three inches, but he was so perfectly made, so beautifully muscled, that he appeared no taller than the average man. His hair, black as a crow's wing and barbered off front and back with horse shears only enough to keep it out of his eyes and off his shoulders, gave him the look of an Indian with some white blood, an impression strengthened by his dark skin and piercing gray eyes. His reluctance to talk, his crouching wilderness way of walking, his superb horsemanship, did nothing to weaken the impression of part Apache or Comanche ancestry. So striking was this Indian look that men who knew him only after his start on the Hondo Canyon ranch, came to call him "that damned Indian," and would not let the legend of his red blood die. Well into the next century there was still old men living in Texas who would swear that Hush Feleen was a "quarter-blood Lipan," a "three-sixteenths Kioway," a "five-eighths Kwahadi," and who would not listen to the actual fact that the Feleens, like most family-proud mountainfolk, could trace their lineage as far back as Plymouth Rock or Roanoke, or as far beyond as the records went.

This dark look of the "breed" exerted a strong fascination on Evelyn Hudspeth. And the considerable difference in their ages did not dim the attraction. The fact of Hush's minority meant little in that frontier time and place. A man, like a woman, was old enough if he was big enough. And Hush was big enough. Also, he and the St. Louis woman were living in an era when a whole nation was growing up overnight. And in that frontier country people took such mates as they could find, where they found them; if a little love and affection developed subsequently, it was accepted as a gratuity. A man did not feel grateful to a woman for her favors, nor did she consider that he should. He took, she gave. It was considered an equal exchange, with no one left owing.

So it was that the Tennessee boy and the Missouri woman made their union and prospered it through the fall of 1876. As Christmas came and the new year turned into the winter of 1877, there was not much that Hush could think to ask for that he did not feel he already had.

True, some shadowy things bothered him still. He had not yet sent for Don Diego and the family. He was even losing some of the more careful ways of speech that he had learned from them. He had not gone into Bandera Town with the woman to get their names on a marriage paper. Neither had he seen that lawyer about making the ranch ownership legally equal. Then there were the nights he dreamed of Ben Sloat 'and of the hole in Howell Hudspeth's belly; of the way Sand Crane's backbone had been shredded and Roan Calf's side torn out, and of the bad sound of the Winchester's butt striking Tall Walker's skull. And further back, before these things, there were the strangled burst of the shotgun shoved in the dun steer's mouth and the sight of Jupe Feleen lying bloody-headed on the dirt floor of the little dogtrot house on the Nueces. These memories made the days restless and the nights wakeful for him; made bothersome times when he was not so certain that all went well for him, and uneasy spells which left him fretful and troubled as to why such remembrances should come back to plague him now that he had found his happiness and was working hard toward his peace of mind and his decent place in the Texas cattle business.

Then the old counterarguments would come and he would feel reassured that he had done right in the long run, and that life had to be fought back at, no matter the hurt, or on whom it might fall.

That *ladino* steer had not worried when it opened up the Morgan mare's flank. Jupe had thought nothing of taking a dogwhip to his firstborn son. Those damned Comanches had robbed and scalped and burned out innocent God-fearing white folks before ever Hush went after them. As for young Hudspeth and that gray-faced pig, Ben Sloat, what right had they to keep him awake? They had both tried to kill him and missed. When he tried to kill them back, he hadn't missed. There were no more morals to it than that. It all added up to the unpleasant fact that it was a world of hard work and no pay for the soft ones. You had to be tougher and quicker and more sure of your aim than the next man. If you weren't, you would never grow old or die rich in Texas. Cut down to simple size, for simple minds, like Hush's, that was the whole truth of it.

With this summation, the Tennessee boy went into the winter of 1877. As an understandable variant of the existing dog-eat-dog packrule of a new frontier's predatory poor, his thinking might have had both moral excuse and working merit. It might have, that was, in a world without women; a world marked "for men only," and meant to be won or lost

96

on the suddenness of a gun, the swiftness of a horse, the certainty of a rope.

But Hush no longer lived in such a world.

Upon his failure to comprehend this fact hung the balance of his future, and Evelyn Hudspeth was not the kind to wait indefinitely for the seesaw to stop.

For her the problem was less involved. It dealt only with three factors: did Hush intend to marry her; did he intend to keep his promise of sharing the ranch's wealth with her; and, regardless of his intentions, did she herself want to share that wealth with him?

But the conclusion was not easily arrived at, and as the new year sped through January into February, Evelyn Hudspeth had not yet made her choice of futures.

For all her hard experience and flinty upbringing, the sheer ardor of Hush's love-making confused her. Had he, during this critical time, given her adequate indication that he meant, as ardently, his agreement to marry her and share the HF connected, their bandit partnership might have flourished and grown respectable, as did several other Texas cattle fortunes of no less sinister origin. But Hush did not do this. And so, on the basis of a misunderstanding brought about by his close Faleen mouth and the southern male's assumption that his actions required no explanations to his spouse, he called down upon himself the unwarranted vengeance of a lonely, strayed woman—one who, treated with only a little more of trust and consideration, might well have changed her own tarnished attitudes in time to redeem and rededicate his.

But it never occurred to Hush to tell her what was in his heart and mind; to reassure her that he meant to keep his word and do it gladly, given only the right time and opportunity. Instead, he went his usual intent, secret-thoughted way; and the Missouri woman, wavering and waiting in vain for him to redeem his pledge, submerged her moment of middle-aged daydreaming and turned on Hush Feleen with the fury of an uncaged tigress.

CHAPTER 20

Throughout the winter months enough riders looking for honest work had drifted on and off the Hondo Canyon range to spread the word that so long as a man didn't care whose cows he marked, provided he marked them with an HF connected, he could go to work for the "damned Indian down on the Medina."

Naturally, what drove off the good men attracted the bad. By late March Hush had a dozen riders who knew what they had been hired for. The new men accepted the same risks as did Iota and the others, and for the same pay—a percentage of the projected illegal gather. The conditions called for a hardcase crew.

The country this close in to Austin City and San Antonio was settling up. Ranges were getting to be well defined, mavericking was being replaced by the newer term, rustling, and maverickers by the time-honored Texas definition, "cow thieves." The penalty under state and local law, however, remained unchanged. If a man was caught with some other man's cow on the ground, or even found off his own range with a running or straight-rod iron under his stirrup fender, it was still shake out the rope and head for the nearest high limb.

Accordingly, the selection of a crew for the HF April gather a full month ahead of the legal dates in Medina and Bandera counties was chancy work. But Hush was satisfied with his choices when, on the evening of March 29th, he called in Iota Jones and told him the soonering of the adjacent ranges would begin on April Fool's day, three days hence.

When the news leaked back to Evelyn Hudspeth, innocently by way of Nocero, the Lipan Apache horse wrangler, she was in a fit frame of mind to do something about it.

The duties of the horse wrangler encompassed about everything beneath the dignity of the regular hands. Having charge of the ranch's *remuda*, or band of saddlestock, was the least of his chores. Care of the "remoother," as the Texas cowboys pronounced it, was regarded as an insult, not an honor, and no normal cowhand would consider undertaking it, short of starvation or senility. Among the wrangler's more important duties, however, was that of assistant to the outfit's cook, and it was in his discharge of this capacity that Nocero picked up the lethal bit of bunkhouse gossip.

Pegleg Pearson, the cook, who had been a tophand until his bronco fell on him and crushed the leg now missing at the knee, was a sanguine and a knowledgeable fellow, and also a considerable talker. He held that it availed a man nothing to be more brilliant than his contemporaries unless he let the latter know about it, more or less endlessly. And just now Nocero was his case in point.

The actual sequence of the ranchyard grapevine was Iota

Jones to Rafer Henderson to Pegleg Pearson to Nocero, who took the message on up to the big house with the armload of stovewood he had cut for "the lady's" kitchen range. Fatefully, Nocero got to the ranchhouse before Hush did, the latter having held up to check the new HF stamp-irons being finished by Tate Lockhart, a true artist in such fancy forgework.

The one-eyed Indian wrangler had taken a liking to the tall yellow-haired "lady" of the big house. She had treated him with more kindness and respect than he was accustomed to in that land of Indian haters. Besides, she was the squaw of the black-haired "boy," and that made her very much *la patronessa*, in Nocero's dark-skinned opinion.

"Him boy heap funny," he greeted her now, as she opened the rear door for him and he moved across the room to dump his wood in the stove box. "By damn, him make me laugh. Got ideas like Indian."

"Now what's he done?" asked Evelyn Hudspeth, suddenly feeling that what would strike a Lipan Apache as riotously funny might curl the hair of a white woman.

"April Fool Day, that the time all damnfool white man make crazy joke on each other, yes? So that him day boy going to start stealing cow all over range. You think funny too, lady?"

"Very funny," said Evelyn Hudspeth.

"Why you no laugh then?"

"It's too much trouble, Nocero. Put some wood in the stove and get scarce. The lady doesn't want to talk to you."

The Apache looked at her from under his shaggy bangs. He put two chunks in the firebox and went back across the kitchen to the door. There he paused, nodding slowly.

"You know something, lady? You good squaw for boy. Tough like bottom of boot, tender like backfat of buffalo calf." He rolled his one good eye, smacked his wide lips. "Him heap man, you heap woman. Me bet make plenty noise on blanket."

She turned pale, but said nothing. The Indian had meant the crude remark as a compliment. But to her it served as a harsh reminder of how far down she had let her relationship with Hush Feleen slide. For weeks she had been trying to quiet in her mind the growing feeling that her partnership with Hush in the original theft of the Rocking H from Avery Hudspeth was moving toward a far more sinister end than the beginning moral wrong done to the old man. Now, of a sudden, the warning instinct had become a cold, hard reality: if she went ahead with him it would mean she accepted equal guilt for the forthcoming illegal gather, the traditional punishment for which was the riata and the gallows limb. The impact of the delayed realization broke the dam of indecision which had been protecting Hush all these months. But she channeled the released doubts with no outward sign.

To the Indian wrangler, still standing by the door awaiting acknowledgment of his Apache *bon mot*, she only nodded and said, "Get out, Nocero. Thank you for the wood," and Nocero had sense enough, savage nose for trouble enough, to scent the unspoken violence beneath her quiet words and to do as she told him.

Left alone, she sank down at the kitchen table, looking off after the vanished Lipan. When Hush came in moments later she was still there.

"What's the matter with you?" he asked. "You look like something the cat dragged in and was sorry for his trouble."

"I'm all right," she said. "I've just been thinking."

"Well, don't," Hush advised her. "That's my job."

"It should have been," said Evelyn Hudspeth, staring at him, and she got up and went out of the room.

What she came to, finally, was the decision to get word out to the Texas Rangers at San Antonio.

She was aware that Hush had been watching her like a hungry lynx since her cryptic comment at the kitchen table two days before. He could not know precisely what was in her mind, but his instincts, wild as those of any outlaw *ladino*, had been set on edge. Knowing this, she realized she could no longer consider going for help herself, but would have to prepare a message and procure a messenger to deliver it.

And procure was the correct word for that part of the plan.

There was only one sure way to turn a man's senses to soapsuds, his will to dishwater. Granted the method, there remained only to select the man.

He would have to be young—the younger the better. As near a boy as was possible to pick from Hush's casehardened crew. Curly—of course it had to be Curly. He was not only the youngest, but the newest. Knowing less of Hush, he would fear him less, lead easier, further, faster than any of the others. Moreover, he was not bright, even for a cowhand; but he was bright enough. And he was big enough and hangdog-looking enough to be obviously the one who would do anything to get his hands on a willing woman's body, or just for the promise of being let to do so. Curly Gilkeson—

slow, stupid, eager, made to order for the San Antonio sneak-out.

Nearing mid-forenoon of the 31st, Evelyn Hudspeth saw her cowboy leading his pony to water at the yard-trough between the snubbing posts. Orders had gone out to get up top mounts for tomorrow's start, and Curly was obeying orders. The St. Louis woman smiled wearily, and went out to intercept him with a forced swaying of hips and straying of eyes which no man, bright or half-bright, could call anything but a personal invitation to put his hands where his thoughts had just been sent.

It was eleven o'clock that night when Curly Gilkeson led his saddled pony up to the harness shed beyond the holding pens. The woman was there ahead of him, smelling of beautiful toilet water and of being still warm from the bed. But when he licked his lips and reached clumsily for her, she struck his hands away and reminded him that he hadn't yet done anything to earn such favors, and that if he was going to get difficult to handle she would have to call out for her husband, and she was sure Curly wouldn't like that.

The slow-witted cowboy said no, he wouldn't, but that he reckoned her husband wouldn't like it either, and so he couldn't see where she would have the nerve to yell out for him, in any case.

"Try me," said Evelyn Hudspeth frostily. Then, instantly melting it with a smile, she held out the letter. "You will have better luck after you get this through to the Rangers at San Antone, Curly. Remember, honey always draws more flies than vinegar when it comes to getting around a woman. Besides, Curly"—she let a little of the frost back into her voice—"my husband would believe *me*, not you."

"He ain't your husband," said the gawky youth. "Not really."

"But he *would* believe me, wouldn't he, Curly?"

Curly thought about that a minute, then nodded. "All right, gimme the letter."

He took the envelope from her and put it in his inside coat pocket. As he did so, he smelled it, perfumed and warm from her breasts, and his breathing grew heavy again.

"I still think I'd ought to get something afore I go. I'm taking a turrible chance." He moved toward her again, and she drew back, fighting to control her fear of him and her disgust with herself, knowing she had to play it out now.

"Curly," she told him, letting a catch come in her voice, "if I led you on to think wrong things of me, I'm awfully ashamed. I thought you offered to help me because I'm a

101

woman and in deep trouble. I guess I just figured you were different from most men somehow. It's my fault, Curly, please forgive me—"

Curly shifted his boots, wrestled manfully with his ugly desires, saw distantly a far light of chivalry shining where before only the near lamp of lust had burned before.

"Damn it all, ma'am!" he blurted, "I ain't said I wasn't going to do it for you. Sure, I reckon I tooken you wrong. But that don't mean you misfiggered me none."

"Curly, oh, Curly—!"

"It's all right, ma'am, it's all right. Now you'd best get back to the house afore he misses you. I'll light out jest as soon as you're clear of the shed. Hurry up now."

"God bless you, Curly. And thank you, thank you *so* much!"

"Don't thank me yet, Mis' Hudspeth. I ain't exactly been there and got back. Go on now, hustle on outen here."

She was already gone and didn't hear his slow-worded answer and its repeated warning. But Curly was used to people walking off before he got his thoughts spoken out, and so he only shook his head and muttered to his horse, "Damn it all, Baby Doll, I dunno, I just dunno—"

Trailing it off, he mounted up and sat the little mustang, looking off into the murky night. Presently he went on passionately between set teeth:

"I will say one thing I sonofabitching sure do know, though. That woman's got the meanest set of lips and wickedest waggle to her seat I ever seen on a human female." He shivered. "Gawd! I guess a man would do most anything short of murder to get his hands on a piece of that!"

"You ought to know, Curly," said a soft voice out of the darkness of the shed's north wall.

Then it went on, more softly still and more pleasant-sounding than ever: "Only why stop short of murder?"

As he asked the low-voiced question, Hush Feleen stepped out from the north wall's shadow and swung the shotgun's muzzles upward.

He kept the shotgun on the young cowboy long enough to let him think he really meant to use it on him, then lowered it and read him his riding orders.

"Curly," he said, "I'm going to let you go. You give me that letter Mrs. Hudspeth gave you and you kick that Baby Doll horse out of here and you keep on kicking her. First light tomorrow I'll track you to the edge of Feleen land. If you're safe gone, I won't follow you. You understand me? Think careful now."

He waited while his meaning sank in on his listener.

He had no real argument with Curly. The dull-witted cow-boy had spoken aloud the literal truth about Avery Hud-speth's long-stemmed mail-order rose. She was the kind al-most any man would stand in line for to get fired on, if getting missed meant gaining a ticket to her bedroom. Curly was no different. But he was not so dumb that he didn't understand the advice to think carefully.

He fumbled the letter out of his jacket and handed it down to Hush. "Shucks, Mr. Feleen," he began, "I never really—"

"Curly," said Hush, "get out."

He raised the shotgun as he spoke, and Curly Gilkeson, thick wits chillingly penetrated, crouched forward and hit Baby Doll with the quirt. The little horse jumped and came down running. She was gone instantly into the prairie dark-ness.

Hush stood a moment, then turned and walked slowly toward the big house. In the kitchen he made a light, sat down at the table and took out the letter.

It was addressed "To the Captain of Texas Rangers, San Antonio," and stated that the writer was being held pris-oner on her own ranch, the former Rocking H outfit in Hondo Canyon on the Bandera-Medina line; that her hus-band and the co-owner of the property, Avery Hudspeth of Live Oak, had disappeared or been done away with and that she, Evelyn Hollister Hudspeth, would make a full state-ment upon release, naming names and formal charges against the guilty. It was signed "Mrs. Avery Hudspeth," and there was a postscript: *Hurry; I am in actual danger of my life!*

There was no mention of Hush Feleen or of the HF con-nected, but Hush failed to mark this peculiarity. For him there was only one fact about Evvie Hudspeth's message that mattered: he had trusted her and she had turned on him. She meant to take the ranch all for her own and she meant to testify against him, Hush Feleen, by way of doing it. That testimony, supported by reliable eyewitnesses—of which there were at least five living within a day's ride, on Pipe Creek—would hang him.

The thought of the rope started a terrible tide of memory flooding up in him. He stood again in the clearing on the Nueces; smelled again the raw smell of the hemp; felt again its cat's tongue rasp against his neck, its choking grip clutch at his throat, the pain of its cruel knot smash hard behind his ear. Then the ice of remembered terror was growing in his belly, spreading its fearsome, familiar cold through him, freezing out of him the final fragment of mercy he might have held for Evelyn Hudspeth.

He got up from the table and put the letter in the kitchen stove and watched it burn until it was only a curl of blue smoke and a wisp of gray-white ash.

Then he went out to the harness shed and got down from its hanging place the small HF jaw-iron he had ordered Tate Lockhart to make up for marking the right cheek bulge of the horse stuff that belonged to Hush Feleen. He took the jaw-iron back into the kitchen and buried it in the banked coals of the stove and stood there for fifteen minutes, fanning the rekindled coalbed with his big hat while the letters of the iron turned from black to yellow to rose. When the color was just right, and not a breath before it was, he took the iron out of the fire and went with it across the darkened *sala grande* toward the foot of the staircase.

CHAPTER 21

"My Gawd!" gasped Pegleg Pearson, sitting bolt upright on his bunk. "What was that?"

"Jesus, I dunno," mumbled Rafer Henderson, rolling sleepily to one elbow. "Sounded like a catamount."

"That warn't no catamount," a third voice said from the dark. "It sure as hell warn't," another voice agreed.

There was a pause of light breathing and hard listening as the awakened hands strained to catch some further sound. None came, and it was Iota Jones who identified what they had heard.

"That cry came from up to the big house," he said slowly. "It was her."

Up before dawn the next morning to see to the loading of his branding irons into the possum-belly steerhide slung under the chuck wagon, blacksmith Tate Lockhart found the saddlestock jaw-iron missing. He returned at once to the cookshack side of the dogtrot where the other hands were still eating breakfast. There were eleven men sitting at the long table in the cookshack when Tate came in and told Iota Jones about the jaw-iron. A minute later, there were only six.

Ab Marquardt, a big, thick-wristed man from the Indian

104

Nations, stood up and said, "It *was* her last night," and he stalked out of the room. He was followed by four other riders, none of whom said anything. The five got on their horses, already roped out, saddled, slickered and bedrolled for the gather, and rode off over the rise directly toward the ford of the Medina, the nearest route off of HF land.

Inside the cookshack no one made a move to go after them. The remaining men just pushed back from their unfinished plates, built up and lit their smokes and sat there saying nothing. They were still sitting there when Hush appeared in the doorway.

He hadn't shaved. His face was tightly drawn. His gray eyes held a bad light. It was plain that he had turned ugly about something.

"You men getting paid to burn brands, or Burley tobacco?" he rasped, scowling at the empty places at the table. "Get your horses and catch up the others."

Little broken-nosed Iota Jones shook his head.

"No, Mr. Feleen, I don't reckon you'd want us to do that. Them men ain't gone ahead to start the gather. They're just gone."

Hush took it like the cut of a whip across the mouth.

"How come?" he asked after an almost interminable five seconds.

"Lost their stomach for the work, I reckon," answered Iota, taking a few seconds of his own before speaking.

"I'll buy that," said Hush. "How about the rest of you?"

Iota looked up and down the table, giving the others their chances to take the question. None did, and he shrugged uneasily.

"Reckon we're still in it, Mr. Feleen."

Hush waited, granting any bunkhouse lawyer among them the time to get up and enter his dissenting opinion. But no one moved.

"All right," he said, "we'll have to move fast now. Things have changed. We ain't only shorthanded, we're cut close for time. Iota, I'll talk to you on the ride out. Let's go, men."

As Hush wheeled to go back out into the graying dawn, Iota spoke. "Mr. Feleen," he asked quietly, "what happened to Curly?"

Hush studied the whole crew, man by man.

"Well," he finally told them, "I don't like this kind of personal asking, but you boys will have it that way and so I'll give it to you." He went on, tight-lipped, the way a man will who wants to get rid of words that don't sit sweet in his mouth or his mind. "Nothing has happened to Curly. I caught him bothering Mrs. Hudspeth and signed his time for him. He's gone and he won't be back, but he's not been hurt."

"How about *her*?" said Tate Lockhart deliberately, and no man in that smoky room missed the deliberate emphasis he put on it.

"She's all right too," replied Hush, checking to the scarcely veiled call. "Any more of my private life you boys like to see dragged out and stomped on before we get to work?"

Iota shook his head, and the others did the same.

Hush went out of the cookshack to rope out and saddle the black mare. When his crunching footsteps had faded safely, Tate turned angrily on Iota.

"Why the hell for did you have to go and say we was all still in it with him?" he demanded. "Goddammit, for ten cents, Mex, I'd cut and drift after Ab and the others. I'm getting chousy as a screw-worm steer about the whole snake-eyed business."

"Yeah," chimed in Rafe Henderson. "Why for *did* you have to speak up for everybody? I was just getting set to—"

"You was just getting set to beshat your pants!" Iota interrupted him testily. "Lemme ask you heroes one simple damn question: Where at was all of you when he invited you to speak up for yourselves?"

The men exchanged guilty, cornered looks and Iota went on.

"Yes, sir—well, I was at the same yellow-bellied place. Now let's don't be playing no more double shuffle with one another. We ain't none of us under twenty-one and we ain't none of us looking for no love letters from the sheriff back home. Remember, we're all in this rustle right up to here." He made a looping motion with his finger around his throat, and the others winced.

"And remember one thing else, too," he added. "Ride almighty careful when you go to pushing that Tennessee *ladino* what just walked out of here."

Then, quickly, before he turned to follow out after Hush, he said, "This boy will kill you if you box him in."

CHAPTER 22

Up to now, Hush had thought to keep on mavericking the ranges adjacent to the HF for another year, going up the trail in the spring of 1878 with somewhere between 2,000 and 3,000 market-quality cattle. Now a new plan was called for.

He could not forever watch the woman. Sooner or later she would slip out word to the law and Hush's great gamble would go down as the posse's rope went up. However, if a man made one swift gather and was gone from the Medina-Bandera ranges before the neighboring ranchers started their '77 spring surrounds, he might solve the entire problem. For one thing, he would be out of the country with their cattle before the ranchers had a chance to come up short in their counts. For the other thing, the woman's story of the seizure of the Rocking H would mean little in a new country—say, somewhere up toward Doan's Crossing on the Red. This country where Hudspeth and his brand were known was one thing; up north was another. Up north, the woman would need paper proof to make him serious trouble, and she didn't have one scrap of that.

Hush made his gather in three weeks of day and night riding.

At the end of that time he had 750 prime animals—all market beef, no feeders or stockers—bunched in a well-broken herd. The whole affair went slick as antelope tallow in a dry hub. There was not even any fuss with the woman to mar the success.

Strangely, life in a spring gather camp seemed to have knocked off the corners of her female ambition. At least Hush thought so. She appeared to quiet down and even to get into the spirit of things after a few days, and wound up the gather working at the fire as Pegleg's assistant, apparently completely changed in her outlook on ranch life and the Texas cattle business.

Seeing the wild cattle worked on the range had had similar strong effects on newcomers to the West before this, but Evelyn Hudspeth was overcome by it about as powerfully as any. At the end of the gather, with the herd held on the south bank of the river and the drive north set to begin next dawn, she sought out Hush and told him the evident shift in her attitude was no false impression—she genuinely did want to stay with him and the ranch. Toward that end she was ready to forgive him if he would do as much for her. They could go on the same as they had originally agreed, staying at the Hondo Canyon spread as legal man and wife, building up the jointly owned HF connected into a South Texas kingdom of grass and water as big as those of Richard King, Mifflin Kennedy, Colonel Goodnight or any of the others. Moreover, Hush had put his mark on her and what other man would want, or think that he could satisfy, a woman who had been with Hush Feleen?

It was heady talk, and Hush was stirred by it. He felt the promises implied in it lift his neck hairs and dry his hungry lips. But he had trusted this woman, and she had betrayed him. What would keep her from doing it again?

"Let it ride, Evvie," he told her. "These cattle have got to go north fast. I'm done in this country, and so are you. We don't dast stop short of Red River, neither one of us."

"What do you mean, Hush," she murmured, "about you and me being done—in this country, or any other country—?"

She brought her body to his, moving her hips demandingly, letting her soft hands slide behind him.

"Hush, tell me—tell me—"

He twisted away from her, his voice slurred with fought-down desire.

"Ask me again at Red River," he said, and turned away and left her standing alone in the April night.

On the night they came to the last camp south of the crossing, Hush settled up the matter of his partnership with the woman who was now calling herself Evvie Hollister.

Ordering Nocero to hook up the buckboard which had brought her to the Rocking H on her bridal night, he took the reins and headed into the settlement at Doan's Store. By his side, silent and very much afraid now, sat his willowy mate.

On the outer edge of the settlement, he stopped the team.

"Get out," he said.

The woman looked at the rutted mud of the cowtrack which ran past the verminous adobe and brush huts of the most famous trading center on the great Dodge City trail and could not believe he meant it.

"My God, Hush," she gasped, "you wouldn't do it!"

"Get out," repeated Hush. "Yonder's the street, start working it."

She still couldn't believe it.

"Hush—" she began, but he interrupted her, low-voiced.

"Evvie," he told her almost gently, "you're a whore. You started on the street, and you'll end up there. Get out."

"Hush, you've no right to say that. I wanted to marry you. I still do."

"And Curly too?"

"He didn't touch me, Hush. You know he didn't."

"You led him on with your body the same as you did me. Get out, Evvie. We're all done."

She knew it was over then. She climbed down and stood ankle-deep in the mud. She was beaten, she could not deny that. And Hush was right—she had stood in the street before, and more than once. The world west of St. Louis was like that.

But she had never stood in the street because she wanted to stand there. As much as any dirt-poor girl, she had dreamed and struggled to improve her harsh inheritance. First deceitfully with Avery Hudspeth, then treacherously with Hush Feleen, she had come within hand's reach of the gold which would buy the respectability she hungered after. Now the Texas adventure was finished, the opportunity lost, the gold vanished. But gutter blood was never bred to quit. Evvie Hollister and Hush Feleen would meet again. When they did—

The tall woman lifted her head, straightened her shoulders.

"You going to give me any money, Hush?" she asked quietly. "You know I haven't got a penny."

"Here," said Hush, fishing in his pocket and flipping her a coin. "Now you got a penny."

It was a cruel, needless thing to add to the punishment she had perhaps earned, and Hush was sorry for it the moment he did it. But he could not call the coin back.

It spun at Evvie Hollister, struck her on the breast, bounced off and into the mud at her feet. She reached down and picked it up. She looked at it a moment, then turned her face up to him and began to speak slowly and distinctly.

"You know, Hush," she said, "I did love you. I did mean to stand by you. In the beginning I believed what Iota told me about Avery Hudspeth having persecuted you unmercifully; I believed, from that, that you were in the right to break him as you did. Then I waited for you to keep your bargain with me about the ranch and the marriage. When you did nothing, I turned against you. That was your fault, Hush. We're two of a kind, you and me. You should have known that."

"No," said Hush, "we ain't two of a kind. When I give my word, I'll die on it."

"Or," murmured Evvie Hollister, "somebody else will."

He swung the team, but the offside horse fouled a tug and began to kick. He had to get out to clear the tangle, and when he did Evvie stepped up to him.

"Hush," she told him softly, holding the muddy penny up in front of him, "I'm going to keep this. It's an 1857 penny and I want you to remember it. You will get it back one day, with interest."

By now Hush was furious. The hard-mouthed anger of the man who knows he is wrong but whose unreasoning pride will not let him admit it, was running in him dark and hot.

"Good luck!" he growled, shouldering past her to get back in the buckboard. "With your talent you'd ought to be able to run it into a fortune inside of six months. And not have to overcharge to do it. Get the hell out of the way!"

He kicked off the brakes, whistled and yelled "hee-yahhh!" at the nervous mustangs. They squatted, jumped, hit into a run. The wheels of the buckboard slewed around, throwing muddy ditch-water up onto the abandoned woman. She stood there motionless, unmindful of the soiling, looking after Hush until the last rattle of whiffletree, the final faint jingle of trace-chain, died away in the prairie night.

Only then, when nothing remained to see or hear of her black-haired Tennessee lover, did she turn and trudge toward the desolate, oil-lit squalor that was Doan's Crossing on the Red River of Texas.

CHAPTER 23

It was a good camp. There was grass and wood and water in abundance. To winter the cattle through would require little work. Therefore the men could be laid off.

It was agreed they would go on up the trail with one of the other Texas herds bound for Dodge City, Iota going with them. This was to let them get some cash money in their pockets and to acquaint them with the problems of the route for the HF connected drive the following spring. Hush figured to lose some of them to the attractions of the big trail town and to the hazards of the long road leading to and from it. But Iota would likely return and with him Tate and Rafer, the three making crew enough around which to build the new outfit.

Meanwhile, he and Nocero would stay on with the cattle, getting up a brush-hut shelter for themselves and a corral and harness shed for their workstock and gear. As soon as they were settled, Hush would go into Denton or Fort Worth and look up the deeded land filings farther out along the Red—say, up on the good grass he had heard about out in the Big and Little Wachita Forks country.

Hush meant to take a mighty different path up here. He was prepared to dig in like a fieldhand to see that he didn't repeat his mistakes on the Nueces, the Guadalupe and the Medina. He had been doing a lot of thinking since the bad parting with Evvie at Dean's Store. The sum of that thinking was that he had been given a second chance—more, really, a third or fourth chance—to start right and stay straight in a clean, new land. If a wrong beginning could be made right by a good ending, Hush intended to try mightily for that good ending.

But that bad beginning haunted him.

He had been wanting to discuss its worries with somebody for a long time, too. But who? Who could Hush Feleen talk to that would listen honest and fair? That was older and smarter than he was? That would answer his questions level and true? That wasn't, in fact, afraid to talk to him?

It was Iota, finally, who got the call.

It was late, nearing eleven o'clock of the night before Iota and the others were due to leave for Doan's Crossing and the Dodge City trail, that Hush found the little cowboy hunched over the fire, with none of the others around. He squatted down on his heels across from him, saying nothing. The pop of the coals and the simmer of the coffee pot were the only sounds for two or three minutes.

"You knew Howell Hudspeth," Hush suddenly blurted out. "You think I done wrong in gunning him down?"

Surprised, Iota wrinkled his friendly brown face.

"I reckon not, Mr. Feleen. He tooken them cows from you, didn't he?"

"He stole my brand."

"It's the same as stealing the cows. Worse."

"I'd like to think so, Iota. It's been on my mind a heap."

The spit and sizzle of the coals took over again. Hush listened to them a minute before he went on.

"I figure these Rocking H cattle we've got here were owing me from old man Hudspeth. If we got a few of the neighbors' cows mixed in on the gather, that's only normal."

"Everybody collects a little of the other fellow's stuff on a spring surround. That's expected."

Hush looked at him.

"But what about Hudspeth himself? I mean what about what I did to him for what he did to me?"

"Well, I say you're right there, too, Mr. Feleen. He strung up your pappy and put rope burns on your own neck you'll take to the last gather. Of course, your pappy *was* working a double loop."

"He was," admitted Hush. "I wasn't."

"That's right. The old man had no call to include you in."

"I sure hope not," said Hush. "I wouldn't want to think he didn't have coming what I gave him." He paused, staring off into the night. "What is a man's life worth, Iota? Five

111

hundred head of cattle. A thousand? I don't know. I only know that these few head we got out yonder"—he gestured toward the bedded herd—"ain't any too much to pay for these." He put his fingers to the rope scars still angrily welted against the bronze of his neck. "But I made my deal with him and I'll call it even and all done. What would you call it, Iota?"

"It's even," said the little cowboy. "Maybe better than even. To old man there's worser things to lose than his life."

Hush returned the nod, knowing that Iota was talking about a man's pride being more important than his life, and knowing he had broken Avery Hudspeth's pride to the last, least bone.

"And how about Ben Sloat?" he asked after a little time.

Iota stirred the coals under the coffee pot, settled back onto his bootheels.

"Ben Sloat," he said, "had it coming in any way you wanted to give it to him."

"You're not saying I gave it to him just the way you would, eh?"

"I'm just saying what I'm saying, Mr. Feleen."

The two fell silent again.

"That brings us to Mrs. Hudspeth," said Hush presently. "You reckon I done wrong with her?"

"I don't think we'd ought to talk abouten you and the woman, Mr. Feleen. It ain't really fitten. There's things that won't stand a straight answer. What's between a man and a woman is one of 'em."

"You liked her, didn't you?" asked Hush.

"Sure. She was a right nice lady."

"You call her a lady. That's sort of funny."

"No, I don't reckon it is. Not the way I see things."

"How do you see things, Iota?"

The wizened cowboy fussed with the coals again, shifted the coffee pot, finally got out his reply.

"Well, let's just put it this way, Mr. Feleen. I've knowed whores I'd take my hat off to, and respectable women I wouldn't spit on."

"I know what you mean," said Hush soberly. "It's kind of a thing where people are more what they think they are, or they would like to be, than they are what they really are. Or something like that. You know what I'm trying to say, Iota?"

"Yes, sir, I do. It's what I meant about Miss Evvie."

They sat still again, watching and listening to the coals.

"I reckon most of us don't get a second chance," mused Hush, "not to mention a third or fourth. Seems to me that I been give a new slate and can write on it just about what I want. Do you see that, Iota? Another chance for me?"

"Yep, I do. You're powerful young, Mr. Feleen. You got the time to do it different if you're a mind to."

Hush nodded intently. "I'm thinking now that I'm powerful of a mind to," he said. "A man's got to fight a little dirty to get his start in a new country, that's only the way the herd drifts. But happen he does pretty good and then don't quit pushing his luck, he's got no more excuses left. I reckon I'm about out of excuses, Iota. I reckon it's time I quit pushing."

Iota studied him a minute. "It's the gal, ain't it?" he said.

Hush flinched, not expecting that. But he stood to it.

"It's her, yes. I can balance out everything except her. I keep thinking I done wrong with her—moral wrong—and the way I'm given to see it, there ain't no more grievous wrong than that."

Of a sudden impulse, then, Hush told Iota all about it: the entire short and stormy history of his affair with Evvie Hollister, their promises, counter-promises, happinesses, treacheries—everything.

Iota sat to the embarrassing end of it without a sign that he agreed or disagreed with Hush, but when the latter had finished and said, "Well, Iota, what do you think?" the little cowboy looked up at him with a worried frown and answered unhesitatingly, "I think you done wrong, Mr. Feleen. It was you broke your word, not her."

That ended it.

Iota saw at once that he had gone too far, had been drawn off guard by Hush's clear need to talk out his troubles. But with this one you had to be eternally careful. He was more like an Indian than was Nocero. His fierce pride and his sense of justice were his whole life. If you touched them or trod on them his dark temper flared, and he either plummeted into a black pit of cold self-control, or lashed out wildly in a rage of eye-for-an-eye vengeance.

For Hush's part, he was in just the state his anxious companion feared he was: squatting there on his heels scowling more furiously by the second, he was "clouding up," as Iota now thought to himself, "and getting set to start raining all over the place."

The threatened storm never broke.

It was forestalled by a pudgy man on a stout bay horse riding up to their fire with a tired wave and saying, "I'm Ed Dempster with the Barse and Snider commission people at Kansas City; we'll buy all you've got, four years old and upwards, forty dollars a head trackside, Dodge City."

They sat still.

Forty dollars a head times 750 head was $30,000.

That wasn't $30,000 next spring, or somewhere in the sweet by-and-by. It was $30,000 this fall, at Dodge City, Kansas, not over sixty days' drive from where they were sitting staring open-mouthed at Mr. Ed Dempster of the Barth & Snider Company, commission buyers of prime livestock on the Kansas City market.

Iota recovered first.

"Get down and come in, Mr. Dempster," he said. "I ain't the boss here, but it sounds to me as though you had arrove with the mortgage money just in time to save the old homestead."

The nighthawks had come in by this time, and their change had gone out to the herd. The other riders, aroused by the commotion of Dempster's appearance, rolled out and joined the group at the fire.

Most of the men knew something about what the Kansas City market was doing. They were aware that, in a manner of cow-country speaking, a $6 steer in Texas was worth four or five times that amount set down in the K.C. stockyards. But that big, range-run, grass-fed native stuff like theirs would fetch $40 delivered in Dodge was startling news indeed. Moreover, Mr. Ed Dempster was the first real live cattle buyer from Kansas City that any of them had ever seen. Now, hearing his offer, their greed rose up like a rubbed cat's back.

Hush had promised each of them five per cent of the selling price on the Hondo Canyon gather. From that, they presently stood to collect $1500 apiece. It was a staggering sum of cash money. When Rafer Henderson muttered an awed, "My God, Mr. Feleen, you cain't beat pickings like them!" he was stating precisely the company sentiment, he and the others naturally assuming that Hush shared it with them. Their shock was only the greater, therefore, when Hush smiled and said to the buyer, "Thanks all the same, Mr. Dempster, but we ain't interested."

"You're not *what*, sir?" challenged the pudgy man.

"No interested," repeated Hush. "If good to medium-good stuff like ours is worth forty dollars a head this fall, it'll bring fifty next fall. And we'll have only half the distance to drive them that we've brought this bunch. Like I said, Mr. Dempster, save your money."

Dempster argued hard, raised his offer $2.50 a head. But Hush wouldn't budge. His riders pleaded with him to take the buyer's raise; when they couldn't penetrate his hill country obstinacy they stalked back to their blankets and sulked.

114

Hush and the jowly commission man were left to share the angry silence with Iota Jones and the muttering coffee pot.

The buyer departed shortly, telling Hush he would be at the Cattleman's Hotel in Fort Worth for the next ten days, should he change his mind about selling.

Hush just looked at him and said, "Don't wait up for me, Mr. Dempster. I'll see you next fall with fifteen hundred head at fifty dollars."

"Forty-two fifty, Mr. Feleen. It's a prime offer and I can't hold it open indefinitely. The market's a little like a fast woman, Mr. Feleen. You got to grab her when she goes by."

"I've had my grabs of the one," said Hush, "and I reckon I can wait for the other."

"Suit yourself," said the buyer. "I've got a soft-legged woman looking for me in Fort Worth, and she *won't* wait. Know what I mean, Mr. Feleen?"

"By heart," Hush answered, and turned his back on him.

It was a night of bad surprises.

The Kansas City buyer had not been gone twenty minutes when another rider loomed out of the darkness. This one was younger and was mounted on a mule. The mule's name was Andy Jackson and its rider was Billie Jim, the quiet one of the Feleen twins.

"At the crossing they told me you was out this way," the wan-faced twelve-year-old greeted Hush. "Back a piece, a fat man on a bulldog bay said it was your fire up here. Whyn't you come back for us like you said, Hush? We uns been powerful lonesome to see you, and a-needing you mighty bad, too."

Hush went over to the old mule, lifted the exhausted boy off him and carried him, already half asleep, over to the fire. There he poured a cup of coffee and said firmly, "Wake up, Billie Jim. Get this down you. Lord, Lord, it's good to see you—"

The boy roused himself, took a swallow or two of the coffee, the strength of the cowcamp blend bringing his tired memory back to where it had interrupted by Hush taking him off Andy Jackson. "Hush, you said you was coming back," he began again, but Hush cut in on him gently.

"Billie Jim," he said, "first things first. What ever you doing up here, boy?"

"It's Jodie Beth, Hush, that's how come we're here. Don Diego said the pore little thing would surely die afore winter, happen we didn't find you to he'p us get her to that doctor in Fort Worth. You know the one, Hush."

115

Hush knew the one. His gray eyes darkened with the twist of his conscience turning in him like a rusty knife. But he held firm and soft-voiced with the boy.

"You say 'we're here,' Billie Jim," he said. "You mean old Diego's trailing with you?"

"Him," answered Billie Jim, "and all the hull rest on 'em. In the burro cart, camped up to Doan's Store, waiting for me to fetch you back."

"Billie Jim," said Hush, "rest easy and don't fret no more."

He had the black mare run in and saddled. He was up on her, taking the river trail for the crossing before five minutes were gone. He caught up with Ed Dempster at the edge of the settlement, spurred the mare past him, swung her hard, blocking the trail. "Changed my mind," he greeted the buyer. "I'll take your deal."

Dempster eyed him shrewdly.

"Great night for sudden shifts in the wind," he smiled. "Your mind's not the only thing that's changed since I left your camp."

"How's that?" inquired Hush sharply.

The buyer merely shrugged. "Market's dropped fifty cents a mile the past ten miles," he said.

Hush kneed the black mare closer to him.

"You telling me you're offering thirty-seven fifty now?"

"If you hurry."

"That's sandbagging," said Hush. "In a poker game it could get you killed."

"Business *is* a poker game, Mr. Feleen. You buy your chips and you bet them to win. I know your situation now. You're whipped."

"How so?" asked Hush.

"I met your kid brother on the trail."

"And—?"

"He told me your family was yonder with a sick little girl needing a doctor in Fort Worth. I figured you'd be along directly. You'd ought to teach the kid to keep his mouth shut with strangers. You can't bluff with a tipped hand."

"I ought to kill you," said Hush. "Any man that would squeeze a deal shut by using a poor little crippled girl, ain't fit to live."

"Don't do me any favors, Feleen!" snapped the fat buyer. He had seen three chance riders approaching and knew he was safe. "I warned you the offer might not hold. As for killing me, it wouldn't pay you. I'm carrying only five hundred dollars. Scarcely a high price for a man's life, wouldn't you say?"

"For your life," said Hush, "it would be overcharging.

But I might take it off you anyway, seeing you just robbed me of five thousand dollars on that price drop."

"I robbed you of nothing. As for the five hundred, I'll be glad to give it to you as earnest money on the thirty-seven fifty offer. What do you say? Take it or leave it, Feleen."

Hush dug a match out of his pocket. He lit it and held it up to his face.

"I say take a good look at me, Mr. Dempster—take a real good look." He let the match burn down and did not drop it even when it smoked out between his thumb and forefinger. "Now, then, Mr. Dempster," he finished quietly, "I'll take the five hundred. You've made a deal."

Dempster gave him the roll of bills, not counting them. He wanted mainly to get away from him now, and above all not to let those approaching riders go by without joining them.

"When can I expect you in Fort Worth to sign the delivery contracts and railhead tally guarantees?" he asked Hush nervously.

"Likely I'll beat you there," answered the latter. "Anything else bothering you?"

"No. Just remember I'll be at the Cattleman's Hotel."

"Sure," said Hush. "Meanwhile you remember something too, Mr. Dempster. It's what you saw when I lit that match just now. You'll be seeing it again one dark night."

"I don't scare worth a damn, Feleen. Save your threats."

"That wasn't no threat, Mr. Dempster. You took me wrong."

Oh—?"

"Yes, sir. That was a promise."

Ed Dempster wasn't lying. He did not scare easily. But he was suddenly very glad the three stray riders were drawing up.

"Evening, boys!" he sang out in relief. "Name your brand and I'll ride along with you. Ed Dempster's the name, and the drinks are on me. Just closed a nice deal with Mr. Feleen, here, but he can't come with us. Got kinfolk to visit out yonder on the drovers' campground. Now, me, I'm for the bright lights, the bourbon and the branchwater. What say, friends, are you thirsty, or just riding through?"

The surprised drifters mumbled that they would be glad to drink his whiskey, or any man's, and the four of them set off toward the dismal light of Doan's Store. Hush watched them go, then spoke a soft word to Muchacha, the black mare. Minutes later, he was with his family.

The reunion got into him lastingly and deep.

In his year of hardship and separation from them, particularly in his bitterness and grief over the death of Arnie and his anger over Evvie Hollister turning against him, Hush had lost true track of what the old Mexican couple and their adoption of him and his brothers and sisters had originally meant to him. Seeing them now, the memory was restored with a rush. And more. When they all greeted him with such pure gladness, and when not a one of them roweled him about where he had been or why he hadn't sent for them, he knew he had gotten farther off on that wrong foot of his than even he had admitted. Clearly, he had had his talk with Iota Jones in the nick of time.

He resolved, then, as he lay down for the night with Don Diego and Billie Bob beneath the burro cart, that he would henceforth refuse to be steered wrong by the storms of pride and temper and outsize ambition which had so far confused him. Moreover, he knew exactly what he was going to do to bring about the change.

First off, he would go into Fort Worth with Jodie Beth, see that doctor and get the little tike made well and strong. Then he would come back up to the Red, put his herd on drive for Dodge, and deliver it to Barth & Snider not one head short. With his part of the money he would return to Texas and, this time, instead of the greedy thinking he had been sickened into by his vengeance against Avery Hudspeth and his lust for Evvie Hollister, he would make the kind of a small, happy, family-shared start he had first dreamed of making in those grand early days up on the Forks of the Guadalupe.

To be sure he stayed with that good and simple idea of life, he would go back to the Nueces *brasada*, never leaving it again.

There in his beloved shinnery, Hush Feleen would be at home once more, amid the remembered sounds of the long-horned bulls talking their deep bass *hablando* to one another as they came down to water, the bark of the fox and the scolding of the vixen, the distant faint bawl of the strayed calf and the answering lowing of the mother cow, the shrill whistle of the mustang stallion and the responding whicker of the mare. There he would stay forever.

There, too, he vowed silently, he would touch no cattle that were not his own, he would work only to care for his brothers and sisters and to provide for Don Diego and Doña Anastasia.

And when, in the due course of those good years thus to come, his neighbors along the Nueces heard the name of Hush Feleen, they would smile and nod and say that it was a good name, belonging to a good neighbor. When that time came it would be the best time of Hush's life. At last he could say to sweet, kind Nancy Hushton and to himself that he had finally done right by the trust she had placed in his hands that sad afternoon of her going away so long ago.

Thus trailed off the tired, hopeful thoughts of Hush Feleen, as sleep closed in on him that late spring night of 1877.

He saw clearly, now, his only true chance. He meant sincerely to gather it to him and to prosper it as a sworn trust.

But between the seeing and the doing, stretched the lonesome, long-miled wheel ruts of the Fort Worth wagon road.

CHAPTER 24

There was no train or stageline to make things easy. It was the buckboard or nothing. In this open, unsheltered vehicle, with Lubelle along to help tend Jodie Beth, Hush set out across the 150 prairie miles to Fort Worth.

The spring rains had been heavy. Half the creeks were still so high that their fords were either outright swimming water or hub-deep slimes of muck and flood debris. It took the better part of a wet, cold week to make the trip, and their small passenger came into Fort Worth badly fevered and barking with the croup.

Their poor luck held. The doctor they sought had moved to Dodge. The physician who told them this got Jodie Beth's chest cold broken but advised them to take extreme care she did not catch another, as her lungs were not good. He would not guess at the nature of her general decline, but affirmed that the doctor they had come to see was, indeed, the only man who might help her. He must tell them that were she his daughter he would feel compelled to risk the journey to Kansas, for there was no other hope for the child.

The second unpleasantness fell when Hush went to the Cattleman's Hotel to sign his papers with Ed Dempster.

Mr. Dempster was engaged at the moment, the desk clerk told him, but had left word that he would be down directly. Would the gentleman please wait?

Battered hat in rawboned, nervous hands, acutely conscious of his lank hair, torn rawhide jacket, frayed rider pants and runover workboots, he eased down on the edge of a store-made lounge chair and began to survey his elegant surroundings. He cast admiring looks at the fine sets of polished steer horns, the elk, buffalo and antelope heads, the bear-hides and panther pelts which, with the French oil paintings, Italian mirrors and glittering Viennese crystal, decorated the paneled walls and ceiling, but he kept shooting glances to-ward the head of the lobby stairs. And presently he was re-warded. Ed Dempster appeared on the landing above—but he did not appear alone. The woman with him was Evvie Hol-lister.

Hush drew in a quick breath.

He had never seen Evvie in her own world, set like this in a surrounding of city things which were as much her home-place as the *brasada* was Hush's. Until this moment he had never rightly understood what Iota saw of the lady in her. Now he did.

Maybe this wasn't *all* there was to being a lady, this acting and dressing the part to the last grand flair, but it was some-thing that was Evvie Hollister's special talent. And it was what lifted her way out of the class of other women you might catch coming out of a cattle buyer's room in Fort Worth, Texas. Hush saw this difference in Evvie now, clear as a fresh sunrise, and for some strange reason it made him feel proud of her.

For her part, Evelyn Hollister returned the feeling. She, now, was seeing Hush Feleen as far out of his natural element as he had once seen her in Avery Hudspeth's paintless man-sion on the rim of Hondo Canyon. And the effect was to make her feel the same nameless pride in him that he was experiencing of her.

To Evvie, it was Hush who made the Cattleman's lobby seem small. He stood out against its brassy background as startingly as would an eagle-feathered Comanche. The room could not begin to match him. Nor, for all his patched work clothes and broken-toed boots, could it make him look the least bit mean or poor.

So Evvie, too, caught her breath, and her eyes were upon Hush as his were upon her, all the way down the spiraling stairs and across the crowded lobby on Ed Dempster's fat arm.

But the little hiatus of time stretched overlong. In its passing seconds a surge of remembered passions and un-forgotten promises flooded up high and wild within Hush.

Of a sudden he wanted to seize Evvie Hollister and strip her of her sinful finery and to hurt her naked flesh with his bare, rope-harshened hands. He wanted to make her cry out in pain and contrition that she was a whore, and worse than a whore, but that she was Hush Feleen's woman who needed and wanted only Hush Feleen, and that she would love him and make love to him today and tomorrow and for as long as both of them should live, or breathe, or feel the burning want of the other's body.

There was a suspended moment then when a word, a smile, the touch of a hand might have changed everything. Hush felt it, and Evvie Hollister felt it. It was there, beckoning between them, and both were yearning to call out and answer it.

But there were too many people in the lobby of the Cattleman. And it took the St. Louis woman and her squat companion too long to make their way to where Hush waited.

The impulse to seize back this golden-haired woman who so possessed him, the impulse which, with one forgiving word might have guarantteed Hush his hopes for a new life, was fought down and brought under icy control. When the couple finally came up to him, the old bad feeling of Feleen revenge had spread through him like a black frost.

It never occurred to Hush that Evvie's presence there in the lobby with the Kansas City commission man might be an innocent coincidence, so far as he himself was concerned. He assumed she knew about him being down in the lobby waiting for Dempster, that she had been lying up with the fat pig in his room, and that to shame Hush and to get back at him in the one way she knew she could—through his pride as a man and as a Feleen—she had deliberately come downstairs with the cattle buyer.

The intent was therefore plain; its consequence inevitable.

Nobody made a fool of Hush Feleen. Not twice in the same lifetime.

CHAPTER 25

It was June when Hush finally got his cattle over the Red and lined out through the Indian Territory for Kansas and Dodge City.

He had seven hands, not counting the cook, when he started from Doan's Store. At the first trail camp inside the Territory he hired on an eighth. His name was trouble and he went to work for nothing, never once letting up on the HF trailherd from Red River Crossing to the North Canadian.

What happened was that the herd got into the habit of running. Nothing worse could happen on the trail.

121

Once a bunch of cattle got the idea fixed in their heads of jumping and running every time a mouse sneezed, there was no way in God's prairie world to break them of it. By the time they had scattered five or ten miles from the bedding grounds it could mean as many days getting them back together again. In the case of the HF herd, it took the better part of two months to drive the 147 miles from the Red River to the Red Hills Crossing of the main Canadian, just west of Fort Reno.

In all, they lost fifty cattle and the herd was so worn from running that a halt had to be called. Delivering cattle like that would break any contract ever written, and they had only one out—throw the herd on graze and gamble with holding it there as late into fall as they dared, then driving desperately to beat the first blizzards to the Barth & Snider stockpens.

All hands agreed to the course and the cattle were crossed over into the fine pasture between the main Canadian and the North Fork, a strip of the greatest grass and water country the Texas cowboys had ever seen.

Here they rested for six long weeks, risking an early snow against getting some of the precious lost tallow grazed back onto their stringy animals.

In his first thoughts of the halt, Hush had figured to push on to Dodge in the buckboard with Jodie Beth. But the little girl pleaded to be allowed to stay with "Uncle Pegleg and the boys." For their part, the men, who had grown attached to her despite the traildrivers' superstition against having children along on a cattle drive, added their arguments to hers and in the end Hush let the matter drift with his grazing herd.

The first part of the HF gamble was won hands down. On that Canadian River grass the Medina and Bandera steers tallowed up like buffalo heifers going into a hard winter. They got back all the weight they had run off, and plenty besides. Moreover, they had lost their spookiness and when Hush ordered them thrown back on the trail in early September they moved out like moolie cows going to the milking barn. Not once in the four days to the North Canadian did they offer to so much as break into a trot. They plodded along as docilely as so many freight oxen, doing their eight or ten miles a day as steadily as though yoked to it.

On the last afternoon, however, they got to the crossing a little late. The sun was low in the west, throwing a bad glare on the water. The cattle would need to face this should it be decided to put them over before bedding them down—the unvarying trail procedure where circumstances permitted.

122

Studying the situation, Hush hesitated. That sun glare might start the herd to running again. He had learned that far back on the drive. In this case it did not seem a matter of vital importance whether the cattle were crossed tonight or tomorrow morning. The river was low, the weather clear, the herd standing still as statues. Why push your good luck? They would cross in the morning.

"Yo!" he yelled down to Iota Jones, waiting below for the signal to hold up, or go on. "We got time to waste a day here?"

"I reckon!" Iota yelled back. "This here's the Cherokee Strip. We got no more than five or six days left to the Kansas line. How's the weather look from up there?"

"All clear!" called Hush. "Throw 'em off and let 'em go!"

He turned the black mare, sending her down off the lookout rise to the bedding flats below. Everything looked just right about that camp. All level, plenty grass, easy water, even wood to hand for the fire. You couldn't beat fixings like that. As far as a man could see, this was the best place they had stopped at since leaving home.

As far as a man could see, this was true. The trouble was that a man couldn't see far enough. Sun glare off a river blinds a human being as bad as it does a cow brute.

It was a happy night around the chuckwagon fire. Cowboy lies and still wilder Texas truths went on until nearly midnight.

One of the men had a guitar, and to the surprise and delight of the crew Hush asked him to play "Red River Valley," and then sang it along with the music in a voice sweet and haunting-lonely enough to break your heart. When little Jodie Beth joined in to sing a high, clear harmony to the last chorus, there wasn't a dry eye among them. It was only when the midnight shift rode out to the herd that the other hands realized they had but a few hours left before the five A.M. roll out.

Shortly, they all sought their blankets, and by one o'clock the camp was asleep. Only the distant eerie whistling and plaintive night songs of the herd guards penetrated the predawn stillness. But in her soft bed of buffalo robes made up behind the driver's box of the chuckwagon, Jodie Beth Feleen stirred fitfully, her slumbers disturbed by uneasy dreaming.

It was a humid night, the warm breeze beginning to bring light spatters of rain on its soft breath. Off to the east and south the heat lightning blinked sporadically. A dozen animals in the center of the herd got to their feet, stood staring uncertainly about them. The nighthawks stepped up their singing, moving their ponies directly into and through the herd proper, talking to the cattle in the lulling monotones of the veteran trailhand. Gradually the spooked animals responded. In twenty minutes they were all down again, their former quiet resumed.

But the third-shift riders didn't like it now. It wasn't the right kind of a quiet this time. It was the kind you could hear if you listened for it hard enough.

The wind lost its softness, took on a cutting edge, shifted from southeast to east, then swiftly to northeast. The sleeping men pulled in their blanket edges, grumbled in their sleep, snuggled to the hard, warm earth.

Pegleg Pearson, older than the others and not so able to take comfort from the rocky ground, got up and looked to see that his banked cookfire was keeping all right. He moved with great caution to be sure he did not bump into anything which might make a sudden noise that 700 listening cattle would hear. Behind him he felt rather than saw a dark shadow. He knew whose it was, and said to him softly:

"*Que dice, hombre?* What do you say? *Hay illuvia o nieve?*"

"Him rain first," answered Nocero. "Then him turn to snow."

"You think the herd will run again?"

"*Quien sabe?* Me *sabe* horse. Me no *sabe* cow."

"Nobody savvies the bastards," grumbled Pegleg. "I'm going to wake up Mr. Feleen if this wind keeps switching. She's coming due northeast right now."

"You get too old," said the Apache. "Worry like squaw. Go back blankets, me watch wind for you."

"You horse-thieving, no good Lipan son-of-a-bitch, I wouldn't trust you to watch a pot boil. You roust me out, instanter, if that wind starts spitting snow, you hear?"

"Me hear," grunted Nocero, and squatted by the fire's warmth.

The gaunt one-eyed Apache drowsed gratefully. The wind had dropped and the heat of the banked fire soaked through him. Presently his head fell forward and did not straighten again. This was a little after one-thirty.

It was five minutes after two A.M. when Jodie Beth awoke from her bad dream, her throat parched, her mouth cottony. She knew where the water dipper hung alongside the chuckwagon barrel, and she got up quietly to go outside and get herself a drink.

At the barrel there was a slight complication. Pegleg had

124

put the lid on for the night and she was not tall enough to hold it up and dip into the barrel.

Back near the tailgate she found a tin cracker-box and Pegleg's huge camp dishpan. The cracker-box set on top of the dishpan would let a little girl step up to get her drink very nicely, without needing to bother Hush or Uncle Pegleg to help her.

The ten year-old placed her wobbly makeshift stepladder without mishap. Climbing up it, she stood teetering at barreltop level. But the lid was wet and slick, and when she lifted it, it got away from her, caromed off the wagonside and banged into the cracker box under her feet. Dipper, dishpan, tin box and thirsty little girl all went tumbling together. Almost before they had struck the ground, the HF cattle were on their feet and running.

They went away from the wind, up the river, to the west, cascading through the sleeping camp—and almost in the moment they jammed bawling and bellowing past the overturned chuckwagon, with the awakened cowboys scrambling for their tethered night horses, the storm broke. Within five minutes no man could know or guess what lay one leap in front of his racing pony.

There was no heading cattle in such weather, and Hush shouted for the men to ride out and get clear, and to let the cattle run until they were through the camp and gone safely on up the river. The men, knowing no more than did Hush what lay to the west and what awaited the cattle up there, pulled out of the herd's way and let it go, more than glad to be called back from such a blind, black run.

Only minutes after the stampede began they were all back in camp, down off their mounts helping Hush and Pegleg raise up the toppled wagon.

Then they were standing in the slanting drive of the rain, in the pale light of the wagon lamp Pegleg had lit to assess the damage to his commissary. They watched while Hush gathered up his sister and held her to his breast, easy and gentle as any mother with a sleeping baby. He held her in that protective, quiet rocking way while the cowboys stood silent in respect. And he held her still in the same way after they had disappeared in the driving rain.

Those men were rough, untutored drifters all. Some of them were wanted by the law back home; others had never had a home, or known a law, or cared about either. They were admitted cattle thieves, working for a boy not yet twenty-one who had killed two white men and three Indians, stolen 750 cattle and another man's wife, and not a one among them would have thought to excuse themselves or condemn him for any part of their joint actions. Yet these same men had hearts and feelings enough to know when a hardcase boy who would not cry outside was weeping inside. And they knew enough to go away and leave him alone with his small dead sister so that he might grieve in private and without embarrassing his pride. And they had gentle instincts enough to do it so it would look as though they had more important things to tend to than standing around in the rain showing sorrow for a spoiled kid who ought to have known better than to get up and go fumbling around for a drink in the middle of a dark cowcamp on a stormy night.

So it was that they went to help Pegleg rig a wagon tarp under which the lot of them could bunch up in the ankle-deep slop until day broke and they could tell what other losses they had taken in that rain-lashed last camp where the North Canadian crossed out of the Cherokee Strip into the Staked Plains.

But when daylight came at last, it only led them to another tragedy.

Two miles west of the HF bedding grounds, the plain broke abruptly to the river, falling off in a straight drop of gypsum cliffs forty to sixty feet high. At the rim of this blind declivity, Hush and his men stood staring down in dull-eyed, dazed bewilderment, unable at first to comprehend the fearful evidence spread below them.

But when their silent-lipped count of the crushed and drowned carcasses of the HF herd lying at the base of the drop-off had been completed, they finally understood what had happened and where it left them on that September morning in 1877.

Of seven hundred prime grass-fat Texas longhorn cattle which had run over that cliff in the dark of last night's storm, something less than fifty head still lived to wander, limping and bawling, along the riverbank below.

The drive was over. Hush Feleen and the HF connected were done for.

CHAPTER 26

It was too late in the year for going on up the trail. And too late to wait where they were in hope that some following herd would come by. There were no herds behind them, and there would be no work in Dodge City ahead of them. Winter was around the corner, and Kansas was a bone-cold country. There was no work in Texas, either; but down in the south of the state, in the cattle country where most of them were from, it was warm. The best thing cowhands cut loose in the face of hard weather could do was follow the ducks—drift south.

When, on the afternoon of the second day a returning crew of Fort Worth drovers came into their camp from the north, it was all the encouragement that was needed. On the third morning Hush stood alone by the deserted cookfire watching his ragged crew of cowboy rustlers jog off down the south trail with the party of honest cattlemen, homeward bound.

As he did, the thought formed that the only thing which separated the virtuous from the wicked was the fact that the former had gotten to Dodge and sold their cattle, while the latter had not. Success, he told himself, fighting down the loneliness and sense of loss which seeing Iota and the others leave had started up in him, was all that mattered to most people. If you made money you were a big man, a worthwhile neighbor. If you didn't make money you were nothing, you were nobody, you were Hush Feleen.

Awkwardly, he returned Iota's wave as the little cowboy paused in the last turn of the trail, seeming half undecided whether to go on or come back and stay with Hush. But as he checked his horse, waiting for some sign from Hush, none came. The tall boy was like an injured animal, Iota guessed, wanting to be alone and to be left alone. He waited a little longer, then sent his pony on after the Texas party.

Back at the dying fire, Hush straightened up. He would miss the little foreman, but in him, even as he waved goodbye to Iota, a new plan was already stirring.

One of the riders with the Texas outfit had told a story, which in later years was to become a rangeland legend, about a man named Charles Goodnight. Goodnight, it seemed, had tried some stocker cattle up in Colorado, perhaps the first Texas cattleman to attempt ranching that mountainous northern range. But the winters had proved too much for the southern cattle and he had packed up his outfit and headed back south, driving his huge herds before him.

This Goodnight was more than a rancher, really. He was a pioneer; he went where the virgin grass was. And he did not go there because it was any better than grass which had been grazed before, but simply because Charles Goodnight wanted to see it wave in the prairie wind the way God had made it. So Goodnight, wending down from high Colorado driving

127

his longhorns ahead of him, came to this very North Canadian River, turned west along it and drove his cattle out of the Cherokee Strip into the north end of the Texas Panhandle.

Drifting southward again, he had looked for and found a place of fabulous virginity—a magic place on the Staked Plains headwaters of the great Red River of Texas; an impossible place where only the buffalo had grazed and the Indians had ridden before the Goodnight cattle came into it.

It was an incredibly beautiful depression in the Staked Plains, protected on all sides by high palisades of rock and weathered earth. In its bottom the clear waters flowed and the thick grasses grew. Its summers were cooled by the canyon drafts, its winters warmed by the walled-in sun. It was a secret kingdom hidden within the heart of the best grassland in the western world; and its name, destined to become as famous as that of its white discoverer, was Palo Duro, called by the Indians the Canyon of No Winter.

The binder for Hush was that all this had happened not ten or twenty or more years ago, but in 1876, the very year before the present one. It was already history, no doubt; but it was history so close that a man could touch it by reaching out his hand.

A well-mounted rider could be in that Palo Duro country in a matter of days. If he were a rider like Hush, knowing longhorn cattle as Hush did, he could take with him this remnant of the HF herd, letting it breed up on the new range, driving its increase on to Dodge whenever in the future the good Lord should say. Out there, a man could find the same honest life and respected name Hush had planned for his return to the *brasada*. Only he could find them much, much closer.

There were some holes in the passing cowboy's story of Charles Goodnight and Palo Duro Canyon. But Hush did not know of these and so they did not deter him. Moreover, the essential part of the cowboy's tale was true: Goodnight had found the big Palo Duro and there was no reason to believe some other man could not find another, smaller "canyon of no winter" in the same virgin area.

Hush was suddenly beset with the idea he was that other man.

While he hadn't the least way of knowing what lay ahead, or how he would manage it alone, when he swung Muchacha and Gato in behind the thin line of longhorn survivors moving westward up the North Fork of the Canadian River, he was absolutely certain he knew where he was going, and why.

All doubts of the Palo Duro decision were left beneath the

128

grassy mound of newly replaced sod which marked the lonely trailside resting place of Jodie Beth Feleen.

He had buried a father, a brother and a little sister in this harsh land. There had been no moral law, no rightful justice in their deaths—only cruelty and heartsickness. There must be no more of that for Hush Feleen.

The shadow of his past wrongs had fallen for the last time across the path of his loved ones. From that day, forward, he would ride alone.

CHAPTER 27

The one-man cattle drive from the North Canadian to the Staked Plains would not have been made but for Old Brimstone.

Old Brimstone was a yellow brindle *ladino* with a black lobo stripe down his back and light-colored *orejano* or "mealy nose" markings around eyes and muzzle. If not the biggest steer ever to come out of the brush in a south Texas pasture cleaning, he was certainly the meanest-looking.

Hush had gotten his rope on him in the surround he and Arnie had made on Pipe Creek. The old devil had broken the rope and nearly killed Hush and the black mare in his stampede for freedom. Under the subsequent pressures of Arnie's death and his own usurpation of the Hudspeth ranch, Hush had forgotten the brindle outlaw. But upon driving back through the Pipe Creek range with the stolen Rocking H cattle months afterward, he had spotted what he thought was a mighty familiar rawboned set of withers and spreading seven-foot horns taking the lead of his new herd.

It was, of course, Old Brimstone, and the gaunt old *delgadito* had not relinquished his leadership of the drive from that day. He became, too, a lead steer as trusted and valuable as any which ever went up the trail. Like Colonel Goodnight's more famous "Old Blue," he was "not worth ten cents, and all the hard money in Texas would not buy him." Indeed, but for him, not even fifty of the HF herd would have survived when the run was made over the gypsum cliffs at Red Hills Crossing. Those fifty which did survive had not gone over the cliffs at all, but had followed Old Brimstone out and away from the main herd just short of the drop-off, and had only gone down to the river the next dawn looking for water.

Thus it was possible, with this wise old leader to guide his small band of rescued seedstock, for Hush to drive the 150 miles into the heart of the Texas Panhandle. His progress was, in fact, halted only by a second snowstorm that caught him in the open sweeps of the Llano Estacado midway between Mobeetie and Tascosa, some fifty miles north of the Goodnight range in Palo Duro.

It was four o'clock in the afternoon of October 4th, 1877, when Old Brimstone stopped suddenly to face into and sample the sharpening rear-quarter wind. Twenty minutes later, howling down out of an innocent-looking bluebird sky, a high-plains blizzard was turning the prairie world dark as night.

It was, in the Texas term of the time, "a blue norther," a flat, driving wind carrying both sleet and snow at such cannonball velocity as to demand of any living thing which dared face it either death or unconditional surrender.

As a south-of-Texas boy, Hush was not familiar with its icy violence, but the axiom, "When in doubt follow the lead steer," had saved more than one trail driver before him, and he had now no choice but to believe in it.

Old Brimstone, after his one alarmed sniffing into the blizzard wind, turned his rump three-quarters to it and began to drift south by west. He plodded only five miles off the buffalo track Hush had been following, but five miles proved enough. At the end of it waited a roughened break of stunted crosstimber which shut off the wind as abruptly as a closed door. Once inside its sheltering stand, the cattle were safe. But the man who came with them was not.

Hush was worn ribby. He had lived off the land for the past two weeks and the living had been scant. When the ice-laden wind of this second storm struck him, it went through him like a sickbed chill. After the first forty-five minutes he lost all feeling, and he was, in fact, freezing to death in the saddle when the brindle steer found the crosstimbers.

He did not remember the branches slashing at his numbed face, tearing at his frozen chaps, seizing the fringes of his frost-rimed coat. He did not hear Gato and Muchacha whicker hopefully when their flared nostrils caught the scent of pony dung ahead. Nor did he hear the answering neigh which came in friendly reply, nor feel the mare begin to move again under him as she went eagerly forward toward the wisp of woodsmoke issuing from the dense thicket just beyond. When Muchacha broke through the thicket to halt and whinny demandingly in front of the snow-caked cowskin tipi which it hid, Hush was slumped motionless across her withers.

130

There Graywing Teal, the outcast Kwahadi squaw, found him when she peered out to challenge the darkening twilight in guttural Kiowa-Comanche.

"*Tou-e mH! hH'-dei-dl a-ha'?* Speak up! Who is there?"

Thus began that part of Hush's life spent with the Plains Indian woman who was to be the second of his three mates. She was not a pretty woman, being short and stocky, with a rather large head and masculine features, after the Comanche fashion. Yet she was attractive in a way which no white woman could match, or would want to. And it was this complete naturalness which appealed to Hush. He felt at once at ease with the Indian woman, and although his feeling for her could scarcely be called love, it was still something stronger than a passing fancy for a dusky smile, or a random passion for a dark body.

It was a fact that "Graywing," as she ordinarily abbreviated her name, saved Hush's life. And Hush realized this and did not shirk the debt. Until the beholdenness was discharged, he was in bond to this Indian woman. If she wanted to consider his gratitude an expression of love, he was not going to disillusion her. Let her think what she would, and be happy. He would do the same. Neither of them was an innocent. Let her look to Graywing Teal's heart; he would look to Hush Feleen's.

His attitude was almost Comanche, and would have worked with an average Comanche woman. But Graywing was not an average Comanche woman. She was a free-spirited rebel against the dominance of the male which was the social rule of her fierce people. If Hush would have made a fine Indian, as charged in so many of the stories which lived after him, then Graywing Teal, his Indian wife for the winter of 1877-78, would have made an equally good—or bad—white woman.

Graywing had been born in the Trans-Pecos buffalo range of the Kwahadi Comanche, the seventh daughter of an aging chief who had yet to sire a son. In her teens she had been sold to a toothless Cherokee by the disappointed father, when her rebellious nature was becoming more of a problem than a seventh daughter of a sonless chief was worth. The Cherokee was wealthy in money and horses, but he was almost four times her age, and he could not cope with his spirited Comanche purchase. Unhappiness had already been growing in their home when Graywing was caught in the unforgivable sin. Her young Comanche lover, who had followed her up to the Cherokee country, began trysting with her at the old man's newly acquired Panhandle horse ranch

131

when the latter would make his periodic treks back to the Strip to attend tribal councils. Apprehended in the last of these assignations by the early return of the old Cherokee, Graywing had been voted the Indian penalty for adultery: banishment from her red fellows for the rest of her days.

Her acceptance of the punishment had been philosophical. She knew the laws of her people. She was already in shame with the Kwahadis. But the Cherokees were Christians as well as Indians. Their doors were doubly closed to her. Her only choice was to live alone in the wild heart of the Staked Plains, and this she had been doing for several months when the October blizzard drove Hush Feleen into her lonely arms.

Her care and affection were boundless in amount and administration. She watched over Hush like a mother. She hunted for him, cooked for him, fed him and babied him as she might a handicapped child. Hush was hardly that, after his first recovery of strength, but he enjoyed the feeling of being wanted by somebody. The fact that somebody was an Indian made no difference. They had a successful mating of both body and mind, took the fullest pleasure from each source without questioning.

The careless recipe suited them both. By the first of the year they had their working arrangement settled into a unique harmony and were free to think of what lay ahead. They had need so to think. The cattle had browsed out the narrow belt of scrub timber which had saved them, and a move to better pasture was urgent. It was in the discussion of this move that Hush first learned of the Cañon Perdido, the lost canyon.

"Do you know," he said to Graywing one fine sunny morning in early January, "where we can move the cattle that they will have winter feed and water? I mean a place that is close by?"

"What kind of a place do you mean, TeihH'nei-kiH?"

She called him that, meaning "Texas Man" in her tongue, all efforts to teach her to say Hush having fallen victim to the guttural Comanche throat sounds. So Hush answered her now, using in turn the formal address.

"I just told you, Kwahadi Woman. A place warm and sheltered with high walls like the Palo Duro. You know the Palo Duro, the Canyon of No Winter?"

"Ah!" she answered, "I know it well. It is a famous place for buffalo in the winter. Three times when I was a little girl the Kwahadis came there for winter meat. But that is all done now. The white man is there. He came last year and chased out the buffalo, bringing in his spotted cattle in their

132

place. The Cherokees say he has a breeding herd of sixteen hundred. They say it will grow to ten thousand, and that because of it the buffalo will come no more to Palo Duro. Do you know some of the old men have said this next spring's hunt will be the last great surround for the Osage and Cherokee people?"

Indianwise, she had run past the point of Hush's inquiry, and he had to return her to it.

"I don't care about the buffalo, Graywing," he told her. "Only about the Palo Duro. Now, will you tell me of it?"

"It is ten miles wide," said the Comanche squaw, spreading her strong arms to show the vastness. "It is thirty miles long and the river goes the whole way through grass which will hide a calf completely. The great walls which rise above the river are nearly a thousand feet high. They shut out the wind but let in the sun. They—"

"Yes, yes," interrupted Hush, "these are wonderful things, but what I ask you is this: Do you know of another place which is anything like the great canyon? I mean a place where our little herd can winter and where it can grow in the winters to come?"

She felt a thrill when he said "our herd" and she didn't know that he thought nothing of having said it that way. Her smile was radiant not only because she could answer "yes" to his question, but because she believed he had just told her that they would be man and wife and equal owners of the increase which would come to their cattle in the other place, the "little palo duro," of which she knew and of which she would now proudly tell her Texas Man.

When Hush heard her description of Lost Canyon, he felt as he had the day he set out from the *jacal* of Don Diego to seek his fortune on the Forks of the Guadalupe. Here was another time of fresh beginnings in a virgin, unspoiled country. Only this "lost canyon" of Graywing's must be incredibly more beautiful than even the Forks of the Guadalupe. According to the Comanche woman, no white man had set foot in the miniature Palo Duro of which she spoke. Its only previous inhabitant had been an Indian. He was a particular Indian, it was true—in fact, he was her recent Cherokee husband, old Samuel Sun Dance—but the aging rancher had left his lonesome canyon home shortly after Graywing had been forced out of it into the wilderness, and it very doubtful the old fellow would ever return. The Cañon Perdido land lay many miles outside the boundaries of the Cherokee Strip, and it could not be legally held by an Indian. Moreover, tribal law forbade subsequent occupancy of a dishonored home. It could be safely assumed from this that

133

old Samuel would not challenge their entry into his forsaken holdings. All that remained to do was strike the tipi and load the packhorse.

On the 5th of January, 1878, Hush roused up Old Brimstone and turned him and his thin-ribbed fellows on the trail for the Lost Canyon country. The course lay south by west; the going stayed open and easy. Graywing rode point on Don Diego's yellow buckskin, Hush rode drag on the black mare. Behind them plodded Graywing's stubby pinto dragging their household belongings on a pole travois.

Nothing occurred to mar the journey. The weather held warm and clear, the cattle went steady as threshing-mill oxen. On the third day the country began to climb and roughen, and on the morning of the fourth day they came out on a windswept mesa and stood looking down into the hidden valley.

Hush sat the black mare and stared, struck dumb.

It was not a valley, properly, but a true canyon, the eroded gorge, apparently, of one of the headwater forks of the main Canadian. But its wearing into the floor of the high prairie was of a gentler, more rounded nature and its depth far less than the thousand-foot slash of the big Palo Duro. It struck Hush on first sight as a valley, and he held that image of it always.

He never knew the name of the bright stream which flowed through its level meadows and timbered draws. Graywing called it Ka-tou, the Sun Dance, after her Cherokee husband, which seemed a pretty and a fitting name for it. In time Hush, too, came to call it Sun Dance Creek, and for some years after him it was still called by that name. Then the name was forgotten, and today in that country not even the oldest man alive has heard of Sun Dance Creek.

Yet by whatever name called, the stream and its lovely canyon formed a rancher's dream of open winters, ample grass and never-failing fresh water. The floor of the depression, as narrow in places as a quarter of a mile, no wider anywhere than a mile and a half, ran perhaps ten miles from its upper reaches to its issuance onto the tableland surrounding it. In all this way there was no side trail which would permit stock to get in or out of it. All a man need do was build his headquarters to block the high end and have his riders watch the lower boundary. He would have, then, a private pasture which would carry 1500 cows and their increase, summer and winter. And he would have it with no more cost than the pay of three full-time hands.

To Hush the vision was staggering.

Coming from a country where it took ten acres to graze a

horned toad, the evident fact that five or six acres would feed a cow and calf the year around was well-nigh incredible. Yet this was what his practiced eye told him would be the case. The grass and water and shelter down there would raise more cattle than he had ever seen. A ranch established in that walled valley would make a man rich within the next ten winters. With market steers already going at forty dollars a head and the stockpens at Dodge City less than 250 miles by easy trails, there could be no question of it. A kingdom was waiting there below him. All he had to do was ride down and take it.

He spoke a Comanche word to Graywing Teal, and put the black mare down the secret entrance trail to which the Kwahadi squaw had guided him. She followed in her proper place, at his rear. Behind them, Old Brimstone blew out through his nostrils and led the wary herd carefully along the narrow descent. Half an hour later the HF cattle were spread peacefully on the valley floor and Hush Feleen was examining the lonely creekside memorial which old Samuel had left to his brief time as the mate of Graywing Teal.

CHAPTER 28

The house the old Cherokee had built for his young Comanche bride beside the waters of Sun Dance Creek was no Plains Indian makeshift of lodgepoles and smoke-tanned buffalo hides. It was a real house made of peeled logs well chinked with moss and mud, and covered by a sod roof laid over heavy joined timbers. No safer, warmer, more snugly hidden place could have been provided for the remaining winter honeymoon of Hush and the Kwahadi girl. Nor, indeed, could a better place have been devised to harbor them for the rest of their lives.

This latter fact was clear to Graywing, and had Hush been as ready as she simply to share the old Cherokee's abandoned home, prospering there in the prairie wilderness, living by their strength and their skills and their combined intelligence, as a man and his woman with no broken prides to repair, no interrupted ambitions to resume, their descendants might still be living on the Llano Estacado and some of the very old men out there might still know where to find Sun Dance Creek and Lost Canyon in the Staked Plains basin of the main Canadian River.

But Hush Feleen was not born to prosper in the wilderness, nor to let an injured pride go unavenged.

Through January and February and into March he and Graywing continued their working arrangement as man and wife. They made a good life of it. When the weather was favorable they would ride out on Gato and Muchacha to explore their own lands and reconnoiter those of Goodnight's J A Ranch outside the Palo Duro. The hunting was excellent, deer and antelope abounding on the plains and along the canyon slopes, buffalo dotting the floor of the sheltered Lost Canyon range. These "curly cows" were thick as gathered cattle that first winter, the J A riders having hazed them out of the Palo Duro to make room for Goodnight's herd. Off them, and the herds of elk drifted down from the Colorado high country, Hush and Graywing lived like prairie royalty. It was "all hump-ribs and backfat," as the old mountain men used to say, and the wild freedoms of the life suited Hush as well as any Kwahadi of the pure blood. He had no complaints with the woman, either, nor she with him. Neither of them asked anything of the other; both assumed their life would continue along its present rewarding level. The first hint that it would not came in late March.

It began with a long ride down to the rim of the Palo Duro, forty miles and more straight away south and east of Lost Canyon. They followed a trail during that ride which seemed by nature made for a purpose Hush believed he had put forever out of mind. Yet with each step of the way the possibilities of it hammered at him the harder: the way he and Graywing were taking from Lost Canyon to the Goodnight spread would make a perfect driveway for getting stolen cattle from the J A to the HF connected. And provided there was a similar natural way to get those cattle up out of Goodnight's great canyon, a man's million might be made in far less than ten winters, or even five. Why, if a man took proper—

Hush cursed, and broke off the thought.

Why was it that his thinking had eternally to be shortcutting the honest trail? He was still very young, and if he worked as hard as he had promised himself he wouldn't ever need to be cutting across another man's forty to get his own piece plowed in time to plant for an ample harvest. No, sir, he had had all he wanted of the long loop and the straight-rod iron; he had seen all he needed to see of the hangman's knot and the mesquite limb. He had the beginnings of a decent life with a woman he could trust, right in the palm of his hand. No man alive knew where they were, no legal or personal pursuit of his killing of Ben Sloat or his breaking of

Avery Hudspeth could possibly trace him here to Lost Canyon. That was the all-important thing for a Hush Feleen to remember. He was safe here. He had covered his tracks into this place. He must never do anything to uncover them.

This resolution was taken on the trail five miles from top-out on the Palo Duro's north rim, but it was only when they were actually there and Hush was seeing that twisting, ancient pathway going down into the Palo Duro, that he realized Graywing had been guiding him to this point from the moment of leaving Lost Canyon. And it was only then that the thought really began to burn in him.

"You knew this trail was here," he said at last. "You knew it all along."

"Yes, I knew. It is the old Indian road. When the buffalo could not be found in Palo Duro, then they could be found in Cañon Perdido. The way we came is the way the buffalo followed to cross the land from the one place to the other. And always the Indian followed the buffalo. Is it not simple?"

"My God!" breathed Hush. "No wonder I kept thinking what a driveway it was! Half a million buffalo walking it out since the Lord knows when. And two hundred years of horseback Indians riding after them."

He sat overlong, frowning down into the canyon. "I can't get it out of my mind," he muttered finally. "God help me, I just can't."

"What is it?" asked Graywing. "What is it that stays in your mind to make your face so unhappy?"

"One thing," said Hush. "One simple damn thing—"

He broke off his words, scowled for a moment, shook his head. It was no use. He knew he should not go down there. But once the idea of how easy it would be had struck him, he just had to go. His mind would never rest any other way.

He clucked to the black mare and started her down the ancient Indian and buffalo trail. Graywing followed him without question, but her mind was uneasy.

The J A riders were not friendly to strangers on their employer's land. They rode a hard line at either end of the big canyon. Large-scale ranching operations always drew cattle thieves. They gathered like buzzards, and like buzzards they had to be kept moving, stirred up, ridden off. For an unknown mounted man to be caught inside the canyon's upper and lower deadlines meant rough handling and fast expulsion at best. At less than best it meant that, were he found carrying either a running-iron or a spare cinch-ring, the mounted stranger stayed on J A land—permanently.

When Graywing decided to speak of this to Hush, halfway down the trail, he assured her they would get nothing worse than the hard warning to get off and stay off the Goodnight range. They carried no straight-rod irons, nor any spare cinch-rings, and they were honest ranchers and residents of the area. There could be no real trouble.

As far as this prediction went, it was reasonable.

But it did not go as far as the grim scene being enacted at the foot of the old buffalo path even as Hush and his Indian wife started down from its top.

There were two of them, tall, tough-looking men, and they were not afraid. They stood straight, laughing and joking with the men who were about to hang them.

The J A riders did not return the laughs nor reply to the jokes. They had caught these two burning a J A steer with a hot cinch-ring held in a pair of shoeing tongs. They had been going on around the J to make it into an O, leaving the new brand to read O A, clean and pretty as though it had been put on with a stamp-iron.

Hush and Graywing rode into the tableau without warning, either to themselves or to the members of the lynching party.

The picture was old to Hush, and wickedly hurtful. It took him by the neck, back to another place. He felt the rope scars on his own throat begin to burn and his hand went up to them instinctively. Graywing saw the dark blood come piling into his face and she was suddenly afraid. But the J A riders did not know Hush as she did, and they were not afraid. One of them, that rarity of the plains, a fat cowboy, squinted at the newcomers leeringly.

"Well, well," he announced, "here's a couple more of them, boys. Rig another brace of halters and we'll hoist all four on the same haul."

Graywing dressed and rode like a man. In her wolfskin winter coat there was nothing revealed of her short hard figure to suggest the feminine. But it was not this mistake about her sex which narrowed Hush's eyes. While similarly set in motion by the fat cowboy's callous order, it was entirely another suggestion which now put the warning Feleen purr in his voice.

"This is my wife," he said to the two men who had started forward with their ropes. "The first one of you sons-of-bitches lays an hand on her—or me—I'll kill him."

He said it softly, the rusted shotgun merely resting on the horn of his saddle, but the two men stopped as though he had struck them across their faces with the swung barrels.

As they did, he raised himself slightly in the stirrups.

"Don't try it!" he barked across their heads at the fat

strawboss and the other two J A hands, and the three froze the creep of their hands toward their revolver butts and stood very still.

"Now the five of you step clear of those boys." He indicated the two rustlers. "And on your way you take those ropes off of them, gentle and easy."

He had not meant to interfere. The sight of the hanging had only sickened him at first. But the action of the fat rider in assuming that he and Graywing were working with the rustlers—precisely the same inhuman carelessness which had nearly strangled him alongside his father—suddenly set his mind aflame. The sinister likeness of this new scene at the bottom of the Palo Duro to the old, terrible one in the darkness of the Nueces shinnery, was too vivid for his unhealed memory to accept.

"Jump!" he snarled at the hesitating J A hands. "Don't you put off on me, you murdering bastards!"

He and Graywing had ridden around a blind turn, squarely into the middle of the group under the gnarled cottonwood. They had stopped their mounts thirty feet from the nearest of the cowboys, forty from the farthest. At that range the twelve-gauge double would disintegrate a barn door, and the J A hands were caught bunched in a space no bigger than that.

They moved as ordered. The rustlers were freed of their arm bonds as well as of the ropes around their necks.

"Where are your horses?" Hush asked them.

"Yonder," said one of the men, motioning toward a clump of artemisia. He broke into a grin. "They're both sensitive. They caint neither one of them abide the smell of incinerating cowhair."

"Neither can I," said Hush. "Let's get out of here."

The two got their horses, swung up and were ready.

"Now," said Hush to the five J A hands, "I'm going to tell you something. My name is Hush Feleen and I live up north on the main Canadian drainage. I mean to ride and ranch in this country. You may see me again. If you do, don't bother waving. Just grab your guns. You understand me?"

"Mister," answered the fat cowboy, "you must be crazy. You got any idee who you're talking to? We're Colonel Goodnight's men. This is the J A outfit. Ever hear tell of that mark?"

"All I care to," replied Hush, turning the black mare.

"Well, you remember it," rasped the other, "for it'll remember you, I'll guarantee you. Them two men was caught changing the brand on a J A steer. They had coming what they was about to get."

Hush stopped the mare.

"What about my wife and me?" he asked stonily.

"Oh, hell!" The fat cowboy shrugged. "I was just talking. You could have cleared yourselves. All you needed to do was speak up. Now you'd best turn them two back to us and ride on out of here the way you come. We'll just act like it never happened."

Hush shook his head. "You'd have to be a better actor than me," he said. "I don't forget that convenient."

"All right," snapped the other, voice coarsening. "If you want to get smart about it, we'll see we don't forget so easy either. Fact is, mister, we'll remember you a spell. I'd say you better ride far and wide of the J A from here out. We catch you again, you'll get what you just spared them two."

"The wind blows just as hard out here on the Panhandle as it does down home," said Hush. "Remember me, boys. Hush Feleen."

He turned to the two rustlers.

"Better collect their guns," he began, then said, "No, hold up. I got a better idea. You!"—he jabbed at the fat man—"mount up and ride along with us. We'll drop you off when we're in the clear. Maybe."

There was no argument.

They were out of the canyon in half an hour. Turning their captive loose, they hit north and west up the Lost Canyon buffalo trail. When its first turn hid them from the released J A rider, the taller of the two rescued men looked at Hush and doffed his big hat to him with a wide-grinned flourish.

"I'm Tom Horn," he said. "This here's my partner, Hi Luck Lewis. We're in the cattle business."

"So I noticed," said Hush. To him the name Tom Horn meant no more than did that of Hi Luck Lewis, so he merely added, "You got my name back yonder. This here's Graywing."

"Howdy, Graywing," acknowledged Tom Horn. "I vow you're the first Comanche I was ever glad to see."

"Amen!" echoed his partner, Hi Luck. "From now on you can call me an Indian lover. I'll fight the first man says red ain't my favorite color."

They were rough men and meant it well. Hush knew that. Moreover, his own sentiments for Graywing's people were not unmixed. He shared the general Texas dislike for Indians, and he saw in Tom Horn and Hi Luck Lewis, beyond forgiving them their clumsy sallies, two champions of a way of life which still appealed to him above all others. The meek might inherit the earth, as Nancy Hushton had always told him, but while they were waiting for their windfall, the

140

likes of Tom Horn and Hi Luck would be living mighty high, fast and handsome. These two were Hush's own kind, he thought. They spoke his language and they did it with a light-hearted courage and good humor as contagious as their grins. There was, in the end, no standing against them.

Before they reached the drop-off into Lost Canyon and eased their horses down the trail to the sodhouse beside Sun Dance Creek, Hush had worked out with them the first details of the most brazen cattle theft in the history of the Texas Panhandle.

CHAPTER 29

It is a matter of record that the J A Ranch was rustled blind its second year in the Palo Duro. It is a matter of conjecture how many cattle were finally lost. So much legend built up around the big steal that an acceptable count never was established. Not so uncertain was that part of the total loss owing to the activities of Hush Feleen and his two debtors.

In the four months covering April through July, 1878, they ran off better than 600 head of choice Goodnight beef. The wholesale thievery worked for three reasons. The J A riders did not know until the fall of '78 round-up how hard their market-age cattle had been hit. Hush and his accomplices never made the mistake of trying to light a branding fire on Goodnight land, rustling their steers clean and fast, never taking any weak stuff that wouldn't stand hard driving. The two men Hush had saved proved to be tophands.

Tom Horn was the best all-round cowboy Hush had ever seen. Hi Luck was only a little behind him. Hush himself could ride and rope with any man alive. The combination was deadly. All it actually wanted, or lacked, of being perfect, was a horse wrangler to keep the hard-worked *remuda* of saddlestock in shape. And even that deficiency was solved when, in early July, Nocero, the Lipan Apache, showed up with a typically Indian greeting.

"Goddamsumbitch!" he grinned happily to Hush. "You hard to find as old man's *pico* on cold morning. Me look everywhere since last snow. You leave no track, not even for Apache eye."

When Hush pressed him about how he had found out where he was, the one-eyed wrangler said he had gotten the

information from a small band of Comanches he had encountered at the Red Hills Crossing. They had been out in
the Staked Plains, they said, and knew the place where the
k'ou-a'-da-kih, the black-haired man, was hiding.

Hush wondered why a chance band of Comanches should
feel he was hiding. He had seen no Comanches and didn't
like the idea that they had seen him. Maybe he had been
mavericking so hard he had become careless. Perhaps he had
been watching so intently for trouble from the J A cowboys
that he had let down his guard against those other riders of
the high plains who did not care how many cattle he stole,
but who would kill him for his horse, or his gun, or his hair,
or, if it came to that, just for the hell of it.

Out on the Staked Plains in 1878, a man didn't forget
about horseback Indians and stay healthy. The Kiowa and
Comanche and Southern Cheyennes were all supposed to
have been rounded up and put on reservations by that time,
but the white ranchers in the territory knew better. As long
as the buffalo were still on the south plains, so would the
horseback Indians be there. And the buffalo were still there.
Maybe it was the last of them in the South Herd, as the
Osages and Cherokees claimed, but they were buffalo.

Hush nodded to himself—the thought of the curly cows
eased his mind. Sure, that was it. The Comanche band had
just been trailing the last of their free beef supply up into
the Palo Duro and Lost Canyon ranges. In passing through
the country they had seen his place, possibly even talked to
his Kwahadi squaw.

But Graywing, when questioned, immediately denied that
she had seen or talked to any Indians, let alone to any
Comanche Indians.

At another time, in less of a hurry, Hush would have
taken warning at her too quick reply. He had asked her only
about Indians; she had added the qualification, Comanche, of
her own volition. But Hush had a herd to gather and get to
market before the new snow flew. He had no time to spend
on Graywing and the matter of her wandering cousins. They
could wait; the herd could not. Those cattle had to be on
trail by August.

Hush's urgency aside, the squaw had a question of her
own which could not wait. She was as big as a barrel. It was
her next to last month, she said, and something should be
done. She would go with Hush and the herd to Dodge City.
There they would be made man and wife by the Christian
Black Robe, so that their son might have a white man's paper
to prove he was entitled to his father's proud name.

To this awkward proposal Hush reacted strongly.

He had not thought of himself in the role of father to an Indian halfblood. He had assumed the child was that either of Graywing's Kwahadi lover or of her Cherokee husband. When the squaw now patiently pointed out that she had seen neither of these others for six months before her Texas Man came to her winter lodge in the crosstimbers, Hush flew into a rage. He still felt she was trying to mislead him, and that she had seen her Comanche young man in those six months. He made the mistake of telling her as much.

The Kwahadi woman looked at him a long time. Finally, and with great dignity, she said to him: "The child is yours, Texas Man. If you will not have him, then I shall take him away from here. Word has come to me that my father who sold me is dead. My disgrace among my people is lifted. I may return to the Kwahadi again. If you say to me that you do not want me, and do not want your son, then I will go back to my people. But if you say that you want us, then my heart will be full again, and we will serve you for all our lives, and we will love you for longer than that."

Hush felt the full shame of her words.

"Listen, Graywing," he pleaded desperately, "I don't want you to go away. But there is only one sensible thing to do about the child. We must wait and see what color it is. If it's mine, I'll stand by it, and by you."

It was a cruel way to put it and Hush didn't think of it in the way it sounded. Fortunately, Graywing saw that he didn't mean it that way. She bowed her dark head.

"You will see, Texas Man," she murmured. "It is your son and you will know him."

"I'll never deny any son of mine!" answered Hush hoarsely, and went out of the house and back to the creekside holding pens where Tom Horn and Hi Luck were branding the last of the stolen J A steers.

They made the drive to the North Fork Crossing without incident, but at the crossing six men who identified themselves as J A reps rode out of the river timber with a terse request for permission to sift the herd for Goodnight cattle.

Hush and his three men—Nocero was along—eased off to one side, Hush telling the J A riders by all means to take their cuts and see what they could come up with. But as he said it, Tom Horn and Hi Luck were moving their horses into flanking positions, kicking loose their scabbard legs, dropping their holsters arms, clearly getting set for a shootout.

It could go either way from that moment.

They had marked all the J A stuff by going very carefully

on around the J to make it into an O, giving them an O A. Then they had added a T after the O A, making a mark which read O A T, which mark they had also put on all the unbranded cattle they had gathered with the J A stuff, the result setting up a most delicate situation for any big company reps who might want to cut their herd on the way to Dodge, the present case being no exception.

The J A reps understood that. If they accepted the O A T brand, fine. If they did not, there was going to be a gunfight.

The J A men were sure these were mainly Goodnight cattle. But the brands were beautifully worked over. There was no way to call them as being blotted, short of shooting and skinning out one of the suspected steers. And that got mighty ticklish. If they happened to pick one of the big slickears, the originally unbranded strays present in any drive herd, things could get sticky. On such an animal the whole new brand would show through clean and clear on the underside of the hide, instead of uneven like a worked-over brand. If they were just unlucky enough to select one of the "honest" animals they would really be in trouble with those hard-eyed bastards watching them so closely over yonder.

In the end, the J A men decided the risk was not warranted. With a larger crew to back them, they would have done it. But six to four—especially those four yonder—wasn't near odds enough to pull a gun on here and now.

They came out of the herd carefully, their leader confronting Hush civilly.

"New outfit?" he asked. "Never heard of the O A T myself."

"They're my wife's cattle," said Hush. "O A T are her maiden-name initials. You want my mark, check the small brand on the left jaw."

"We done that," said the rider.

"What did you find?" asked Hush.

"An HF connnected."

"That's me. Hush Feleen."

"That," said the rider, "I've heard of."

"Reckoned you had," nodded Hush. "Now, mister, we're going to put these cattle on across. We still got a ways to go and September's staring us in the eye. You got any more to say?"

The J A rider did not throw in. "Feleen," he said quietly, "we think those are J A cattle and we mean so to report them to Colonel Goodnight."

Hush shrugged.

"By the time you do," he said, "they'll be hung up in the

cooler at Kansas City. Now you going to move back, or ain't you, mister?"

The J A rep nodded to his companions. The five swung their horses off the trail. Hush waved to Horn and Hi Luck to start them moving. Old Brimstone bellowed, raised his tail, took to the water like a spaniel after a down duck. The water was low, the crossing better than half wading. All the cattle were over in thirty minutes.

The J A men sat with Hush watching it to the last cow. Then their leader said, "All right, boys, let's go." Checking his horse, he called back to Hush. "I've got a message for those two hands of yours, them tall boys yonder. You tell them we got orders to shoot them on sight on J A land. They would be real wise if they never rode back down this trail."

"How about me?" Hush grinned, well pleased with himself and the way things had gone. "A man don't like to feel left out."

"You," said the J A man, not grinning, "we're going to hang."

On the far side of the river they noticed a neighboring campfire winking through the murky twilight. After the cattle were down and quiet, Hush and his two hands rode over to exchange the time of day. It had been a long winter. Horn and Hi Luck, particularly, were hungry for some conversation other than that with Hush and his Kwahadi squaw, both of whom were Comanches when it came to small talk. But the pleasure was not to be theirs alone. When Hush rode up to that small fire beside the Dodge City Trail, he enjoyed one of his rare moments of real emotion.

There, walking bandy-legged out to meet them, was a dried-up wisp of a man with a brown face and broken nose, whose glad cry of recognition warmed Hush all over.

"Lordy, Lordy, boys!" called out Iota Jones; "it's Mr. Feleen!" Then, almost overcome, he said to Hush: "Get down, get down, boy. I'm happy enough to see you I could cry. We all thought you was done for."

"So did I," agreed Hush, swinging down and taking his hand. "Is that Tate yonder? And old Rafe?"

"Sure is, Mr. Feleen. The three of us been up to Dodge with a big bunch of Lazy Jaybird beef for Mr. John Blocker."

"Paid off now and heading home, eh?" queried Hush.

"Well, heading home anyways," grinned Rafe sheepishly. "We're done busted flatter than a schoolmarm's chest."

Hush looked at the three of them, a sudden thought forming.

"Well, boys," he said, "you come to the right place. I owe you each fifteen hundred dollars on them seven hundred head we never got to Dodge. Now I got a chance to pay you off. We got another seven hundred bedded yonder, and they *are* going to Dodge."

"You giving us the chance to throw in with you again, Mr. Feleen?" asked Iota warily. "At fifteen hundred dollars each?"

"It's what I'm owing you, ain't it, Iota?"

"Shucks, Mr. Feleen, you ain't owing us nothing."

"Iota, you three want to help me get this new herd up to Dodge, or don't you? I ain't running no charity raffles."

"By damn," drawled Rafe, "I ain't got nobody waiting Christmas dinner on me down home."

"Me neither," said Tate. "And I'd dearly love to get another shot at that damned faro dealer at the Long Branch."

"I cain't stand agin a stompede," grinned Iota. "Sign us on."

"You're signed," said Hush. "Meet Tom Horn and Hi Luck Lewis," he added, waving toward his still mounted companions. "They're working the herd with me."

Iota's jaw dropped, as the two tall riders stepped down.

"My Gawd, boys," he said to Rafe and Tate, "this here *is* Tom Horn."

"Well," acknowledged the latter, moving forward with his wide grin and ready hand, "it sure is nice to be remembered."

"I should think so!" enthused Iota. "Can you beat that? Tom Horn, himself, right here and real as a rifle bullet!"

Tate and Rafe edged forward to shake hands and stare at the famous adventurer whose name was already a legend up and down the Dodge City trail, or wherever cattlemen might gather at either end of it. A good spurring was given Hush over the fact he had worked all winter with such high-class help and hadn't known it.

Tom Horn allowed that this innocence of Hush's was what he had enjoyed most about being with him. It was a rarely agreeable thing, he said, to meet up with a man who'd been so busy being onery himself, he'd had no time to keep up with the meanness of others. The good feeling continued as all hands went over to the O A T herd and built up a reunion fire that had the prairie lit up for an arrowshot all around. There was only one small jarring note, and that came after Iota, Rafe, Tate and Hi Luck had turned in and Horn was starting out to relieve Nocero on night guard.

Hush followed him over to his horse and told him he had something to tell him, seeing as how he had found out he was Tom Horn.

146

The tall rustler at once turned edgy, standing away from his mount and dropping his gun hand. "What's that, Hush?" he asked softly.

Hush told him about the J A man's warning, adding, "It didn't make much sense to me then, but it does now that I know who you are. I reckon they spotted you where I didn't."

"I reckon," said Horn. "So what about it?"

"So likely you had best take their advice and keep drifting north. The J A's a rough outfit. They fight fair, but they fight hard."

Tom Horn nodded thoughtfully, his hand easing away from his gunbutt. "Likely you're right," he said. "We'll think it over."

"I would," answered Hush, and turned back to the fire.

Six days later they made Little Arkansas Crossing in the Cherokee Strip near the Kansas line. From there, the rest of the way to railhead was like driving down a road. Good grass and water and level ground, not a Jayhawker, Texas fever inspector or roadbrand cutter the entire distance. In Dodge they hit a high market and Hush sold his 700 cattle at $47.50, the top of the 1878 drive. He walked out of Ed Dempster's trackside office shack with $29,350 in a Barth & Snider draft on the Mastin Bank of Kansas City in his pocket, the buyer's fat hand patting him on the back in congratulation for letting bygones be bygones, and for such a timely late fall drive of superb quality cattle.

"By the way, Feleen," the commission man called after him, as Hush started off, "I ran into an old friend of yours the other day. Working the bar up to the Alamo. She don't look too good these days. Maybe you could see that some of your boys threw a little business her way."

Hush came around on his heel, his gray eyes turning icy.

"Is *she* up here?" he asked quietly.

"She sure is. Like I say, though, she's not doing well. Looks old as hell."

"In a year?" said Hush unbelievingly.

"Well, she's still got her shape, mind you. But she's no chicken. When a woman's her age, working a town like this one, a year shows heavy as lead. You just don't get the trade the young gals do, nor the prices. A man's going to spend his hard-earned money for a woman, he wants one that don't remind him of his mother."

"She's barely thirty," muttered Hush. "My God, that's not old."

"It is in her business," said the other. "Be sure you get

that draft deposited right away, Feleen. This place is rougher than a last year's cob in cold weather. Don't let it separate you from your stock money."

"Thanks," said Hush. "But save your worries. I'll be back next fall with fifteen hundred head. You can start making out the draft for that right now."

He started off again, hesitated, turned back.

"Say," he asked, "you know a good lawyer in town?"

"Sure," answered the buyer. "Abel Nathan, across from the Dodge House. Smart as hell. He's a Jew but he's honest. Does all the Barth and Snider business at this end. Why for you want a lawyer, Feleen?"

"To keep me out of jail," answered Hush, and stalked off up Front Street toward the bright lights.

CHAPTER 30

After depositing the Barth & Snider draft, Hush took a wallet full of bills and went to see Lawyer Nathan. The latter proved to be a smallish, older man whose simple dignity and disarming manner drew respect from the guilty, trust from the cynical, and confession from the conscience-stricken. Hush, finding himself in all three categories, decided to put his faith on the line along with his money.

On the occasion of this first visit, however, he warily confined himself to informing the attorney that he owed a debt of considerable amount to a certain lady of the town. The lady was currently down on her luck and could use some assistance through what might otherwise turn out to be a very rough winter.

Hush counted out $5,000 in hundred-dollar bills, and placed them on the office desk, saying quietly, "See she gets this without knowing where it come from."

"Her name?" asked Nathan.

"Hollister," said Hush. "Evvie Hollister."

The lawyer nodded slowly.

"Now, I will guess, Mr. Feleen, that you want me not only to give her the money—it's a great deal of money, you know—but also to assist her in investing a goodly part of it. As well, I am imagining you will want to know if the effort goes prosperously, or poorly. And it is essential that I do not disclose the source of her original good fortune. These are close to your wishes in the matter, Mr. Feleen?"

"As close," said Hush, "as a barbershop shave."

"You understand," added Nathan, "that this is a somewhat unusual request and may entail complications beyond my professional abilities or, for that matter, ethics."

"You're a lawyer," said Hush confidently.

Abel Nathan inclined his head, a touch of sadness in his smile.

"To most people," he said, "that means I will do anything for money. However, in your case, Mr. Feleen, I shall do my utmost to make a reality of the popular fancy."

"I don't care how you spell it, Mr. Nathan, just do it."

"It shall be done. Now, do you have any ideas how we might best advise the young lady? Anything at all which occurs to you as being a feasible investment for her particular talents?"

"A what kind of investment?"

"Workable, Mr. Feelen."

Hush thought a minute, then nodded.

"She's spent her whole life in dance halls and such. I reckon some sort of cut-glass and gaslight place would be the answer."

"She could do much worse," Abel Nathan agreed. "In Dodge City not all the fortunes are being made in cattle. I know of a place which can be leased reasonably. It is not far down the street from the Dodge House."

"Down Front Street?" asked Hush.

"Well, no, a bit around the corner, you might say."

"Across the tracks?"

"In a manner of speaking, yes."

"All right; fine. You sure you ain't unhappy about taking this job on, Mr. Nathan? I know it ain't exactly high-class business for a man like you."

"Thank you," said the lawyer, spreading his hands. "I agree it is not, Mr. Feleen, but I am not buying into the business we have been discussing. I am acting solely as your agent in a legitimate transfer of funds. I am morally convinced of my own position, sir. There is no statute forbidding sin in Dodge City, Mr. Feleen."

"God knows it don't look it," grinned Hush, and reached out and took the other's proffered hand.

That was all the contract they made. Five minutes of straight talk and a handshake completed the fateful agreement, and Hush was gone down Front Street seeking out his remaining creditors.

The new owner of the Lost Canyon Ranch had never felt more certain of himself nor of his future than he did that early September evening of 1878. When he had paid off his five hands their $1500 each, including a $500 bonus for Nocero, and the $5000 put to Evvie Hollister's account, he would still come out with $16,750 deposited in the Cattleman's National Bank of Dodge City to the name and to the free-using credit of Hushton Hatterson Feleen. Maybe some other shirttail-poor Tennessee boy had come further, faster, but Hush doubted it. A year ago tonight, dead lost in an early fall blizzard with fifty head of mixed, sore-footed stocker cattle 250 miles from the railroad; tonight, walking down the middle of the widest street west of Kansas City, or even Chicago, with money in the bank, a kingdom of the world's finest grass awaiting him in the Palo Durito, his debts all discharged, or about to be, and the evening yet young and inviting before him.

There just wasn't much of any way you could better a run of luck like that. Not, the good Lord knew, when you still lacked some days of being six months over twenty-one years old.

He met his boys in front of the Lone Star Dancehall, as agreed, and gave them their cuts of the herd-money. The Indian, Nocero, disappeared at once, but the others insisted on buying one for the boss. Hush, on top of the world and feeling mighty tall about it, declared that twenty-one ought to be old enough for a man to take his first hard pull at the tiger's tail, and went with his men into the Lone Star.

There was a lean-to tacked on one side of the main hall to house the bar. This proved low-ceilinged, dark and smoky, half filled with hardcase customers and stinking of sour beer and bad whiskey.

Iota reckoned nervously that if they had wanted to travel first-class they should have gone to the Dodge House, the Alamo or the Long Branch, where the cattlemen and other honest crooks hung out. Hush said it was all right, he didn't mind second-class, but he wanted to get his drink and clear out. He hadn't got a room yet, and Ed Dempster had told him that the Dodge House was full of dudes from Iowa and Minnesota on a tour from Kansas City to see the "Sodom of the Arkansas." It was the last trainload of tourists for the season—that is, for the season when the Texas cowboys were still in town—and a room was harder to come by than a sure cure for saddlegall.

They lined up at the dingy bar, Tom Horn insisting on standing the first ten rounds. Hush noted the way in which two or three of the local patrons seemed to pull away from Horn and give him room. He didn't think much about this, but was surprised when some of the other customers did the same thing for him. The barkeep's face wasn't exactly lit

150

up with welcome either, he observed. But the bottle came out readily enough and was spilled into the six glasses.

There were the usual salutations as the whiskey went up in a toast to Hush Feleen and the financial success of his O A T trail drive. Somehow, though, the words rang hollow and too loud, and of a sudden Hush realized the other men in the dim-lit room had stopped talking and were listening.

A glance up and down the long bar showed the latter gathered in two groups at either end of the mahogany, a clear space of at least ten feet flanking both sides of his own party. Hush put down his whiskey untasted.

"What's the quarantine about?" he asked the barkeep. "Your customers sensitive to the smell of Texas cowdung?"

"Whaddya mean?" muttered the other. "Ain't the whiskey good?"

"The whiskey's as bad as you can buy," said a quiet-spoken voice behind Hush. "But that isn't what Mr. Feleen means, is it, Mr. Feleen?"

Hush came around slowly.

Tom Horn and Hi Luck followed his move, their hands dropping toward their holsters. But when Horn saw the foppishly dressed, mild-looking man with the derby hat and Malacca cane standing there, he broke out his best grin and said, "Why, hello, Bat. You still trying to stay honest?"

It wasn't a common name, Bat, and it didn't go with a common-looking man, and from the dudish attire and the dull wink of the pewter star on the flowered vest, Hush knew he was staring at the notorious William Barclay Masterson.

That fall of '78 the famous Dodge City deputy was twenty-two years old, only a few months Hush's senior. He was possibly five feet eight inches tall, and not heavy. On the street you would have guessed him for a bank teller or a whiskey drummer—anything, in fact, except a gunfighter of frontierwide reputation. Yet there in the smoke and haze of a cowtown barroom, his coat opened just enough to show the butt of his gun and the glint of his badge, his steady eyes watching you while he waited for you to reply to his probe, he looked like what he was.

However, Hush had no great regard for gunfighters, famous or ordinary. He showed as much, now, in his calculated answer.

"You don't hardly look old enough," he said to Masterson, "to go around getting smart with strangers. Not, anyway, with this stranger."

The deputy shook his head. "You're no stranger, Mr. Feleen. Your reputation has run ahead of you. As for my being too young for this kind of work, look what you yourself have managed to accomplish and in even less time. Ah, no, Mr. Feleen, I think we're well enough met."

Hush's eyes narrowed. "What do you want of me?" he asked watchfully.

"Five minutes of your time."

"For what?"

"A walk to Mr. Earp's office."

"Wyatt Earp?"

"The same. Mr. Earp's marshal of Dodge these days, in case you hadn't heard. Charlie Basset's Ford County sheriff. Billy Tilghman's chief deputy. I'm second assistant to the dog-catcher."

"Meaning what?" said Hush.

"Meaning move," answered Masterson.

Hush looked at his companions and Tom Horn advised him quickly.

"Best do what he says, Hush. There's no bucking the law in this town no more. Not if Wyatt says there ain't. You go along. We'll see you back here when you're done."

The slender deputy shook his head once more.

"No, Tom," he said in his gentle voice, "I don't think you will be here when Mr. Feleen gets back. Wyatt asked me to tell you he would be pleased if you would just keep moving. You and Hi Luck both. All right?"

"Sure thing, Bat. We'll think about it first thing tomorrow."

"He meant tonight, not tomorrow."

"Aw, come on, now, is that any way to treat an old friend?" said Horn with a grin. "You boys surely have suffered shortitis of the memory. You call to mind that time up in Deadwood when me and you and Wyatt took on them four—"

"Wyatt says you got sixty minutes, Tom. He didn't say anything about no time up in Deadwood."

The good-natured outlaw knew the quality of the law and its officers in that time and place. He hitched up his gunbelt, downed his whiskey, and accepted the order to move on with the easy grace that was his to the last tragic day of his life.

"Well, boys"—he smiled at Iota, Tate and Rafe—"it's been grand, and don't think it ain't. Still, all good things got to end sometime. Me, I got a sudden hankering to go north. Up Wyoming way most likely. I been hearing about the good grass and high pay up in Johnson County. Reckon I'll give that country a looking over while I'm about it. You coming, Hi Luck?"

"Not north, sure as hell," said the other cowboy. "Why don't we head back to Arizony? We was doing fine down

152

there. We can go to scouting for the cavalry again. What you say, Tom? It's for certain a better winter country than Wyoming, and that Army pay ain't the worst in the world."

Horn had been a scout for the Army against the Apaches for the past two or three years. In the last six months he had been famed Al Seiber's right-hand man. The scouting for Seiber and the cavalry were the only honest work he had done since running away from his Missouri farm home at fifteen. The thoughts of Arizona's high sunny plateaus and pungent juniper flats came to him strongly with his partner's words, and directly he nodded his agreement.

"Likely you're right, Hi Luck," he said. Then, prophetically, "Wyoming will wait, I reckon."

"That's an even money bet," drawled Hi Luck. "Let's ride."

The two tall men—rustlers, army scouts, folk heroes or whatever—went out the door of the Lone Star with a careless wave and a last grin at their recent friends. If Dodge City saw either of them again, the record does not list it. Certain it was that Hush never did.

When they were gone he looked after them a thoughtful moment, then turned to Bat Masterson.

"All right, deputy," he said. "Let's go see the marshal."

Wyatt Earp was a different kind of man and a different kind of lawman from Bat Masterson.

There was precious little of gentleness or humor about him. Although he, too, was soft-spoken, the quality of his talk was not the same. What he said stuck in a man's mind. Moreover, while Hush had not cared for Bat Masterson a little bit, he found himself understanding Wyatt Earp and even warming toward him in a strange way.

What the marshal of Dodge City told him, however, was not warm.

Word had gotten around town, he said, that the much-talked-of herd of late-season beef driven in from the Staked Plain by young Hush Feleen had been rustled out of Colonel Goodnight's Palo Duro pasture. As far as Wyatt was concerned, situations of this nature did not interest him, ordinarily. But Goodnight was a mighty big man. As far as the rustling of his cattle went, he figured, the Colonel could no doubt produce a self-cure. He had been in the cattle business a long time; he knew it was a hard business, and Wyatt knew he hired hard men to carry it out for him. It was, in fact, the general foreman of the J A, come to town with a herd the month before and still in Dodge on company orders, who had come to the marshal's office that same evening and suggested that Earp have a little talk with young Feleen of the O A T and the HF connected.

"Now, Feleen," Wyatt concluded in his slow, careful way of talking, "I've heard other things about you that we won't go into. I've said what I have to say to you and you may take it as a sort of friendly first warning. With this added bit to remember."

The big marshal paused, studying his visitor with eyes as gray and disquieting as Hush's own. Then he said very quietly: "I don't give no seconds."

CHAPTER 31

Hush returned at once to see Lawyer Nathan.

When he had told him of the warning from Wyatt Earp as to further rustling, and the veiled reference to other past wrongs which might lead to law action, the little attorney asked him quietly if it was true he had stolen the herd he had brought to Dodge. As quietly, Hush answered him.

"Mr. Nathan," he said, "Marshal Earp didn't accuse me of stealing those cows. He only said he had heard I did. You're apt to hear the same thing, but not from me. What I want from you is legal paper to that land out there in Lost Canyon. You get me the grass, I'll worry what to put on it."

"As you will," Abel Nathan agreed after a long pause. "But I will not defend you, boy, if I am brought to believe you are guilty. Our contract depends on good faith from you."

"I'm not asking you to help me steal livestock for a living," said Hush, relieved. "Just get me title to those meets and bounds on that Cañon Perdido range. Besides," he finished with another of his quick-flashed smiles, "don't worry about defending me, Mr. Nathan. Out in this country cow thiefs never get into court."

Assuring him he would look to his land titles with every legal care, the lawyer then told Hush he had some further information which he thought might be of interest to any cattle-owning land holder faced with possible range possession rights.

The information proved to concern one "Bobwire" Bailey, an advance man for the Barb Fence Company of DeKalb, Illinois, manufacturers of the new-fangled barbed wire which was catching on with the farmers and small ranchers of the settled country to the east, and which Bailey was trying to peddle to the far western owners of the really big grass. When Hush saw the patent drawings of the short-barbed, doubled-strand wire which Bailey had left with Nathan, his eyes narrowed with excitement. Here was his answer, legal or otherwise.

The Lost Canyon range, closed off at both ends with Bailey's cat-clawed fencing, would make a cattle kingdom he could hold against all comers. Furthermore, he could afford the price of walling off his Staked Plains empire. Selling at 20¢ a pound at its introduction in 1875, the wire was now down to 4¢ on the open market, and for this particular shipment of sample wire sitting on the siding at Dodge City, Bailey would take 2¢ and sign the sale in twenty minutes.

When Abel Nathan saw the fire rising in Hush's eyes he told him the most interesting part of the deal was yet to come.

"Bailey was sent out here," he explained, "to sell the product to Colonel Goodnight. The idea was that to get the wire in use on such a large and famous ranch would open up the entire western country. But the J A apparently wants nothing to do with closing off its pastures. Goodnight's man here in Dodge, Coke Bancroft, says the Colonel not only won't have the wire on his own land, but will fight to keep it off anyone else's. Goodnight seems to feel the barbed wire will bring ruin to the big cattleman. He has a dozen J A men in town with Coke Bancroft under orders to watch those 'bobwire' cars down at the siding around the clock. This will explain, of course, why the wire is down to half price with no takers. I've an idea you can acquire the entire shipment for whatever fraction of 2¢ per pound you care to offer."

Nathan spread his hands, pushed back his chair.

"Well, what do you say, my boy?" he asked Hush, getting to his feet with the question. "Do we send for Bobwire Bailey, or bow wisely to Coke Bancroft?"

Hush rose in turn, teeth flashing again in a smile.

"You take care of Bailey and the bobwire, Mr. Nathan," he said. "I'll handle Bancroft and his J A boys."

Hush knew what he needed and how to go about getting it. It was nearing ten o'clock when he set out along Front Street to recruit his wagon guards.

By midnight he had hired six Texas trailhands of the right kind, men who had the look of the *ladino* about them and who were beginning to wish mightily that they had gone home to the shinnery with their friends and partners who had trailed up to Dodge with them earlier that summer. They were not any of them gunmen in the fanciful sense. But they all owned guns and had worn spots on their trouser legs where their holsters had been before they came to Dodge, and where they would be again when they left it.

To these half-dozen homesick *cimarrones* Hush offered $100 cash and the winter's keep at his place out on the Panhandle in return for their services as chaperons to his wire wagons. He would hire teamsters; all they needed to do was ride along.

None of the six took more than thirty seconds to accept. They all knew of Coke Bancroft and the J A riders being in town to bluff out any buyers for the Barb Fence Company's new "calf-gutter" wiring. Yet not a one of them but felt $100 was ample fee for risking his life to side Hush.

As Texans and as trail drivers, they never had liked quarantines. Beginning with the early tick-fever deadlines and ending with the later anti-Texan discriminations of the Kansas sodbusters, it was in the trail breed to resent being told where they could and where they could not go.

Right now, if this black-haired kid with the Tennessee mountain drawl wanted to take a line of freight wagons down to the Staked Plain, and that bear-sized Coke Bancroft had told him he would never get across the North Canadian with them, why hell, there was only one decent thing for a man to do—go fetch his horse out of hock down to the livery barn and saddle up for an early start.

Coke Bancroft was a huge man, taller than Hush and forty pounds heavier. He had a voice to go with his heft, but he was never loud with it. It was simply that so deep a growl had to be heard. And every hand with the six-wagon Feleen train loading at trackside next morning heard it.

Coke came alone and on foot down to the freight siding where the flat cars were that carried the Barb Fence Company's spindles of thorned wire. He walked straight up to Hush and rumbled unheatedly, "I'll give you a friendly piece of advice, young feller. Don't try it."

"Well," responded Hush, "that's one way of looking at it."

"How's that?" asked the older man.

"Being friendly," said Hush.

"But it ain't your way, is that it, boy?"

"That's it, Mr. Bancroft."

Coke's massive jaw had the look of headstone granite, but he was not a vicious man. He had seen many a hardcase kid come and go in his time, and he was old enough to be this one's father. Childless himself, he now felt a twinge of compassion, even a stirring of liking and of wanting to help this fierce-eyed mountain boy with the Apache-black hair and the soft southern voice.

"Boy," he told him at last, "I do wish you would dwell on it a little. I don't want to take you on. You haven't gone so far but what you can't back up. But if you keep coming our way, boy, you give me no choice save to be waiting for you."

Hush didn't take the suggested time to think.

"Mr. Bancroft," he answered at once, "you better wait with your eyes open, for I'll be along directly."

"Boy," said Coke Bancroft, eying him quietly, "we'll be there when you are."

Two hours later the wire wagons were loaded and rolling. By high noon they were hull down to Dodge City and by nightfall were twenty miles south.

The following days went equally well. The road was dry and hard, the rented Wright & Beverly Company mules big and fast-stepping. The new model Murphy wagons leased from the same Dodge City firm were loaded in good trim, and moved as easily as Concord coaches over the level prairie. In all the way down to the North Fork there was no sign of Coke Bancroft and his J A riders.

But mid-afternoon of the fifth day, still some miles above the North Fork Crossing, they raised sign of some other riders just as interesting.

It had been four years since the power of the Southern Plains tribes had been broken at Adobe Walls and Palo Duro. What little of the red man's will to fight pitched battles remained had been given the death shake by a party of forty buffalo hunters from Dodge in March of '77, when the latter attacked and scattered the last major encampment of "wild Indians" south of the Arkansas River. But those hardy white souls who worked and lived out in the empty solitudes of the Staked Plain had not quite forgotten the recent power of their red brothers, and for ugly reason.

Having learned they could no longer gather in large groups, the Indian marauders had operated the past three or four years in smaller bands of the kind Nocero had talked with at Red Hills Crossing the previous summer—the band which had told him where Hush was. These small raiding parties meant nothing to a well-armed white party such as Hush's, but they meant everything to the lonely settler, the one- or two-wagon freighter, or the unescorted stagecoach run.

In the present case, to whatever party they had just caught on the trail ahead of the HF wire wagons, they had already meant death and destruction. When the black smoke was coiling skyward as it was up there beyond the rise, it was too late for anything but pursuit and punishment of the red killers.

Pausing now to shade his eyes against the slant of the sun, Hush snapped as much to Nocero, who had galloped up to join him. But the Apache horse wrangler grunted and shook his head. "Sumbitch Comanche too quiet," he said. "Maybe somebody still alive up there. Better so you me go see, boy." Hush shot him a hard look and said, "You, me, and about half a dozen others!" and stood up in his stirrups to wave forward the wagon guards.

When the men had come up he led them on a digging run for the top of the grade which hid the stageroad from them. Sweeping over the rise, their speed was only increased by the sight which met their eyes.

A quarter-mile away an old-style Conestoga freighter was burning alongside the road. Drawn up opposite it was the southbound Dodge City stage. It was this latter vehicle upon which the Comanches had just renewed their attack as Hush and his men burst over the rise.

The Indians, angered perhaps at being interrupted short of firing the stage, did not at once break and run, but hung back long enough to let the feared Texans get almost up to pistol range before wheeling their mustangs and fleeing to the west. This boldness allowed Hush to recognize two of their number, and Nocero to recognize all of them. The white youth had to reach back two years to make his memory connection; the Lipan Apache needed only to return to the past summer.

"By God!" yelled Hush, pointing to a tall brave and a squat, thick-bodied one riding in the rear of the retreating raiders. "I know those last two birds from somewheres!"

Then, even as he said it, he remembered from where.

Those two were part of the bunch he had trailed out from the Nueces shinnery to get back Gato for Don Diego and take Muchacha for himself. The tall one was the one he had thought he'd killed with the rifle butt, the one he'd heard the others call Tall Walker, the one who had wanted the black mare for himself. His short, fat friend was the one named Big Belly, the one who had preferred Gato to Muchacha and who had sworn he would have the yellow gelding, one way or another.

As these bits of backtrail flashed before Hush's mind, he heard Nocero yelling back to him between running shots.

"Sumbitch! Me know all them Comanche bastard! And me know from where. Those him same Kwahadi band me see at crossing. Same ones tell me where you hiding in Cañon Perdido!"

Hearing this, Hush had a sudden dark and fearsome wonder rise up in him, but he forced it down again.

The Comanches were the nomads of the South Plains; to wander was their way of life. That Tall Walker and Big Belly and their friends might not be wandering was a distinct possibility but a very unlikely one. As he had dismissed the matter of Graywing denying seeing the Kwahadis at the ranch, Hush now dismissed his own thought and its attendant fear that they might be following him as womanish imagining. As usual, there was more important work to hand than fretting about shadows on the trail. The flaming Conestoga and the apparently lifeless stage still remained to be investigated. Toward them, the Comanches having drawn out of even Winchester range, he now swung his grim-faced Texas crew.

The freight wagon took only a glance. It had been soaked with coal oil from its own cargo and fired, with its scalped driver left slumped across its high dashrail. The stagecoach waited beyond, with no sound coming from it. Hush and his watchful riders went slowly toward it.

They could see the bodies of three passengers, one with his rifle still poking out the window. Up top, the driver hung over the seatbox siderail, not moving. His shotgun messenger lay sprawled behind him in the ruck of the roofdeck luggage. Hush pulled in the black mare ten feet from the nearside windows, his men reining in behind him.

He waited through a several seconds, giving any shocked survivor still possibly alive and hiding in the bottom of the Concord time to get his senses back so that he would not come up firing blindly when hailed from the outside. Then Hush called out low and clear:

"Hello the coach—anybody in there?"

A few more seconds passed.

Then a small pair of gloved hands slid over the sill of the rear window. A pale face followed them up to stare, big-eyed, at the startled cowboys.

"There's me," said the girl in a tiny, wavering voice, and fainted dead away.

CHAPTER 32

The driver was dead. The shotgun rider, hit twice in the chest, was dying. Inside the coach the man with the rifle was dead, shot through the head. A second passenger lay stretched on the floor, not a mark on him. He was a fat man, and had apparently died of heart failure from fright. The third man was superficially wounded but had bled all over the seats and collapsed from shock. The girl was unhurt.

Hush put the shotgun rider and the other wounded man in the number-one wagon, and buried the three dead beside the trail. He pushed the work, for it was growing late in the day. With both the J A riders and the Comanches to worry about, a man had better get parked early and tight.

He turned the dazed girl over to Iota, thinking very little about her. She was a fair-skinned, thin young thing, not over seventeen, and still too wrought up to get any sense out of. Accordingly, Hush ordered her put in the number-six wagon and forgot about her. He had his entire line straightened out and rolling thirty minutes after she had raised her head above the Concord's sill and quavered, "There's me."

By five o'clock it was twilight and he had reached North Fork Crossing, parked his wagons and put out Rafe and Tate as pickets.

When it was dark, and before the moon got up enough to be a problem, he and Nocero slipped out of camp and went across the river on foot. They found Coke Bancroft's crew hidden about a quarter of a mile below the crossing, just off the trail in heavy brush. The J A men were sitting in the dark with only a small chuckwagon and a shielded bull's-eye lantern to mark their camp. Their saddle horses were on a picketline run between two cottonwoods at least fifty feet away from the chuckwagon. The wagon team was tied to the tailgate.

When he saw the picketline, Nocero nudged Hush.

"White man damn fool. Tie pony all on same rope. *Ish-ke-ne!* A boy child could do it."

"Como se dice?" whispered Hush. "A boy child could do what?"

"Steal him pony like fish on string. Heap easy, *wagh!*"

"By damn, it might work at that."

"Him work. Sumbitch, boy, you go back hitch up wire wagons. When you ready to go, you make one long howl like lonesome wolf. Me do rest. *Ho-hah!* Him bastard good joke, yes?"

"I hope so!" muttered Hush fervently. *"Cuidado, amigo."*

Nocero didn't reply to the warning, and Hush, looking around, saw why. The Indian wrangler had already disappeared, quick and silent as the night breeze now stealing up from the river.

Turning to go himself, he cocked an ear toward the J A men.

"Well, anyway," he heard one of them say, "with this wind rising it's a centerfire cinch we can hear them if they try a night crossing."

"Maybe," said a second voice. "But I still think we ought to double the guard up yonder. Damn it, I ain't been easy since we seen them Comanches three days back."

Hush recognized the second voice. It was that of the fat cowboy who had tried to hang Tom Horn and Hi Luck Lewis in the Palo Duro. He thought he recognized the first speaker as well—the sparse-worded head rider of the J A reps who had stopped the O A T herd at this same crossing on the way up. Granting both guesses, it figured that Bancroft had as many as eighteen, twenty men with him now. Those were rougher odds than he had expected, and Hush's angry scowl darkened.

Obviously, this trap had been long planned for him. The wire wagons were only a handy excuse. They had been waiting to corner and kill him, regardless. They hadn't been sharp enough to catch him stealing J A cows so that they could string him up, Texas style, which was to say more or less legal. No, they had to gang up on him and do the job, Mexican fashion, dry gulching him like a damned two-bit horse thief or a flat-hat sod farmer. Well, all right, by God, if they couldn't do it fair and they wanted to play "get the guts" with Hush Feleen, they had come to the right man. They would find that out before they were many hours older. Why in God's name was it that people were forever putting off on him? Why couldn't they just let a man alone? Damn their lousy murdering souls! Damn them to hell!

As the old blind-proud anger rose in him, Hush heard the J A trailboss answering the doubts of the fat cowboy.

"You may be right, Stub," said Coke Bancroft. "You go along up and set with Wes at the crossing. Go afoot and careful. We don't want that Feleen boy getting onto us."

"You don't need to tell me that twice," replied the fat hand. "I owe him one on my own. He's loco as well as crooked. He ought by rights to be shot on sight, same as a hydrophoby skunk or a hoss full of jimson weed."

"He's got a mean-wild eye, sure enough," agreed Simms Bettis, the lean-jawed leader of the rep band. "When we was sifting them O A T steers of his it was like cutting up a fresh-gutted buck in front of a starved wolf. Horn and Lewis was full of hell, but not mean. That Feleen kid, he looked light-eyed and bad-nerved as any lobo ever whelped. I never was so glad of anything in my life as to see him ride off across this here damned river with our cattle. Believe me, boys, he could have had seven hundred head more of them for all I would have tried stopping him. He's bad to the bone, and the bone's rotten too."

"Yes," said stolid Coke Bancroft, "he's the kind that will kill you. It's no more complicated than that."

"I met two fellers in Dodge, said their names was Les Mason and D. J. Pettigrew, claimed they knew him from down on the Nueces," offered one of the listening cowboys. "Seems this kid's old man took to marking cows that wasn't his and was caught and swung for it. The kid hadn't been mavericking with his pap, but was with him when this here rancher that Mason and Brown was riding for down that way came up to the old man with one of his steers on the ground. Well, it seems that—"

"Never mind the rest of it, Red," broke in Coke patiently. "It'll keep till this winter. You'd best get along, Stub."

The paunchy hand got up and said nervously to the interrupted storyteller: "What the hell happened? Don't tell us they strung up the kid too."

"That's the spooky part of it," nodded the other cowboy. "They did."

"Cow hockey," observed an anonymous hand out of the dark.

"Gospel truth!" insisted the red-headed cowboy. "This here rancher's name was Hudspeth. Him and his son Howell strung up them Feleens side by each and left them swinging in the wind. Them fellers Mason and Pettigrew swore to it."

"Pure cow chips," said the invisible cynic.

"Would have said the same thing myself," agreed the storyteller, "up to last week in Dodge."

"What about last week in Dodge?"

"Well, this here Mason and Pettigrew they said if I didn't believe them I should look inside Feleen's shirt collar happen I ever got the chance."

"So?"

"So last week in the Long Branch I got the chance. He come in there Tuesday night collecting that pack of brush wolves he's got riding wagon guard for him. I got a good look in good light, and mister, believe me he's got 'em. Rope burns, by Gawd! Old and faint-scarred, sure. But they're rope burns, boys, and they wasn't put there by nothing but the high hemp!"

"All right, all right," rumbled Coke. "Let's forget Feleen and his daddy. Move out, Stub. Time's a-running."

The heavy-set cowboy went to the wagon, got his rifle out of his bedroll and started up the trail for the crossing. As noiselessly as though he were the departing rider's shadow, Hush drifted after him, cut in behind him, and followed him off through the dark of the river brush.

Back at the wagon, another of the J A cowboys who had been in Dodge with Bancroft spoke up in belated defense of his friend.

"You can't rightly blame old Stub," he said. "I hearn a story about that Feleen kid too when he was up yonder. Seems he shot the belly out of that young Hudspeth. Done it with that damned shotgun he always totes. Then he run the old man Hudspeth off his own ranch and stole every damn head of stock he had. Drove 'em all up the trail and lost the whole bunch in a nightrun over them gyp cliffs west of here. And that ain't all neither."

The cowboy took a breath and plunged on.

"You ever hear tell of Ben Sloat? You're blamed right you did. Best gun, likely, between Abilene and Tascosa. You know what that Feleen kid done to Ben Sloat? Roped him, by Gawd, and drug him to death." Another quick breath scarcely interrupted the excited cowboy. "You think there ain't more? Huh! Seems he onct went out after a passel of Comanches to get back a stole hoss. Wasn't even his own hoss. Jumped 'em all by himself, kilt three of 'em with the shotgun, beat another two nigh to death with a riflebutt. No, sir, by cripes, I sure don't blame old Stub. That Feleen feller would give a Cherrycow Apache the creeps. He's colder-blooded nor a froze snake."

Coke Bancroft shrugged.

"Now, Pinky, slack off there. You can hear anything you want from a bunch of whiskied-up trailhands. Especially about a tough kid like Feleen. It's mostly the liquor talking."

"I dunno," said Simms Bettis. "The whiskey goes in, the truth comes out."

"Pinky, them two hands say where they got their information?" Coke asked. "I mean other than out of the bottle?"

"Sure they did. Claimed they worked for young Feleen, and for old man Hudspeth before him. There was two of 'em. One heavy-built feller named Tate, one string-bean boy called Rafe."

"Still bushway," said the nameless hand out of the dark. "Straight uncut steer manure."

"And whiskey talk," reiterated Coke.

"Could be," agreed the amiable Pinky. "Gawd knows that Dodge City sheepdip would shake loose the one-eyed Egyptian sphinx."

"Apparently you'd ought to know," said Coke. "Let's leave

off the augering, boys, and turn in. Feleen ain't going to try anything tonight."

"Reckon he ain't," said Simms Bettis. "You figure he'll throw in or fight in the morning, Coke? We got him outnumbered near two to one. The teamsters'll stay out of it."

"Him?" answered Coke. "Simms, he's been outnumbered all his life. His kind don't know there's any other way than outnumbered. Nor they don't want it any other way. He'll fight. And for keeps."

"Yeah, I guess. I just thought he might back off if we gave him the chance."

"No," Coke said, shaking his big head, "I happen to know for sure that he won't."

"How come you to know for sure?" asked Simms Bettis.

"Because," Coke growled, calm and steady, "we ain't going to give him the chance."

The J A trailboss pulled his blankets closer, shifted his broad hips to find a kinder piece of dirt, relaxed and almost got to snoring. Presently the lonesome cry of a stray lobo came downwind from the crossing. Coke sat up.

"You hear that wolf, Simms?" he said to Bettis, bedded nearby. "Must be crazy to prowl that close to Feleen's camp."

Simms Bettis had a better ear for night sounds and was reaching for his boots. "Might be crazy," he said shortly, "but that ain't no wolf. That was Injun talk."

Coke heaved up his square bulk to join his quicker companion, but both were too late. From the picketline came a hair-raising Apache yell, followed by the stampeding drive of the saddlestock trying to run over each other in their panicky rush to get away into the dark. Stumbling around the chuckwagon, Coke and Bettis were in time to get knocked flat by three ponies that had broken free of the picketline. From the ground, they saw the rest of the J A saddlestring being led off at the gallop by a single Indian mounted on Coke's own bay. And even as they lay there with the sounds of the stolen horses still echoing through the camp, they could hear the distant shouts of the wire-wagon drivers urging their mule teams into the water at North Fork Crossing.

"Goddammit!" yelled somebody on the other side of the chuckwagon. "What happened to those bastards supposed to be on guard up there?"

"Whatever it was," came Coke's voice, "it'll keep. Come on, we got to catch up these free ponies or we'll be left plumb afoot."

Still arguing and cursing the stupidity of themselves and

their outposts at the crossing, the hands spread out through the brush. But the night was windy and dark and the three mustangs were all the way spooked. It took half an hour to get them gentled down to where their bridle reins could be grabbed. By that time every one of the J A cowboys had calmed down enough to know that Hush Feleen and his six bobwire wagons were well across the North Fork and safely started up the south-bank road into the Panhandle. Naturally, they knew they could catch up with those mule wagons on their three recaptured mounts. But what the mounted three of them were going to do with the black-haired *brasada* boy and his six hired toughs when they did catch them, was something they didn't know. Phlegmatic Coke Bancroft, for one, knew they weren't going to do a blessed thing with them, and he was man enough to admit it.

"Boys," he announced, "he's outmarched us. Ain't no use going after them wagons, our three to his seven. Simms—"

The serious-faced cowboy stepped forward. "Yes, sir?"

"Put the team to the chuckwagon. Go on up to the crossing with the rest of the boys and see what's happened to Stub and Wes. Me, Horgan and Dade will trail out the horses a ways. With the Indian towing so many head, there's a chance he'll get them scrambled. It's a chance we got to run out."

"All right," said Simms Bettis. "Good luck."

Coke and his two men mounted up and rode off to the south, quartering through the patchy moonlight for a sight of Nocero, or of his trail away from the camp. They cut a trackline and had it going for about twenty minutes, but lost it on a stretch of hardpan two miles west of the south trail. They gave it up and spurred back for the crossing.

There the news was no better.

Feleen himself had stalked and stuck up Wes and Stub with the shotgun. Herding Coke's sentries across the river, he had tied them up and left them with the wounded men from the Dodge stage, comfortable by his own camp's abandoned fire. Then he had hooked up his wire wagons, given his wolf-call signal for the Apache to run off the J A picketline, poured the leather and the language to his mules and was gone across the North Fork just as quick and slick as that.

Coke Bancroft stood there without a word.

This getaway from the J A trap at the North Canadian was going to be repeated many a long year around the ranch stoves of the Staked Plain. The big billy goat of the affair was going to be Coke Bancroft. He was the one who had gone soft-hearted and let the kid get out of Dodge with the wire in the first place. He was the one who had been so bull-headed sure he had him penned up there on the North Fork he couldn't possibly slip his bobwire wagons over the Canadian and get away to the west. He was the one that was going to get the credit for letting that newfangled fencewire into the Panhandle. And he was the one that was going to have to get Hush Feleen, or quit his job and get out of the country.

Coke was no blusterer, not even in his own mind. He knew the blues were in the middle of the blanket between him and the soft-talking owner of the HF connected. He didn't duck the play-out.

To Stub Judson, the fat cowboy who was just finishing giving his excuses for the fiasco at the guardpost by the river, he said:

"All right, Stub, you all done? If so, have you or any of the others got any more to say about me signing a full confession and taking the next boat out of New Orleans?"

"Don't know about no others," the embarrassed cowboy said gruffly. "I'm done."

"So's this poor devil," called over Simms Bettis, who had been looking after the lung-shot stage messenger. "He's cold as potter's clay."

Coke only nodded his massive head. "All right, we'll put him under first thing in the morning. Meanwhile, everybody ease up. We've been made fools of. We might just as well admit it and keep going. Feleen's luck can't last forever. We'll come up to him in time."

He looked around to see if there were any dissents. When none came he went on, "Now is there any last little thing's been forgot or overlooked in the excitement—?"

Only headshakes went around the circle of his listeners, then came a gasp from the lightly wounded stage passenger.

"My God, yes, the girl!" he cried. "There was a young lady on the stage with us. Feleen left her here with us when he pulled out. She must be close by. Any Blake was her name. Good Lord! Miss Amy—! Miss Amy—!"

He staggered to his feet calling the girl's name into the darkness beyond the firelight, but Coke Bancroft reached out and took hold of him, gentle and quick.

"Set down, mister," he said. "If she's around here we'll find her. Scatter out, boys. Poor thing's been in a Comanche surround, she might just have lit out afoot, loco-ed. Ride out a good wide piece. Hop it and look sharp."

Simms Bettis and two more of the men got on the three horses and scattered. They were back in an hour, all reporting the same thing.

"She's gone," said Simms Bettis flatly.

The men looked at one another, the same uneasy thought forming in the minds of several of them.

"By Gawd!" blurted Stub Judson, "I betcha she was still starey-eyed shocked, and clumb right back inter one of them Feleen wire wagons!" The others nodded their wordless agreement to the guess.

Finally, it was the slow-speaking Coke Bancroft who said with a sort of rough softness: "I surely hope she didn't do that. Happen she did, poor little thing, she'd have done better to have stayed in the stage."

"She's gone," repeated Simms Bettis darkly. "Either with Feleen or with the Comanches. And where's your difference there?"

The J A cowboys looked at him, shaking their heads. None of them answered him.

CHAPTER 33

That was the way Amy Blake came to Lost Canyon Ranch. It was the way, too, in which Hush Feleen found the third woman in his life.

Whether through numbed instinct or conscious intent, the girl had clambered back into the number-six wagon of Hush's train, as Stub Judson had guessed. And somewhere between North Fork Crossing and the drop-off into Cañon Perdido Hush and Amy fell in love—real love.

For Hush the feeling was utterly different from the body hunger he had known for Evvie Hollister, or the creature rewards of his winter and summer with Graywing. It was a sort of superlative mixture of both passion and calm. It left a man fired with the want to have, yet cooled by the knowledge he would get. The girl, a delicate ash blonde of natural beauty and shy manner, was the kind who grew more desirable each day, while at the same time becoming clearly more obtainable. She was the type of woman no decent man would touch short of marrying her, and the type he could be sure would want that touching after he had. Hush found the combination irresistible, and long before the wire wagons reached the mesa above his hidden canyon ranch he was deeply in love—a kind of love he had never known.

As for the girl, it was reasonable to assume that to an eastern child the lean, sun-bronzed good looks of Hush Feleen—tall, soft-drawling, romantically garbed in the high

167

boots and fringed buckskins of the frontier—would present a dangerous attraction. That infatuation rather than true love might be the likely result of being with him did not occur to Amy Blake. Or, if it did, it was disregarded.

From the moment her violet eyes came up above the windowsill of the ambushed Concord, they never quit following Hush. Like the dark-faced young master of Lost Canyon Ranch, she proved unable to distinguish between rational action and impulse, or to control either. But unlike him, she had no taint of wildness in her. This softness, coupled with the unseasonably warm nights and white moons of the autumn drive into the Panhandle, devastated Hush.

True to his idealization of her, he did not try to touch her, but he returned her shy stares and schoolgirl blushes with a stricken mountain boy's ardor that burned more fiercely than any adult lust. By the afternoon of the tenth day from the crossing, when they had reached the top-out above Cañon Perdido, the matter was completely talked through and settled between them: when they reached the ranch Hush would dispatch Nocero to Red River to guide Don Diego and the family up to Lost Canyon; the old man would bring with him a padre of the True Faith, and when all was properly arranged Hush Feleen and Amy Blake would be married.

Graywing did not meet them at the foot of the canyon trail, nor was she in the yard of the sodhouse beside Sun Dance Creek.

In the bedroom alcove curtained off from the main room by a hanging buffalo robe, Hush found her and the answer to her failure to greet him on his return. The Indian woman was in labor.

Hush quieted her glad cries of relief at seeing him and told her everything was all right; that she must rest and not excite herself. Presently she slowed her Comanche greetings and asked Hush in halting English:

"You bring Black Robe from Dodge City, Texas Man?"

"I never said I would," Hush answered, feeling the shame of the situation rise in him. "I said we would wait and see about the baby."

"Aye, I know, I know. But when a woman loves a man and is bearing his child—"

"Oh, Lord!" groaned Hush. "Don't say that, please don't say that." He paused miserably, the knife of memory turning in him. "Listen, Graywing," he went on, the feeling that her trusting looks left inside him growing more desperate, "I want to do all I can to help you, whether the kid is mine or not. You're wanted here, and you're welcome. Do you understand that? The place and everything on it is half yours—you're legal half-owner by the white man's law—I made it that way for you in Dodge City. You and I've been over a lot of trail together. I'm not forgetting what I owe you, you hear me?"

"I hear," answered the Comanche woman, "and my heart bleeds."

Hush got up from the bed and paced the alcove.

"Dear Jesus!" he said to himself. "How can a man make her understand?" He wheeled back to the bedside. "What do you want of me, Graywing?" he asked. "I can't marry you. I never led you to believe I would, or wanted to. We've had a good life together, now what is it? *Tou-K'a'm!* Speak up!" he insisted, dropping into the harsh Comanche gutturals. "Tell me, Kwahadi Woman, what is in your mind. It is more than the Black Robe, more than the marriage paper."

Graywing looked away from him, her dark eyes dull with the pain of the new life within her, and of the old life, without.

"I heard the wagons come into the yard," she said. "I heard the men and the mules, the complaining of the wheelspokes, the squealing of the axle hubs dry for a dubbing of antelope tallow. I heard you and your voice which stirs my heart, the crunch of your boots on the small creekstones, the sound of the doorstep beneath your entering stride, the call of my name from your lips, all of these dear things I heard.

"And then I heard another thing, a thing that was like a buffalo lanceblade in my side, and my heart began to cry out and to grow cold and to die within me.

"I heard this gay and happy sound from outside the house, and I did not want to believe my hearing. I told myself it was the murmur of the stream playing tricks with my eagerness to see you. Surely, I said, it is the laughing water which welcomes his return as I do. Surely, I told my heart, he will take me in his arms and tell me the same thing. But when you came in and I asked you about the Black Robe and you said you did not bring him, then I knew that it was not our small stream laughing out there.

"*TeiH'nei-kiH*, it was your new woman."

Hush dropped his head. It hit him deep, the way he deserved it, but he had to stand to it.

"All right, Graywing," he began, "let's talk with our tongues straight. You have guessed the way it is. There is a new woman out there and I have brought her back to be my wife. Her name is Amy, and I love her. As soon as Nocero can get back from Red River with my family and the Spanish Black Robe, we are going to be married.

"Now, please, that don't mean you have to leave, or that we won't treat your child like our own. It don't even mean that I don't love you in a different way from the new woman. But the new woman is of my own blood. She is the one to be the mother of my sons. I don't want you to go, and Amy don't want you to go. We have talked of you and we both want you to stay and make your home with us, if you want to. We are going to build a big new house up the stream a ways. This little house can be yours for as long as you want to live in it. But if you want to go, you will always have a home here when you need one, and you will have all the money that is coming to you through the years from what your part of the ranch pays. That's my mortal promise, Graywing."

He stopped, waiting for her to flare up, to strike back at him wild and strong, the way a man would expect from her heathen kind. But she did nothing like that. She only turned her face to the wall and bit her underlip to keep from crying out in the pain of her labor.

Hush's face contorted with pure misery and he said to her in low-voiced Comanche:

"Now you understand that I make these plans and do these things because I love the new woman in the same way you loved your Kwahadi young man before you were sold to the old Cherokee. We're no different, you and me. We love fierce, we love strong, our hearts are wild and free and we cannot tell them what to do. Now you know I speak the truth. It is a different kind of love between this woman and me, from the love there was between Graywing and the Texas Man. You know what I am saying, so why do you torture me by not answering?"

He sat down on the side of the bed again, and took up her dark-skinned hand.

"You will find your own love of this different kind again," he told her. "You will find it as I've found it, among your own people. When you have done this, then you will know what it is I've been trying to say—that my heart is good for Graywing, always, but that it is not hers to keep in the forever way."

He looked down at her, softening his voice, putting his calloused hand on her warm shoulder.

"Graywing," he said, "now will you please tell me that you understand this and that you believe me?"

For a long time she said nothing; she did not even move.

When her reply came at last, it came in deep-toned Kiowa-Comanche dialect, its words as well as its thought pure In-

170

dian. Hush remembered that answer to the last day of his life.

"I understand what it is that you want me to do, Texas Man," said Graywing Teal, "and that is all that I understand."

She took her hand from his and kept her face to the wall. Then she spoke, with no more of the sound of useless tears softening her voice.

"Good-bye, Texas Man. You have said it, not Graywing. Now I must tell you how it will be. Your fine big house for the new woman will never be finished. You will never live in it with her. Before the third snow from this time shall melt, only the buffalo will wander where your cattle now stand in the Cañon Perdido."

CHAPTER 34

It was when Hush went back in with Iota and Amy Blake to help bring the baby that he first understood the seriousness of Graywing's parting words. The alcove stood empty. The Kwahadi squaw was gone.

He at once took Nocero and the six wagon guards and fanned out through the nearby bottoms. He reasoned that in her condition the Indian woman could not go far afoot, but an hour of looking, ranging as far as the hilly footings of the canyon wall, disclosed no sign of the missing Comanche woman. It was not until the next morning's daylight allowed the one-eyed Lipan to pick up and run out her trail from the alcove window to the timber behind the sodhouse, that the mystery of her disappearance was solved.

In a clearing a half-mile from the house, her moccasin prints merged with the marks of the hooves of several unshod ponies. Among these latter was one set of hoofmarks which the Apache wrangler remembered. They were those of the pony ridden by the tall brave whose band had known where to find Hush Feleen hidden in Lost Canyon.

There was no question of it, Nocero said. The Kwahadi woman had gone back to her own people. This band had been waiting for her, and they had picked her up and taken her with them. There were no moccasin prints leaving that clearing, only pony tracks. Graywing Teal had gone to have her child where the color of its skin would make no difference.

Hush did not miss Nocero's deliberate allusion and knew

171

the Apache had not meant him to miss it. It was plain Nocero didn't hold with such white seducing of Indian women, and when Hush took him up on it he did not flinch.

"Squaw tell Nocero that him your baby she got in belly," he said. "That make it your job take care of baby."

"Damn you," growled Hush, "I know what my job is. And I wasn't trying to get out of it, you hear? I told her to wait and we would see what color the kid was."

"Squaw no care about color," said Nocero. "She only care about baby and baby's father. If you baby's father, then him your job know how squaw feel. You old enough make baby, you old enough take care of him."

"God damn it!" flamed Hush, more helpless than ever. "How am I supposed to know if I'm the baby's father? Or how a squaw feels?"

"You know in here." Nocero tapped his dark chest. "Your own heart no lie to you, *schichobe*."

"Now hold on there, Nocero," objected Hush. "Don't give me any of that 'old friend' bushway."

"No bushway. You my *schichobe*, you my old friend."

"I give up," said Hush. "You damned Indians are all alike. Trying to talk sense to you is like arguing the Republican ticket in Tennessee. The hell with it! Just forget the whole thing."

The Apache bobbed his horse-sheared bangs.

"Sure," he said, "me forget. But Kwahadi woman she no forget. You wait. You see. She come back one day pay you off. Comanche bad Indian. Got bad temper. Never forgive white man. You find out one day."

Hush shook his head, sobered by the warning, but not believing it.

"Most Comanches may be that way," he agreed. "But Graywing was different. She was more like a white woman the way she thought. I know her. Maybe she's hurt right now because of Miss Amy coming here, and maybe she's acting like an Indian sure enough. But she'll get over it. She's happy-natured at heart. She'll come to see I meant to treat her square. No, you're plumb wrong; she won't be back."

Nocero only looked at him. He gave him a long, hard stare, then said, almost sadly: "What happen you, boy? You no think like Indian no more. You no hear what Nocero tell you no more. Why you change?"

"What the devil you getting at?" snapped Hush. "You got something to say to me, say it straight out."

Once more the Apache wrangler eyed him at length, before nodding with regretful finality.

"Goddamsumbitch, boy, me already tell you but you no listen no more. Too bad, *schichobe*. Me sorry for you."

Nocero started southward for Red River that same night. He struck the Red at the Forks of the Wachita in four days, and next morning arrived at the abandoned cowcamp he and Hush had set up for the winter of '77 on the east bank of the Little Wachita River. There, still dwelling in the mud-and-brush *jacal* where Hush had left them to await his return, he found Diego Santimas and the three Feleen children.

They had passed a hard winter of hunting and living off the country, and the toll had been heavy. Only the past week Doña Anastasia had put down her burden and asked for a padre to be brought to her. There were precious few priests in that north of Texas parish, and the only one Don Diego could locate was Father Garcia, a Jesuit army chaplain at Fort Arbuckle up in the Chickasaw Strip. The devout Doña Anastasia had lived by sheer faith until the twins could get up to the fort and back, fetching the padre in the burro cart, and it was on the morning of Nocero's arrival that she was being laid to rest.

The Apache waited respectfully out in the brush until the Spanish Black Robe had made his ritual signs in the air over the closed grave, then rode his lathered pony on in and pulled him to a halt in front of the *jacal*.

When the family heard his message it was as though the sun had come out on a gray, cold day. Father Garcia, very pleased, made some more signs, and announced that this was the circle of life eternal, that when some good soul went away another took up its burden and carried it along for the next traveler, and so on forever. Thus it was that the faithful son of the departed mother was sending for the family for which she could no longer care. It was God's will; let them all pray in happiness and gratitude once more in the name of the good woman who had gone on:

"Memento etiam, Domine, famulorum famularumque tuarum, qui nos praecesserunt cum signo fidei, et dormiunt in somno pacis—Remember, O Lord, thy servants and hand-maids who have gone before us with the sign of faith, and sleep the sleep of peace—Amen."

That winter of 1878–79 in Lost Canyon was as wonderful a time as could come to a human being. Certainly it was the high time of happiness for Hush Feleen and for those who looked to him.

To begin with, an early snow trapped Father Garcia in the canyon, keeping him at the ranch through Christmas. It was

173

the first gaily celebrated Christmas Hush and the other Feleen children could remember. The peculiar mixture of fiesta and sober religious ceremonies which only the Mexicans could blend so delightfully, was highly contagious. The enthusiasm of the ebullient Jesuit and the sly wit of old Don Diego caught up and carried away the sober-sided Feleen brood. Not only was the sodhouse on Sun Dance Creek transformed into a place of gaiety with decorations as bright and cheery as a store-bought Christmas card, but all of its inhabitants, save the agnostic Hush, had been joining Father Garcia at prayers before the good-natured priest had been in the canyon a week.

As for Hush, he had never been able to pray out loud or in front of others, and he made no pretense of doing so now. It was not that he didn't believe in God, he told Father Garcia, but more that he didn't think God believed in him. Nothing in his life up to now, at least, had shown him that the Lord was anything but against him. As for his present good fortune, he wasn't going to start totting up his chickens too early. If everything continued to go as it had since the family had come up from Red River, why then there would be a time for learning to pray and for listening to the priest's arguments for believing. Meanwhile, he would keep right on putting his faith where he always had—in Hush Feleen.

So it was that Father Garcia, blessing the entire family and charging Hush to keep thinking about the Power above his own, left the ranch during an open spell in early January to return to his duties at Fort Arbuckle. And Hush and his new wife, his foster father, admiring twin brothers and handsome young lady sister all settled in for the late snows and for the promise of a deep-grassed spring to come and a golden summer to follow on the Llano Estacado.

There was reasonable prospect of fulfillment. Hush finally had his start, the good start so long delayed.

True, there were fewer than one hundred head of cattle in Lost Canyon bearing his original HF-connected brand. But they were honest cattle, they were his cattle. From their small number, the safe winters in the canyon would guarantee a big calf crop. His new wire strung across the two ends of his domain would keep his little herd intact and tamper-proof. What was bred and raised on the HF would stay on it. It could not wander away and it could not be rustled by the cow thieves who soon would be swarming in to get at Goodnight's huge herds.

The whole thing, too, could be a family operation. The twins, now fourteen, were big, rawboned boys and would make good hands in another year or two. They were, in fact, already easily the equal of the average hand, thanks to Don Diego's early training. With Nocero to handle the *remuda* and Iota to handle Nocero, the HF could run a thousand head and never need to hire another man.

Indeed, the ranch was already running as strictly a family affair. The wagon guards, along with Tate and Rafe, had decided it might turn off a pretty long winter after all and had gone down home to Texas, in the same open spell which saw Father Garcia on his way. Since then a month had passed, the late snows had come, the deep winter quiet had fallen over the Staked Plains. Nothing happened to disturb that stillness. March melted into April, April gusted and showered into May, May bloomed and burst into June.

So began a summer that Hush had never dreamed could be.

It went so swiftly and so happily by that he scarcely knew it had been. But with the canyon cottonwoods turning flame and russet and the high blue days of October graying to the whistle of November's winds, he knew that in some magic way a year had gone. He knew, too, that it had been the best year a man's memory might dare treasure. In it he had learned to love his violet-eyed child bride as only a lonely, hunted *ladino* could love such a trusting, needful creature as Amy Blake Feleen. In that summer, too, Hush had rediscovered the rewards of having his family about him, and the forgotten pleasures of doing for others instead of for self. When, nearing their second Christmas, Amy told him she was two months' pregnant, Hush reckoned his cup was as full as that of any man.

Later that night, standing alone under the stars in the still December air outside the door of the sodhouse on Sun Dance Creek, he admitted as much.

"Thank you, Lord," he said, speaking softly, with face upturned. "I reckon you're really up there. You've finally made me believe it. I'm happy now, like other folks. And grateful, Lord, deep-down grateful—"

Then, dropping his head and saying it out loud and firmly: "God forgive me for all I've done. Amen."

From that time on, Hush did not mark a cow he could not reasonably consider his own, and did not burn a brand other than his HF connected on any animal. He kept at the hard work, and as the months passed he began to show a return to the thoughts and acts of kindly Hushton compassion which had characterized his Tennessee boyhood. Lubelle, now a striking girl of seventeen, and the husky twins felt keenly this going back to remembered tenderness, this return of the old, gentle-natured Hush they had known in the days after their mother's death. All three responded to this warmth of feeling; and the winter, thus begun in rising spirits and determined hopes, turned smoothly into the new year, and moved swiftly toward the second spring. All went normally and well with Amy's pregnancy; the cattle prospered, the weather stayed open and bluebird clear.

Then, in early March, the sun disappeared.

For twenty-one days the blizzard held, sweeping the North American plains from Canada to the Red River of Texas and driving before it, down from the unprotected ranges of the high north country, the second largest drift of western cattle in the history of frontier ranching.

From as far east as Nebraska, as far north and west as Montana and Wyoming, the bawling longhorn horde came wandering before the merciless wind. Day after day they piled into the Panhandle, seeking out its warm draws and wooded crossbreaks and, above all, its deep safe canyons like the Palo Duro and the Cañon Perdido. In the three weeks of the monstrous drift no less than 50,000 northern cattle lodged in and around the southern pastures of the Staked Plains; and of these, some five or six thousand head passed into Los Canyon.

At first, when the starving, snow-caked cattle began to pile up against his new wire fence at the south end of the canyon—the north end not yet having been closed—Hush did nothing about it. He knew the brutes would quiet down and spread out on his rich grasslands as soon as they realized they had outdrifted the blizzard and were safe. Then his cattleman's eye began to get the better of his charity.

Among the constantly arriving cattle were many full-grown slickears and strong big yearlings which had never known the bite of a smoking iron. The numbers of these unbranded animals ran as high as one in four of the total drift. The arithmetic was too obvious to be ignored by Hush. He saw his great opportunity, weighed it carefully in the scales of his new morality, and found no conflict in the resulting balance.

Rightful ownership of these unmarked drift cattle could never be established. If they were allowed to stay with their branded mates they would only be thrown into the community cut of the next summer sifting which the reps of the northern companies were bound to stage down on the Red or the Canadian for the purpose of getting back what few they could of their storm-scattered herds. As Hush saw it, his Lost Canyon shelter and wired-off grass had saved all of the five or six thousand head on his place, branded and un-branded alike.

Now, if a man should turn loose four or five head of the branded for every one of the unbranded he kept, he would be doing all anybody could rightfully expect of him by way of honoring the claims of those northern owners. They would be lucky to get back that much of their lost cattle, and could thank Hush Feleen that they got back any at all. He could have opened his south wire and let them drift to hell, but he hadn't done that. He had done what he humanly could to save the stuff which came into his canyon. He saw, then, and finally, no reason why he should not take what the Lord had plainly sent him.

The moral decision reached, Hush moved quickly.

It was the 29th of March, 1880, when he cut the wire on his south fence and started checking the branded animals through to freedom on the adjoining, million-acre J A range.

On May 3rd, five weeks later to the day, he began branding the first of 972 unmarked cattle which had remained on Feleen land when the barbed strands were twisted back together again.

CHAPTER 35

Before a folklore trail vanishes altogether, it begins to grow dim. The track of Hush Feleen fades abruptly beyond that long-ago spring of 1880. From that point, only the barest bones of his harsh story lie scattered along the lonely path.

It is known that late in the summer of that last year he appeared in Dodge City with a trailherd of approximately a thousand head. He sold on the excessively high market created by the winter's great loss of northern cattle, and received somewhere between $60,000 and $75,000 for his snow-drifted herd. The money, whatever amount it was, never left Dodge City.

The story goes that on the hour of starting back down the trail for his Lost Canyon Ranch and the waiting arms of Amy Feleen and little three-months-old Nancy Ann, Hush's long string of *ladino's* luck ran suddenly, lethally short.

He met Evvie Hollister on the street in front of the Lady Gay Theatre. He had had a few drinks and the night was young. Before the next day's dawn began to gray the littered alleys and back streets of Dodge City, Hush Feleen, who never before had gambled a dollar or tasted more than a mouthful of hard liquor, had lost to the gaming tables of the trailtown's newest and most glittering bordello $50,000 in hard cash and was staggering down the center of Front Street.

The bordello's name? The Painted Lady. Its sole owner and proprietess? Evelyn Hudspeth Hollister.

Deputy Marshal Lowe Wayman found Hush unconscious in an alley at 8 A.M. The only money he had on him was a punched 1857 penny hung about his neck on a ribbon from a lady's perfumed camisole.

By nine o'clock it was common news that he had shot and killed a faro dealer in the Painted Lady in the four A.M. anger of a losing game, preceded by two hours upstairs with the leggy blonde mistress of the house.

At ten o'clock, sobered and whiskey-sick, he faced the new Ford County sheriff, William Barclay "Bat" Masterson. He was given an hour to leave town, on unconditional advisement never to return to it.

After thirty minutes with Attorney Abel Nathan, he agreed in part to Masterson's ultimatum. He would go, he told Nathan, but would be back some other summer with a new herd of HF cattle. He still had the Lost Canyon Ranch, his horse, his rope, and the old rusted shotgun. And he was still Hush Feleen.

There the matter rested, as far as Lawyer Nathan's record of it went.

Some few other scattered bits and pieces of his last visit to Dodge City are remembered by the old men.

With him when he came up with his drift herd were his sister Lubelle, and the twin brothers, Billie Jim and Billie Bob, and all three children had been put on the Santa Fe cars for Kansas City and a winter of real schooling at the Sessions Academy. Also with him was the aging Diego Santimas, who had come to chaperone Lubelle and the twins during their Kansas City stay. Iota Jones and the Lipan Apache horse wrangler, Nocero, had stayed behind to help Amy Feleen get moved into the new house, run the ranch and tend its tiny new mistress, Miss Nancy Ann.

It was shortly before high noon of September 27th, 1880, that Hush left Dodge City for the last time. He departed alone and unnoted. He did not even have with him his faithful black mare, Muchacha. She, with Gato, the swift yellow gelding, had been left behind on the ranch for the riding enjoyment of Amy Feleen in her continuing explorations of her husband's hidden empire in the Llano Estacado.

178

This aloneness of Hush's only lent speed to his flight from the disaster at Dodge, gave solace in the delusions of his return to his loved ones in Lost Canyon.

He had been a fool, and worse than a fool. He knew that now. But he also knew one other thing above all else in his crushing hour of defeat. As long as a man had the love of his woman, the laughter of his child, the firm hand of his friend, he still had the makings of the main chance within his grasp.

And all of these three things waited now for Hush Feleen in the fine new home which stood so proudly on the grassy rise beyond the small sodhouse on Sun Dance Creek. All he had to do was to go back there to Cañon Perdido and start rebuilding his wasted strength on those waiting foundations of love and faith and friendship which no wicked, vengeful woman could ever take from him.

This philosophy of final desperation might yet have worked for the black-haired Tennessee boy, might yet have written a different, less sinister ending to the history of Hush Feleen. It might, but for one innocent error in its wishful logic. Hush had forgotten a fact as old as the memory of man—the dark fact that the stored angers of a bad woman betrayed, were as the pleasures of heaven to the tortures of hell, measured against the saved-up furies of a good woman scorned.

Hush had forgotten Graywing Teal.

CHAPTER 36

The last brief part of the story is Nocero's.

The Apache wrangler was away from the ranchhouse on Sun Dance Creek when the Comanches came. He was up on the mesa hunting some strayed horses, and that is the only reason there was anyone left to tell what happened that dark day in early October.

A cold storm, half snow, half rain, had begun to drive in ahead of the black weather moving down from the north. Turning his back to it and coming up to the canyon's rim about five in the afternoon, the one-eyed Apache suddenly threw up his head and sniffed the draft working up from the valley below. It was bad, stale air, the kind that always started to move a little before a heavy storm in that country. But it was not that quality in this air that bothered him; it was the rank odor of the wet, burned wood that came to him upon it.

Nocero stiffened.

To a horseback Indian the smell of a homestead burn-out was different from all the other smells of woodsmoke. When the white man's buildings were fired they sent up an acrid odor which stung the nostrils in a way no redman could miss. In this case the Apache knew, before he slipped from his pony's back to belly-up to the canyon's edge, what he would see smoldering there below him.

It was the new house, the one not quite finished, and into which he had helped the slim girl and the young baby move only the week before; this as a surprise for the tall young husband when he got back from Dodge City with the cattle money and the several small things needed to complete the new place. But there was nothing left of that place now, save its gutted cedar walls and smoking sawlog sills. Nocero knew what else he would find down there, though, when it was dark and he could safely approach the charred timbers.

With night, he went on down, and he was not wrong about his grim certainty. The story lay as though painted on a tribal buffalo skin in bold Kwahadi symbols. To the Apache, reading it was as simple as looking at it.

The slim mother lay across the baby's cradle, her long pale hair matted with the blood from the ugly wound made by the riflebutt which had caved in her skull. The little one, being a girl child, had been picked up by its heels and its brains dashed out against the charcoaled doorframe. In the opening of the door, huddled the scalped body of the small broken-nosed cowboy, Iota Jones.

That was all. Nothing else in the new house had been touched or taken.

The coal oil for the fire which had destroyed its roof and seared its walls had been brought up from the old sodhouse below. From that older house, too, had been taken some bright cotton dresses and trading-post jewelry given Gray-wing Teal by her toothless Cherokee husband, and left against her return by Hush Feleen in the bedroom alcove of the sod place.

The only other things missing from the ranch were the two horses which had been in the saddlestock corral with the old mule, Andy Jackson. The two horses were Hush's fine black mare that he had taken from the Comanches, and Diego Santimas's good yellow gelding, Gato. As for the mule, what Kwahadi would bother with such trash, when there was treasure like the black and the buckskin to be had?

The last thing was the matter of who it was that had come here and done this to the one the Comanches called K'ou-a'-da-kiH, the Black-haired Man. This, too, was easy to read.

Among the dozens of pony prints in the freezing slush around the ruins of the big house was one set that Nocero knew well. And in the melted mud inside the ruins, close to the body of the slim girl and the overturned cradle, there was a set of moccasin prints made by soft squawboots of the kind Kwahadi women wore. *Dah-eh-sah,* there were your bringers of death, then—Tall Walker and the returned squaw, Graywing Teal—along with Big Belly and five others.

When he had studied these signs left behind by the Comanche avengers, Nocero said aloud to the brooding silence in Lost Canyon: "Sumbitch, boy, too bad you no listen to Nocero. You my *schichobe,* boy. Me always remember you in here." Speaking these words, the Lipan wrangler put his dark hand over his heart. Then he turned away toward his waiting pony.

As he did so, he heard from the canyon trail the sound of steel striking on rock and knew a shod horse was coming down from above. Quickly, he went with his mount back into the shadows of the creek willows, crouching there with his hand held over his pony's muzzle so that he could not whicker when the strange horse came up.

The stillness grew heavy.

The light of the stars boring through a rift in the cloudbank overhead reflected off the snow to touch the ruins with eerie phosphorescence. Against this glow the Apache saw the tall, spare figure of the approaching rider stand suddenly forth.

It was the black-haired boy, Hush Feleen.

He came up to the ruins and got down and went inside them. When he came out he walked around the ground outside, and on down to the old house; then back up to the new one again, just as Nocero had done. He made no sound at any time: not when he saw his murdered wife, not even when he stared down at his mutilated child. It was only when he had finished his silent, slow study of everything there before him, that he turned away from the blackened sills and began to laugh.

It was the most terrible sound Nocero had ever heard.

When the gaunt Apache heard it, he did not go out to his friend as he had thought to do after giving him his needed moment of grief alone. Instead, he stole down along the banks of the stream and when he was safely away from the empty-eyed creature that had been the black-haired boy, he mounted his shaggy pony and sent him due south away from the whistling cut of the snow driving down from the canyon rim to cover the dead embers of the big new house on Sun Dance Creek.

That was nearly the last of it, then.

The real last of it, the actual words spoken in final settlement of the score against Hush Feleen, went to a stolid, steady-natured man who had said he would have those last words and who, in the strangely ordered way of such things, did have them.

It was in mid-February of that same winter of 1880-81, four relentlessly cold months after Hush's departure from Dodge City, that a band of J A cowboys out looking for storm-drifted cattle came upon a bearded, bone-thin mavericker at work in the upper Palo Duro. The man had a J A steer down and tied, and a fire going, a running-iron heating in its windblown coals.

None of the cowboys knew the rustler. Neither his unkempt wild-animal look nor the rough, cracked sound of his voice was familiar to them. They recognized only that he was a man whose mind had failed, or had never been normal to begin with.

He was clad in a filthy combination of city-tailored buckskins and crudely handsewn varmint pelts. His bleeding feet were bound up in feedsacks and strips of green cowhide. He wore no hat, and carried only a rust-choked, broken-hammered shotgun for which he had no shells. His mount was a gray-muzzled old mountain mule, his saddle an ancient high-forked Spanish heirloom.

The man was as unaccountable as his outfit.

He never said a word to the J A cowboys from the beginning to the end. Why he had roped that lone steer to burn some unknown brand over the existing Goodnight mark, the riders were unable to determine. To their every question his answer was the same—a soundless brute showing of white teeth through the matted hair which hid his entire face, save for the falcon bridge of his nose and the blank wolf's stare of his gray eyes.

In the end, of course, there was but one thing they could do with him.

They did it with the quick, guilty clumsiness of men who knew that what they did was wrong, and who only hoped that why they did it was right.

When it was over, they got on their snow-caked ponies, took the old mule in tow, and rode away from there at a kicked-up lope. They did not talk to one another, nor did any of them look back.

Sometime after supper that night their youthful leader sought out the homeplace foreman. He found him alone in the main bunkhouse, and for some reason he felt glad for that. Probably it was for the same reason that he shut and barred the door behind him, so that none of the other boys would come in on them until his business with the foreman was done.

"Here," he said, handing the latter a grease-stained piece of thin paper, folded and refolded and grimed with the finger smudges of a hundred lonely, out-trail campfires. "I found it on him and figured it might tell who he was."

"You didn't look at it?" asked the big man quietly.

"No, sir," said the hand. "Didn't care to."

His companion understood that, and said so. Then he frowned and added, "Somebody's got to, I reckon."

"Yes, sir," said the young cowboy. "That's what I thought."

The big man turned the paper over, opened it slowly, thick fingers moving with respectful care.

For a long time he looked at the words which were written there. They burned themselves into his mind, and went with him to the end of his life:

> "Hushton Hatterson Feleen, firstborn son to Jupiter Aurelius and Nancy Hushton Feleen; Wheeler's Ridge, Slashpine Township, Holden County, Tennessee, Apr. 17, 1857. May he walk tall and talk soft all the days of his life."

But to the young cowboy who had brought him the paper he only nodded slowly as he refolded it, hiding its soiled secret.

"It's a book page," he said, his broad face creased in the squintlines of far-off thinking. "Appears to be torn out of a family Bible. Old wrinkle-thin paper. You can most see through it, like a cigarette shuck. There's some small printing here at the bottom says 'Tabernacle Press, Shiloh, Tennessee.' Then under that there's a cross and a head of Jesus with sparks of light shining around it."

The young cowboy looked at him, puzzled. "That's all?" he said.

The older man got up and went across the room to the woodstove. He stood over it, turning the paper for a last time in his big hands. Then with a final deciding nod he took off the lid, crumpled the paper, and dropped it into the firebox.

It caught, flared into flame, shriveled, and was nothing

183

but a curl of silvered ash, all in the little space of time he took to answer the waiting cowboy.

"That's all," said Coke Bancroft, and unbarred the door and went out of the J A bunkhouse into the winter night.

Will Henry was born Henry Wilson Allen in Kansas City, Missouri. His early work was in short subject departments with various Hollywood studios and he was working at MGM when his first Western novel, *No Survivors*, was published in 1950. *Red Blizzard* (1951) was Allen's first Western novel under the Clay Fisher byline and remains one of his best. As Fisher, he tends to focus on a story filled with action that moves rapidly. His many novels published as Will Henry tend to be based deeply in actual historical events. Under either name, as a five-time winner of the Gold Spur Award from the Western Writers of America, Allen has indisputably been recognized as a master in writing gripping historical novels of the West.

Bill Henry was born in from Albany, N.Y. in Kansas City, Missouri. He was thirty-two years old when he accompanied with... to the... of... in the West... was... occupied... and... first visit... under the Clay... from the... and... was... the best available... he goes... At... it was... filled... within the... the year of... by... many levels... within...